Fifteen Minutes

Luke Fetkovich

Copyright © 2013 Luke Fetkovich

Hardcover ISBN: 978-1-62646-465-0
Paperback ISBN: 978-1-62646-466-7

All rights reserved. No part of this publication may be reproduced, stored in a retrieval system, or transmitted in any form or by any means, electronic, mechanical, recording or otherwise, without the prior written permission of the author.

Published by BookLocker.com, Inc., Bradenton, Florida.

Printed in the United States of America.

The characters and events in this book are fictitious. Any similarity to real persons, living or dead, is coincidental and not intended by the author.

BookLocker.com, Inc.
2013

First Edition

To my Grandma F.

who taught me the game of life

and

to the players, managers and staff

of the

2011 Penn State Football Team

WE ARE...

Table of Contents

Game On - Chapter 1 9
Battle in the Blizzard - Chapter 2 17
3 + 86 = 7 - Chapter 3 22
Thompson's Tangle - Chapter 4 31
The Shoe Room - Chapter 5 40
An Unexpected Arrival - Chapter 6 47
St. Bruno's Academy - Chapter 7 56
The Lodge - Chapter 8 61
Deifer Hall - Chapter 9 72
Roster Revelations - Chapter 10 83
The Yellow Slip - Chapter 11 90
A Seventh Floor Startle - Chapter 12 101
Cowboys & Coyotes - Chapter 13 107
A Night at Retone's - Chapter 14 113
Fifteen Minutes - Chapter 15 124
The Crypt - Chapter 16 131
The Homecoming - Chapter 17 143
Pizza & Poodles - Chapter 18 149
Where the Hash Marks End - Chapter 19 160
The Dream - Chapter 20 164
The (End)Zone - Chapter 21 170
A Tale of Two Halves - Chapter 22 178
Second-and-5 - Chapter 23 185
The Waiting Room - Chapter 24 193
The Final Minute - Chapter 25 199
Afterword 207

Thanks to...

Aliesha Walz, for her editing expertise

Shane McGregor, for his quarterbacking insight and analysis

Dan Sowash, for volunteering to be on the cover

Steven Linden, for the photography

My dad, George Fetkovich, for the cover design

You, because you're reading this

and the following people, who all made a meaningful contribution to this story, whether it was NCAA transfer rules, game play rules, concussions, medical research or creative advice. Thank you, because you made this book possible:

Pat Foley, Bill Lindley, Dave Materkowski, Ryan Retone, Steve McKaveney, Dave Safin, Fred Fox, Chris McCahan, Geoff "Regata" Sebastianelli, Luke Slagel, Jevin Stone, Kirk Diehl, Brad "Spider" Caldwell, Scott Campbell, Tony Mancuso and Matt McGloin

Also, a big shout out to my family and friends, for their continued support of this project and all the challenges that come with it

And finally, thanks to the Booklocker staff for formatting, printing and distributing this story to the world

Game On
Chapter 1

"Tell me a fact, and I'll learn. Tell me the truth, and I'll believe. But tell me a story, and it will live in my heart forever."

--Ed Sabol

"Adam."
The voice came from somewhere in the back of his mind.
"Adam, it's game time, man."
Slowly, he slipped back into consciousness. A tall boy donned in shoulder pads and tight pants stared down at him. He clutched a helmet in one hand.
"Wha—? Did I fall asleep or something?" he yawned.
"Nah, you were actually abducted by aliens," the boy answered.
"Yeah, they just left. Said they wanted to come back and see you after we win the national championship, though." This time it was a lanky player with dreads. He threw a wet Gatorade towel at him and added, "Get your ass off the floor."
Adam Dorsey threw the towel aside and sat up. He was lying in the middle of the locker room with football gear, athletic tape and plastic water bottles carelessly strewn about the floor. His teammates huddled over him and chortled as he rubbed his head. His own shoulder pads proved to be an uncomfortable pillow.
"I don't remember...who are we playing?" the first boy asked.
"Nobody important, Chris," the teammate with dreads answered. "Just another Mountain Valley team. Nothing special."
"Yeah, I agree, Deion," Chris replied sarcastically. "It's only the game that's going to win us the conference title and get us into the national championship. And it's going to have the draft analysts buzzing about you this offseason," he added, pointing at Adam.
"Oh, *and* it's against Michigan," Deion added as an afterthought.
"Shut up, guys," Adam protested as he rubbed his eyes. "Can't you cut me a little slack today? I know who we're playing."
"Then why aren't you getting ready for warm-ups?!" Deion laughed, gesturing towards the other players and their newly-donned game outfits. "Quarterback drills are starting in ten minutes!"

"What?!" Adam cried, scanning the cavernous room for the clock. "Oh *shit!* Why didn't somebody wake me up?"

"Because we were having too much fun taking pictures of you snoring with your mouth hanging open," Chris chuckled as Adam began stuffing on his gear.

He took one huge gulp from his Gatorade bottle, threw it back into his locker, grabbed his helmet and headed for the door. He didn't even glance at anyone else in the messy room as he brushed past.

"Hey, Adam! You snore like my grandpa!"

"Shut up, Bowser."

"Adam, I think your hair got messed up a little—"

"I don't want to hear it, Jamal."

"Adam, are we going to win today?"

The quarterback stopped just before the door. He stared at the floor for a moment. It was such a simple question, but at the same time it was extraordinarily difficult. Some days the answer was easy, and others it was a little harder. But it was always the same. It was *always* the same. And there was no reason to change that now.

"Yes, Joey. We are going to win today," he told his center softly, without even looking up. Then he turned and left.

* * *

"And welcome to Sunset Vale, Pennsylvania, where we are preparing for an outstanding football game between the Keystone State Gargoyles and the Michigan Racers in the 2012 Mountain Valley Conference Championship Game!" an off-screen voice exclaimed as sports channel SportsNetwork streamed an aerial shot of the massive stadium. An early December snowfall had blanketed the field and stands, so that the Gargoyles' midfield logo was barely visible in the fading afternoon light.

"Corey Cousins here with Mike Mays," the younger ex-coach announced, flashing his short blonde hair and charming smile to the TV audience. "And Mike, what's not to like about this match-up?"

"You sure are right, Corey," the older, play-by-play commentator Mays replied. He provided a stark contrast from Cousins, with a gray mustache and heavy build. "The Gargoyles have clearly been the best team in the conference this year, and the Racers haven't been far behind. We've got a 12 – 0 team featuring the nation's most prolific passing attack going up against an 11 – 1 squad with one of the premiere defenses in all of college football. Folks, this is what it's all about, right here. This game has received a ton of hype over the past few weeks, and it shouldn't disappoint."

"And with that, let's remind our viewers what the stakes are," the color commentator Cousins added, and a flashy screen flew onto the broadcast.

Current BCS Rankings

RANK	TEAM	BCS AVG.	RECORD
1	SCU Sharks	.9968	13-0
2	KSU Gargoyles	.9463	12-0
3	Michigan Racers	.9124	11-1
4	Texas Tornadoes	.8879	11-2
5	Miami Gators	.8342	12-1
6	Arizona Coyotes	.8331	11-1
7	New England Clams	.7954	11-2
8	Ohio Valley Bears	.7822	10-2
9	Florida Hurricanes	.7126	10-2
10	Alabama Arrowheads	.6508	10-2

"Now, the Southern California Sharks have already won the Pac-West Conference Championship Game and have effectively punched their ticket to the national championship," Cousins went on. "Keystone State will certainly clinch the No. 2 spot with a win today. But if Michigan wins, they are expected to jump Keystone State in the standings, meaning they will make the trip to the Texas Dome instead."

"High stakes indeed," Mays agreed as the two commentators were shown once again. "And let's not forget, the winner of this game will take two of the past three MVC championships."

"Well, Mike, you don't win titles without great leadership at the top, and these two powerhouses have very accomplished head coaches. On one sideline you've got Paul Eberly—already a legend at Michigan. His defenses have finished with a top-10 ranking every single year since he took the job. And this year's defense has a chance to finish No. 1 with a good performance today."

The broadcast showed the Michigan coach walking the sidelines and brushing snowflakes out of his hair as the kicking teams warmed up.

"But you know what, Corey? With all that Eberly has done at Michigan, it's hard to believe Randy Thompson has done even more at Keystone State."

"It's simply astounding, Mike. When he was hired eight years ago, this football program was in shambles. They needed a new direction—a new energy—and Coach Thompson has provided that to an amazing degree. Under his watch, the Gargoyles have an outstanding 91 – 16 record, with two national championships, two Heisman winners and four MVC conference titles. And in addition to all of that, the man is 6 – 1 in bowl games.

"Sure, there have been some hard times. Everyone knows about the recruiting violations three years ago, and many people question some of his coaching tactics. But his supporters counter that he wins games, and any little indiscretions pale in comparison to the success he's brought this Gargoyle team."

"And it's not just the victories, but what he's brought to the program on a recruiting level," Mays added as another chart appeared on the screen.

Quarterbacks at KSU under Randy Thompson

NAME	YEARS AS STARTER	CAREER STATS
Kyle Stafford	2005-2008	12,342 passing yds, 87 TDs, 29 INTs
Derek Bridges	2009-2010	7,103 passing yds, 62 TDs, 17 INTs
Adam Dorsey	2011-2012	7,582 passing yds, 64 TDs, 11 INTs

"Keystone State has been an offensive juggernaut since Thompson's arrival, and the numbers just keep getting better," he continued. "Adam Dorsey boasts great stats to begin with, but if you separate the two years you can really see his progress. He chalked up 28 touchdowns and seven interceptions in 2011 after he took over for injured senior Derek Bridges. This year? He's got 36 TDs against just four picks while leading the Gargoyles to an undefeated record—undefeated. Corey, the Heisman ceremony is just a week away, and if he can pull out this win, he has a great shot at claiming that trophy."

"He would certainly deserve it, because both teams know how to play some 'D,'" Cousins remarked.

"Should be tough sledding for both quarterbacks," agreed Mays, turning to face the camera. "It's No. 2 vs. No. 3 coming up next on SportsNetwork."

* * *

Snow was falling heavily by the time Adam jogged onto the field. The student section erupted in cheers as he emerged from the locker room. The dividing wall showcased banners reading things like, 'DORSEY FOR PRESIDENT,' 'WE BELIEVE IN #3' and 'YOU CAN'T SACK THE DORSEY ATTACK!' But he didn't pay any attention. He loved it last year, when he was just starting out. Now it was old news. He didn't need his fan base telling him how good he was.

"ADAM!"

He glanced through the snowfall to see quarterbacks coach Pat Peterson rushing towards him, his glasses askew and his disheveled gray hair sticking out from beneath his winter cap.

"Sorry Coach, I—"

But the words barely left his mouth when he realized his coach wanted him for a different reason.

"No, no. I don't care about your warm-ups. You're scheduled for a pre-game interview with SportsNetwork, and they've been looking for you!" he explained, gesturing towards a small group of reporters on the sideline.

"Aw, I gotcha Coach."

He turned and headed towards the reporters, dodging a few footballs that sailed past from the kicking teams' drills. He noticed a sexy sideline reporter with a fluffy fur jacket and microphone, and hoped she was doing the interview.

"Hi, Adam. I'm Jennifer Rush," she said as he approached. "Thanks for your time."

"No problem," Adam grinned back. "I do this all the time. I'm used to it."

Before he knew it, Jennifer was talking to the camera five feet away, and Adam realized they were on the air.

"Thanks, Corey. I'm here with Keystone State starting quarterback Adam Dorsey, who has been enjoying a phenomenal year on the field. Adam, what do you think has contributed most to your success this season?"

"I mean, I'm really good," he answered without thinking, as the microphone was stuffed in his face. "I've been winning games since junior high, and I've got a 77 – 10 record overall, so I guess it just comes naturally. When you've got an arm like mine, you can pretty much do whatever you want."

"A couple of your teammates are poised to break some school records this year, specifically Chris Cook and Deion Carter," Jennifer continued. "How has that arm of yours helped them succeed?"

Adam paused. "Well, they're breaking records because they get to play with me."

Jennifer pursed her heavily-lipsticked lips. "But in terms of team camaraderie, is there some special connection you have with those wide receivers that has helped the chemistry between you three?"

"Oh, yeah, definitely," Adam replied as he grasped what she was looking for. "Me and those guys were in the same recruiting class, and we both arrived at Keystone State that spring before our freshman year. You know how it is when you first get to a new school—you don't really know anybody. So me,

Deion and Chris kind of bonded together and formed our own little group, because we were all in the same boat."

"So you and those two receivers have been pretty close since you first came to KSU?" Jennifer prodded.

"Yeah. We started throwing together after spring practices, to kind of get a feel for each other, you know? And that continued into summer work-outs. So that whole spring and summer we became really close, not just because of our positions as wide receiver and quarterback, but also 'cause we felt like we needed each other to survive up here...that really started our friendship. And now I'm still throwing to those guys, just in front of a hundred thousand fans," he finished.

"Adam, one more question. Do you three still throw after practice?"

"Yeah, all the time," Adam explained. "It really does help with team commodery, or whatever you call that stuff."

"Thanks, Adam. Back to you, Corey."

He was slightly disappointed about ending the interview with Jennifer, but he snapped out of it and reminded himself there was a game to play. Fans were screaming for him in the nearby student section, but he ignored them and jogged towards the quarterbacks.

The three other signal-callers were warming up near midfield, and Coach Peterson instructed him to throw with back-up Danny Thompson.

"How'd the interview go?" Danny spat through his face mask as he hurled the cold football at Adam.

"It would have gone better if she'd asked me out on a date," he replied grudgingly.

"Hey, at least you actually *get* to do interviews," his back-up pointed out. "Me? Nobody ever wants to interview me, even though my dad's running the show."

"Yeah, and if he wasn't running the show, you wouldn't even be here, so quit complaining," Adam shot back as he caught another pass.

"So why don't you leave early for the draft? If you end up winning the Heisman, you'll be a top-10 pick!"

"Yeah, but three national championships as a senior is a hell of a lot better than one this year as a sophomore. Trust me, DT. I'm going to be a top-10 pick when I get outta here, and I'm going to make boatloads of money, and I'm also going to win lots of Super Bowls...just not this year."

"But my dad wants—"

"You're full of it, DT. Your dad might be the head coach, but that's only going to get you so far. He's in this business to win football games, just like I'm in this business to win football games. And you're not part of the plan. That's just how it is."

"Aw, go *fuck* yourself," Danny shouted, and he chucked his next pass so off-target that Adam had to jump up and tip it out of the air. DT was storming away, and for a second Adam wondered where he would go, but it didn't matter. A whistle blew in the distance.

Well, what's wrong with telling it like it is?, he thought as he jogged towards the huddle. *What do I owe him? I don't owe him anything. Sorry, DT. It's time to wake up.*

The crowd was on their feet, applauding them even though he could hardly see the surrounding stands through the snowfall. He gathered in the end zone with his teammates, and the applause from the fans seemed to come from the swirling snow itself as it whirled around their outstretched arms.

"OK, win on three!" offensive coordinator Tim Bauer declared as he stood next to the mountain of hands. "One, two, three, WIN!!"

Their shout echoed away, answering the fans' cheers. The huddle broke. The crowd's roar reached a peak.

He was jogging through the tunnel back to the locker room with his black Gargoyle helmet clutched firmly in hand. The cheering grew more distant as they made their way beneath the support beams of Keystone Stadium, fading into a low rumble that seemed to make the surrounding structure tingle with energy and anticipation.

"Heard you got asked about your buddies in your pre-game interview," the player next to him said as he reached his locker.

Adam turned. Joey Callahan was grinning at him with that boyish look he wore so well.

"Eh, they don't want to hear about your fat ass," he joked.

"I heard it from one of the trainers. They were watching the broadcast on the TV in the training room. She asked about your relationship with Chris and Deion, and you didn't even mention me!"

"Look, she was asking about them, not you," Adam chuckled. "What was I supposed to say? 'Oh, and by the way, I'm really good friends with that fat kid that plays center?'"

"You told them the whole story about how we throw after practice!" Joey persisted. "Come on, Adam, you left out the best part! About how you and Deion and Chris decided you needed somebody to snap the ball? About how I was a freshman too, and I didn't have *any* friends until you found me, and wanted me to snap balls with you guys? And then how you helped me fit in up here, when I'm from a small high school and a small town? And we became really close, just from all of that happening that first spring?"

Adam nodded as he cinched up his laces. "OK, so I left out the best part of the story."

Joey just laughed. "I'm teasing you, Adam. You know I don't really care. Centers never get any attention. It's always the wide receivers and the quarterbacks that get that. I'm used to it."

"Next interview," Adam chuckled. "Next interview, I'll talk about you."

"You do that."

Randy Thompson had burst into the crowded room and was striding purposefully towards the clearing. He was wearing his usual teal Gargoyle ball cap over his square face and prominent jaw (even though it was barely 30 degrees). His black team polo was tucked into his pants, highlighting his bulging muscles and strong build.

Adam and Joey took a seat on the locker bench. If they hadn't known the man in front of them, they might have thought he was a boxer ready to knock out his opponent, the way he was pacing about the room now.

"Alright, men! Shut your mouths and listen up. There ain't no game bigger than this," he declared. "This, right here, is our chance to prove how good we are to the rest of the country. Everything we've worked towards the whole season, everything we've accomplished...men, it don't mean a damn thing if we don't win this one."

He paused, a blazing fury in his eyes, and pointed towards the doors. "That team over there wants to intimidate you. That's how they win games—by winning the battle in the trenches and breaking their opponent's will. They want to beat you down and force you into mistakes, until you finally give up. But ya know what?! They don't know what you're made of! They don't know what's about to hit them! So you *show* them!!" he screamed, pausing only to take a breath. "You run them over! You outmuscle them and beat them at their own game, and you don't stop until they run home crying and screaming to their mommas! You show them whose house this is!!"

Everyone was on their feet now, ready to give their head coach a rousing applause.

"SIXTY MINUTES OF HARD-NOSED FOOTBALL, RIGHT NOW!! LET'S GET TO WORK!!" he spat.

"Hey! HEY!" Adam screamed, when it was apparent that Coach Thompson had finished. He'd given pre-game speeches before, but this one was extra special. "When I came here three years ago, I came here to win a national championship. Now, I can. This is the time—right now. We've *annihilated* 12 teams so far, but we still have two left. The first one wins us the Mountain Valley Conference, the second one wins us the national title. Now just like Coach said, let's go out there and kick some ass!"

There were shouts of approval from his teammates as everyone put their hands together one last time.

"MVC champs, everybody!" Adam cried as he looked around at Chris, and Joey, and Deion, and all his other friends and teammates who were about to win him his first conference title. It was finally here. He almost couldn't believe it was finally here!

"One, two, three, MVC CHAMPS!!"

Battle in the Blizzard
Chapter 2

"It was an ideal day for football – too cold for the spectators, and too cold for the players."

--Red Smith

The roar was always loudest when you ran out of the tunnel.

The captains would lead the way through the damp concrete passageway, followed by the other players and assistant coaches, with Coach Thompson bringing up the rear. Then they would come to a long tunnel with the exit molded in the shape of a giant Gargoyle, painted to look like the patina monsters of Gothic cathedrals. Its jaw was frozen in an endless roar, with the bottom half sunken into the ground so that the team could burst from its mouth.

The team mascot and captains would gather just inside the stone fangs. Then they would wait for the band to finish playing the school anthem, and the color guards would raise their teal and copper flags high and rush onto the field—that was the signal to go.

The tumultuous cheer from the fans was deafening. Adam felt like he was charging out to war with his fellow soldiers, or maybe like a gladiator sprinting from the bowels of the Coliseum.

"Welcome back, folks! We're just getting underway here in Sunset Vale, as the Gargoyles have won the toss and deferred their choice to the second half," Mike Mays announced as the broadcast resumed. "OK, here we go. The anticipation and hype is all over, and we're off!"

The student section jumped up and down on the bleachers brandishing pom-poms. The crowd noise reached a peak as the place-kicker raised his hand high into the snowy air and ran forward, sending the football spiraling away towards the gray misty atmosphere above...

Adam knelt near the field as his teammates rushed past him, his helmet at his side. He waited just long enough to see the Michigan return man get tackled at the 25. Then he turned, walking purposefully along the sideline without talking to anyone. There was too much energy inside of him to just stand. He had to walk around and get at least some of it out, until he could finally take the field.

"And the senior running back takes it in for the Michigan touchdown!" Mays announced a few minutes later as the Racers capped an impressive drive.

Adam swore under his breath. They were losing, and losing was something he hated more than most people.

"Hey, why don't you do us all a favor and quit the team?" he jabbed at defensive back Darius Frazier as he jogged off the field. "Go play ping pong or some sport like that...you know? Maybe something where you don't have to tackle? Because you can't tackle worth shit."

"It's my bad, Adam," Frazier muttered through his face mask.

"You too, Porter, you big baby," he went on as defensive tackle Terrence Porter panted his way to a halt beside him. "You can't even get off your block against their freshman! I saw you out there. You all looked like shit, and that's why we're losing. How come I'm always the one that has to save our asses? You know, we'd probably be 2 – 10 without me, the way you guys have played all year."

"Now here's something you don't see every day," Corey Cousins exclaimed from the booth. "It looks like Adam Dorsey's having a little heart-to-heart talk with some of the defensive players after they gave up that score."

"You know Corey, this just shows how much of a leader Dorsey has become in his second year. What do you think he's saying to his defense right now?"

"He's probably telling them to keep their heads up and keep fighting," Corey surmised. "He's probably letting them know that it's just one score, and there's still the entire game left to come back strong. That was always my mentality as a quarterback, and I know that's what I'd be telling my teammates. You win as a team, you lose as a team, and if Adam is anything like me, he's hammering that home to his defense with that little chat."

"But offensively, this is a huge drive for Dorsey and his side of the ball," Mays continued. "With this clock-eating Racer offense, the Gargoyles aren't going to get as many drives as they're used to."

"You can't understate the importance of every possession."

Adam jogged onto the field with his teammates 150 feet below the commentators. He could barely make out the yard lines under the light frosting of snow, but he didn't care—it brought back some of his favorite high school memories of playoff games in November and December.

Fifteen seconds on the play clock.

He surveyed the Michigan defense. They were in their base formation, playing man coverage. This was the best part of quarterbacking right here, down by a touchdown with the home crowd at his back. Sure, it wasn't always fun when a 300-pound lineman took him down or he threw an interception. It wasn't always fun or easy, but *damn*, was it his favorite thing.

Ten seconds.

The play call was simple—a quick slant across the middle. His intended target was Jaden Hall, a shifty little wide receiver from Florida. The actual pass was only a short gain, but Jaden could always dodge linebackers and pick up extra yardage.

"Set...HUT...Hut!"

The football was in his hands again. He surveyed the field as his linemen shuffled around him, diverting his eyes from his intended receiver until the very last moment. Jaden made a skilled cut to the inside, and the defensive back was just a tad too slow...

Adam delivered a perfect pass right to the numbers on his receiver's chest. Maybe it was the weather, or maybe it just wasn't his day, but Jaden's gloved hands closed on the ball for a split-second before it bounced away over his shoulder...

"And Dorsey's pass is...INTERCEPTED by Michigan at the 35-yard line!" cried Mays. "And he's going to run it back. Oh, what a move there! And he runs it back all the way for a touchdown! *What a play!*"

They were running the wrong way. Everyone was running the wrong way. Adam stared in disbelief as he relaxed his muscles. It was a perfect pass. How? *Are you kidding me?!*

"What an incredible turn of events this is!" Cousins exclaimed as the broadcast showed an instant replay. "Look at this! Dorsey isn't even bothering to run the Michigan player down! Most quarterbacks will at least make an attempt at catching the intercepting player when something like this unfolds, but Dorsey looks like he's been struck dumb. He just stands there while the other 21 players go running in the other direction. Mike, he looks like he's insulted that this is even happening."

"Well, 99 percent of the time that's going to be a completion for a good five to ten yards. But Corey, that ball is extra slick out there today, and sometimes it bounces the other way," Mays commented. "So now the Gargoyles are down by double-digits, and this is going to be a different kind of challenge for Adam Dorsey and this explosive offense. You saw the way he reacted to that pick. Well, he's going to have to shake it off and keep his team focused here, or things could get ugly fast."

"And losing by double-digits is something this team hasn't experienced," the ex-coach remarked. "You know, we're talking about a quarterback who won most of his games in high school, came up here, took over this team last year and went 10 – 2 with a win in the Beach Bowl. Now they're 12 – 0, and most of those contests have been blowouts. Dorsey is a guy who's experienced success, but it's success that's come easily for him. You're the starting quarterback for one of the biggest programs in the country, you've got a rocket arm, and your team is winning. That's all been there for Adam Dorsey, but success doesn't just come with talent. It comes with sacrifice and perseverance.

"We mentioned how Dorsey has become a leader for this team. That's unquestionable, but what *is* questionable are his credentials for leading a team through this kind of test. And with the way this offense has cakewalked through the rest of the conference, I just can't say how they'll respond against this top-ranked defense."

The Racer fans were screaming in the far corner of the stadium, but everyone else was too quiet. It wasn't supposed to be this way, Adam thought angrily. Their own fans were always the ones screaming, every other home game this year...

"The extra point is good, and the senior linebacker has just added seven to his team's lead!" Mays announced. "It's the Michigan Racers 14, the Keystone State Gargoyles nothing halfway through the first quarter. We'll be right back."

* * *

"What happened?!" Adam hissed angrily as he caught up to Jaden in the locker room an hour later, slamming his fist against the frame of an empty locker. He'd cornered him in a small alcove where a set of extra lockers had been placed for injured or red-shirt players.

They were trailing 17 – 3 in the biggest game of their lives, and he wanted answers.

Out in the main room, Coach Thompson was in a frenzy as he kicked wadded-up balls of athletic tape, screamed at the top of his lungs and threw anything he could get his hands on. Most of the players were getting taped up, changing their wets socks, slurping down chicken soup and fruit, or just flat out trying to avoid getting hit by whatever object their head coach had in his hands. No one wanted to sit there and stare him straight in the eye as he yelled a thousand different criticisms—poor coverage, lousy-ass tackling, too little emotion, running the wrong routes, butterfingers, brains filled with cotton candy, babies, diapers, his 92-year-old grandma (who he apparently thought would be a better alternative to their starting middle linebacker), his taxes, the broken water pipe in his basement and, for some reason, his bloodhound named Devil.

"It was slick," Jaden replied as he and Adam hid behind the dividing wall. "I don't know what else to say."

Adam felt like he was about to explode. *"But it was a perfect pass!* You always catch the ball on that route—*always!* Why did you have to go and screw it up now?!"

Jaden lowered his eyes as his quarterback stared him down. "Listen, Adam. I'm not perfect, you're not perfect. We can't just stand here and yell at each other, we have to work as a team—"

Fifteen Minutes

"But that was a perfect pass!" Adam reiterated angrily. "I did my part! That interception wasn't my fault, it was your mistake! *You* didn't catch the ball, and that's what the problem was! Now, we've *got* to win this game today, so all I'm asking is that you make sure that doesn't happen again! Because we've got to play a perfect second half to come away winners here, Jaden, we've *got* to!"

He waited, expecting more out of his receiver and refusing to believe it was that simple. And Jaden did go on, but it wasn't what he was anticipating.

"You know we trust you, Adam? All of us wide-outs? We trust you to get us the ball. So you gotta have that same trust in us. You can't let one little mistake get to you. Just trust us back. That's all *we* want. You think we aren't trying our best, when there's a spot in the national championship on the line? Come on, man!"

Adam just shook his head in frustration. "No, no, don't give me any of that sappy feel-good crap, Jaden! That's not gonna win us the game. You catching my touchdown passes is gonna win us the game!"

Jaden rolled his eyes, as if to say, *"Honestly? No shit!"*

"But Adam, what I'm saying is, you gotta keep your poise when things get tough. Just because my pass got intercepted doesn't mean I ain't trying my hardest, you know?"

He couldn't take any more.

"Yeah, yeah, I know," he spat sarcastically, and pushed Jaden out of the way as he stormed back to his locker. He looked up as he entered the main room and dodged a flying tape ball from Coach Thompson. It whacked Jaden right in the nose, and the little receiver rubbed it uncomfortably as he slumped to his own locker.

"And where the *hell* did you two come from?! Making out in the back room, I guess? Sit your asses down and hear me out! Ya just missed my entire speech about how we won the Super Bowl back in '94! We came back from a 14-point halftime deficit, just like you pansies have gotten yourselves into right here! So buckle up and get ready to win this game, or yer gonna have the worst December of your pathetic little lives! What time is it?!" Coach Thompson roared at the head equipment manager, spit flying from his mouth.

A short man with a hat and glasses leaned his head out of the equipment room window and looked up at the digital countdown clock.

"Three minutes, Coach! You know it's right up there if you ever need it."

Coach Thompson glared at the little man dumbfoundedly, like he'd just realized the clock was even there.

"Thanks, Brad," he muttered in a softer tone. "Three minutes...damn. What the hell am I going to do with three minutes? I can't think of anything else to yell about."

3 + 86 = 7
Chapter 3

"Gentlemen, it is better to have died as a small boy than to fumble this football."
--John Heisman

Every team loses.

If you're good, then you'll win more games than you lose. If you're really good, then you'll win almost all of them. You might even go undefeated, but when the next season comes around you'll lose then. It's inevitable.

Unless you are Adam Dorsey.

If you are Adam Dorsey, you line up under center with a tremendous amount of talent and skill. You are determined to squeeze every ounce of that talent out of you, doing every last thing possible to ensure that next first down, and then that next touchdown. And you don't let up until that last second ticks off the scoreboard, and your team has won.

It's true that Adam Dorsey isn't perfect. He is 22 – 2 as a starting college quarterback. But he lies awake at night, thinking that those two losses could have just as easily been two wins. He thinks about the interception in the fourth quarter of the first loss—the tipped ball that wound up in the hands of the defensive back. Then the fumble with two minutes left in the second. Neither of those were truly his fault. If it weren't for his teammates, he would be 24 – 0. Undefeated.

He remembers lying in his bed and crying after that second loss—the one that put the national championship out of reach for good. He hated crying. If his girlfriend Kelsey ever saw him doing that...well, he didn't want to think about it.

That would never happen again. Because that was when he vowed never to lose again. And ever since that game, Joey had asked him the question before they went out for warm-ups, and the answer was always the same...

"Teal 18! Teal 18! Set...*HUT!!*"

The Michigan defense swarmed around him once more. The powerful stadium lights made the black helmets of his teammates shine like giant eight balls. Deion's flashed by in a streaking blur as he cut across the middle of the field and caught Adam's pass for a gain of 15.

He walked calmly to the new line of scrimmage, not celebrating, not happy...not yet.

"Dorsey takes the snap from center and hands it off to running back Jamal Harris," Mike Mays exclaimed. "Harris runs to the right...looks like he's trying to get outside and turn the corner...now wait a minute, folks. Harris stops and throws a lateral back to Dorsey, who's got all the time in the world to throw..."

The excitement in the announcer's voice grew with every passing second. Even he could sense it was a touchdown before the ball ever left the quarterback's hands.

Adam Dorsey let it fly, hurling a perfect spiral into the air as Jaden made the final cut on his route. The wide-out was too quick for the defender, and by the time the ball arrived he was miles ahead.

"And that's wide receiver Jaden Hall coming down with it in the end zone, and the Gargoyles have their first touchdown of the evening!" shouted Mays as an explosion of cheers erupted inside the stadium. "A 47-yard touchdown strike from Dorsey to Hall with 8:35 remaining in the third quarter!"

Adam ran down the field to high-five his receiver. "Now, that's what I'm talking about!" he screamed. "That's how we get it done, man!"

"Did I make up for that interception yet?" Jaden had to ask as they trotted off the field.

Adam really wasn't sure why, but he smiled to himself. It was easy to hide with his helmet and face mask on. "Just keep catching those footballs, man, and we'll win this thing."

And so the waiting game began again for the offense. Adam squatted on the sideline as the kickoff team rocketed the football back to Michigan, hoping that his defense wouldn't allow any more points.

Fourth down.

Chris ran the punt back to the 28. It was a long way to the end zone, but Adam didn't care. As long as he had the ball in his hands...

"And Dorsey finds Deion Carter in the back corner of the end zone for an 8-yard touchdown pass!" Mays announced ten minutes later. "What an impressive drive by the Gargoyle offense to end this third quarter. Folks, we've got a good one here in Sunset Vale as the score is all tied up, 17 a piece."

"You know Mike, we've talked about how this Keystone State team needed to show they could respond to adversity, and they've done that to this point. But now the Racers need to show they can take a punch and still win the fight. We could be in for a wild fourth quarter."

Corey Cousins could have saved his breath, because the 20 million people watching on TV weren't about to budge. They waited to see Michigan and Keystone State trade three-and-outs, and then watched as the Racers drove to their own 20 and kicked a field goal. Then they saw a calm but determined Adam Dorsey walk onto the field after the clock-eating drive.

He looked up at the scoreboard. It was 20 – 17 with 5:53 left. Do or die? Maybe. Actually, yes, he decided. They needed a touchdown. A field goal would only tie the game, giving the ball back to Michigan for a possible winning score as time ran out.

"Grenade! Grenade!" he audibled, checking his teammates' positions to his left and right as the hungry Racer defenders stared him down.

Jamal Harris ran it for a gain of five on first down. Deion caught a screen pass on second, but the Michigan defense stuffed it after a gain of three.

Third-and-two.

Coach Peterson was calling for a run up the middle. Adam stared. That wasn't going to work, he knew it. The Racer front seven was too solid. He thought about running over and arguing, but the clock was ticking and they couldn't afford to burn a time-out.

"Pony, pony, pony!" he shouted as he read the new defensive formation, changing the play from a run to a pass. He could only imagine what Coach Peterson was thinking right now...

He'd called a play-action pass. Adam coolly faked the hand-off to Jamal and scanned the field with his nerves tingling.

He thought he had him. Chris had run a slant to the middle of the field and looked open. He fired the ball, putting his faith in his talents and trusting—no, hoping—that it would zip perfectly over the head of the Michigan linebacker and come down in his receiver's arms. But the linebacker reached up and got just enough of the football that it changed direction and wobbled through Chris's fingertips.

Adam glanced to the sideline and saw Coach Peterson rip off his headphones in frustration. That was a telling sign—Peterson rarely got mad during games. He was the definition of composure.

His teammates were leaving him. They were jogging off the field for the punting unit.

"No, no, no, get back here!" he screamed angrily. "We're not going anywhere!"

He practically dragged his offensive tackle back to the spot of the ball, and he was about twice his size. "Fourth-and-two," he yelled fiercely. "Fourth-and-two. Jamal, *stop staring at the sideline! Fuck* the coaches! We've busted our asses all year for this!"

Chris and Deion and Jaden had all lined up and were waiting for his play call. They trusted him...at least *they* trusted him...

"Rocket reddy 28 blue!" he screamed, checking his teammates' positions as the play clock counted down to 10...five...

Whistles were blowing left and right. Joey and the other linemen relaxed and stood up. Adam swore under his breath and kicked the frost-covered ground. Time-out.

"Dorsey, what the *hell* are you thinking?!"

Coach Peterson's ill-tempered expression bore down on him 30 seconds later.

"We have to go for it, Coach."

"And it looks like Dorsey and his quarterbacks coach are having a heated discussion on the sideline," Mike Mays commented. "An interesting decision here, Corey."

"Yeah, Pat Peterson might be Adam's favorite assistant coach, but it looks like the two are at odds right now. It's interesting, Mike, because Peterson was a big part of the reason why Dorsey came to Keystone State. He's the one who recruited him and promised him big things as a part of this offense. And it's been a fun ride for both of them so far, but it looks like they're having their differences with this play call."

Adam glared into the eyes of his coach as he argued, and knew that Pat Peterson the savvy recruiter had been replaced by Pat Peterson the conservative play-caller. Their relationship had gone from good to great over the past year, and it was probably a testament to the pressure of the situation that Peterson was so reluctant to put the ball in his star quarterback's hands.

"Adam, what did I tell you during film study? *Take what they give you!* You're not taking what they're giving you right now! You're trying to force the issue, and it's costing us!"

"You called for a run up the middle on third-and-two! And in case you haven't noticed, Coach, we've gone 0-for-2 with that play so far! See, I've been keeping track! We'd be punting anyway!"

Coach Peterson looked something between outraged and speechless. "We can't risk giving them the ball at midfield! There's four minutes left. That's plenty of time for us to get the ball back! We've still got two time-outs!"

"It doesn't matter where we give them the ball! There's only four minutes left, which *means* that once we punt, and they run it up the gut every single down, they'll run out the clock and it's game over anyway! We *have* to go for it! It's our best shot!"

Peterson just stared at him, his mouth half open as if he wanted to speak but could not.

"Let him go for it."

The gruff voice belonged to Coach Thompson, who had been watching them casually with him arms crossed 10 feet away. The quarterbacks coach turned and glared incredulously at his boss. Adam could tell he was buckling under the pressure and was about to give in.

"He's your starting quarterback. Let him win the damn game."

Adam was almost surprised that the same man who had thrown a fit at halftime could look so composed now, but it gave him a sense of confidence. Coach Thompson liked to lose his temper, but he had spent 16 years as a head coach, and he wasn't stupid. He knew what they were up against with the Racers' clock-eating offense, and he knew that his quarterback provided him with the best chance to win the game. *Smart man*, Adam thought. But he couldn't get too full of himself—not now.

"Rocket reddy 28 blue!" he repeated two minutes later, and the entire stadium seemed to hold its collective breath. "Set...*HUT!!*"

Now, in the most pivotal play of his football career, the snap of the ball seemed to happen in slow-motion. He watched as the defensive linemen and linebackers all blitzed towards him in a frenzy. He felt the presence of the relentless defensive ends closing in...

Jamal Harris was supposed to pick up a block for him. *Man, I hope he's doing his job*, he thought for a fleeting second.

Chris was open. It was the same route they'd tried on the previous down, but with the linebackers blitzing, he was more open this time than last. All he had to do was place the ball so that his teammate would catch it and not the defender...

Instinct overwhelmed him. A tiny gap had formed between the struggling linemen, but with the opposing ends nearly grabbing his jersey it seemed like a chasm to Adam. He tucked the ball and ran.

He wiggled through the opening, but hands were pulling at him. Something tugged his cleat for a fraction of a second; he kicked it free. Almost there, almost to the first down, but time seemed to have halted...

He fell forward as strong hands grabbed hold of his ankles and pulled him towards the ground. Someone came crashing in from the side as he fell, and the football popped from his grasp before his knees hit.

Adam slammed onto the cold grass with empty hands and looked up to see the frozen ball rolling away. He reached out and desperately swatted it towards him, tucking it beneath his chest just as more hands swooped down, clutching at his arms and torso.

There must have been three players on top of him, at least, and he had no sense of who anyone was or how many of his teammates were there with him, fighting off the opponents. All he could think was to protect the football, as fingers and elbows nudged and pounded their way under his chest, searching and grasping. He held the football so tight, it felt as though he were clutching his soul.

He was sure the whistles had blown by now, but he could not hear or see anything in the dark mass of bodies. So he lay there, pinning the ball to the chilly grass surface with his chest and inhaling the aroma of sweat, turf and stinky shoes.

"Folks, we may as well take a commercial break while they try and unpile these players!" Mays joked as the overhead sky cam showed a dozen athletes—some wearing blue jerseys and others teal—bunched together just past midfield. The referees began pulling players off the pile one by one, slowly revealing Adam.

"Yeah, and even if Keystone State recovers this fumble, it might be Racer football," Cousins pointed out. "They look very close to that first down marker."

"It will be a close one," Mays affirmed. "But I believe I saw Dorsey regain control before he was lost beneath that pile. Interesting decision to run for it, though, with a couple of wide receivers open downfield. Don't you think, Corey?"

"I'm not sure if Dorsey saw that Jaden Hall was open. But it sure looked to me like he was going to throw the ball to Chris Cook. That would have been an easy catch for him too."

"And you would think, with all the games these guys have been through together, and all the records they've broken this year, that Dorsey would trust his receivers to pick up this crucial first down," added Mays. "But with Cook missing on that last attempt, I'm not certain that didn't factor into his decision."

Adam was finally able to stand and give the ball to the referee. Every muscle in his body ached, and the fact that they had to measure for the first down didn't make him feel any better. The nose of the football beat the down marker by two inches, and he felt as though an invisible weight had been lifted, freeing him to go and finish the game.

A SportsNetwork assistant with a red hat and headphones was walking onto the field. That meant there was a commercial break.

"I was open."

Chris was glaring at him.

"I would have caught that ball. You know I would have caught it."

Adam suddenly realized he couldn't look one of his best friends in the eye. "Don't worry about it. I got the first down."

Chris wouldn't go away.

"I got it. Don't worry," he repeated.

"Why didn't you throw that ball to me? You were eying me down for like five seconds. I saw you. Why didn't you throw it?"

Adam felt a twinge in his stomach, and he knew it wasn't associated with the tension of the game.

"Tell me why you didn't throw it."

"Uh…your favorite play. The deep bomb down the sideline. You've got the height advantage on their defender, and we haven't called that one yet. Let's do that next."

Chris glared.

"I'll go ask Coach Peterson right now. There's no way he'd say no, not on first down."

"The winning touchdown pass? Alright, fine. You can make it up to me that way."

Adam nodded half-heartedly and shrugged his friend off with a sigh of relief. He ran to the sideline and met his quarterbacks coach, who was all for it.

Seconds later, Joey snapped the ball on what would be their last offensive play of the game.

Adam grasped the football with a renewed sense of confidence. He watched the play unfold before him as if he were a mere overseer, only there to ensure that everything went according to plan, and that there was no unblocked linebacker racing towards him and no cornerback smothering No. 86 on his way to the end zone.

Of course there wasn't.

Chris made a brilliant cut and raced down the sideline. The deep safety couldn't possibly reach him before he crossed the goal line…

After a game so physical, so emotional and so intense, it was almost ironic the way the football gracefully sailed through the night air in a perfect spiral.

The fans rose to their feet while the ball was still ascending. The ones in the first row leaned over the handrails with their heads craned for a better look. There was a fleeting moment of silence before a thunderous roar of approval echoed around the field.

Adam ran after his teammate with his fist raised. It was 45 yards, but his feet were so light that it felt like 10. He nearly jumped on Chris as they met in the end zone, the stadium lights casting a warm glow over the scene and the fans screaming wildly. Coach Thompson had to stop the whole team from running onto the field, and so they were greeted by one high-five after another on the sideline. His teammates thumped him on the back as he pulled off his sweaty helmet, and he felt like he'd just returned from a far-off battle as the hero of some ancient war.

Before he even realized what was happening, the game was over. They were free.

Those last three minutes flew by faster than any other game in his life. The Racers desperately tried to mount a scoring drive from deep in their own territory. And as the last Hail Mary fell incomplete at the 10, another roar erupted from the crowd and the celebration seemed to begin all over again.

"And that's it!" Mays announced to the television audience. "The Keystone State Gargoyles have won the contest, 24 – 20, and are going to the national championship for the third time in six years!"

Adam could see it now—thousands of KSU students jumping up and down in their apartments and dorm rooms, with empty soda cans and beer bottles littering the floor and the TVs blasting loud as the sportscasters announced that Keystone State was still, indeed, the team to beat in college football.

"All season long, people pointed to the Gargoyles and Sharks as the most complete teams in the country. Well, they've both proven themselves today, and we're in for quite the national championship, don't you think, Mike?"

"No doubt about it, Corey! And how about Adam Dorsey? Heisman winner?"

"He sure has established himself as the favorite with his performance in the second half," Cousins remarked. "What a quarterback. What a team. What a game!"

Down on the sideline, fans were stretching their arms over the handrails to give he and his teammates high-fives as they paraded towards the locker room. People were taking pictures of him, of the scoreboard, of the aftermath and the celebration that *he* had caused. There would be a more exclusive celebration tonight, after the media frenzy died down, but that was only a small thought now—he had to claim his prize first.

"Jaden! Jaden, get up here, man!" he called through the crowded locker room ten minutes later.

The scene was nothing like the somber gathering at halftime. He was pushing his way through a crowd of media members and KSU administrators, fighting to get to the tiny and somewhat claustrophobic clearing in the middle. The Mountain Valley Conference commissioner was there, holding a three-foot trophy in his arms. Chris and Deion and Jamal Harris were already waiting with their MVC Champs hats donned.

Everything was a whirlwind as they were presented the trophy. It felt like the Oscars, the Olympic awards ceremony and the post-game coverage of a Super Bowl all rolled into one. Cameras flashed as the commissioner gave a short speech, and Adam hoped the whole world was watching as he lifted the trophy high, then passed it to Jaden, Chris and Joey. Free safety Darius Frazier triumphantly lifted it over his head. Then he passed it to linebacker Lukas Bowser, who grabbed it simultaneously with their other top defender Terrence Porter.

A reporter from SportsNetwork interviewed him right then and there— What was it like? What did this mean to him? What was he thinking when they were down 17 – 3? He couldn't even think, so he just blurted out words like, "awesome," "great" and "amazing experience." This really was an amazing experience. He'd never felt like this before, not in junior high or high school or college. Even when they won the state championship, it wasn't like this...

As they walked downtown on the way to Terrence Porter's apartment an hour later, fans cheered and waved and ran up asking for pictures and autographs. The bars were absolutely hopping. Drunken students with beer cans in their hands meandered down the sidewalk singing fight songs. People were shouting and applauding him from their apartment balconies. It felt like Mardi Gras had come to Pennsylvania.

His girlfriend of two years was waiting in the apartment lobby, and she gave him a long kiss as they embraced. Kelsey Stuart smelled like vanilla, with her long golden-brown hair flowing over her shoulders and a teal Gargoyle claw-print painted on her cheek. No doubt she had been in the front row of the student section hours before the game, staking her seat with friends and cheering him on even as the fell behind by two touchdowns.

They walked up the stairs together, and he received another standing ovation as they entered the spacious apartment. There was more alcohol here than he could ever dream of (and not the cheap stuff you found a frat parties either).

Adam found the perfect spot on a giant leather chair in the living area, and he lost track of time as the night wore on. More people showed up. Deion and Chris were here, and so was Jamal Harris, Joey, Darius Frazier, Lukas Bowser and his girlfriend, *plus* his girlfriend's friend...he had a feeling there were lots of girls here, but that was definitely OK if not planned in the first place.

Hours passed, and he slouched lower and lower in the plush chair as the empty beer bottles piled higher and Kelsey ran her fingers through his hair.

Terrence came over, sat on the couch and asked if they wanted anything else to drink.

"Yeah, yeah," Adam replied. "Whatever, bring it over. So where were you in the first half, huh? I told you your big fat ass couldn't sack their quarterback!"

Terrence laughed out loud. "Took me a half to warm up."

"Yeah, I knew you'd get him," Adam chuckled. "I knew you would, Big T. You were great."

Everyone had been great—hell, they'd played almost as well as he had. Did he finally have a team that respected him enough to give him their best, each and every game? It sure felt that way as his teammates came and went and the hours blurred together. And he was their leader, their king, as he sat here on his throne with his queen. Soon he would lead them onward in battle, on to the national title game and the Southern California Sharks as they completed their quest to conquer the college football landscape.

Nothing could stop him now. He would go undefeated for the rest of his college career, he was sure of it as he threw yet another empty bottle onto the nearest table. He was invincible, the greatest college quarterback ever, a No. 1 draft pick for sure. He had won it all—the treasure was his—and he sure as hell deserved it. Every last bit of it.

Yes, he had won...

He had won.

Thompson's Tangle
Chapter 4

"What the hell is going on out there?"

-- *Vince Lombardi*

His phone was buzzing.

Adam slowly became aware of his surroundings as warm rays of sunlight crept in through the brown curtains.

He got up on all fours, scanned the room with his head throbbing, and finally located his phone on the nightstand.

"Fuck," he whispered to himself as he stumbled off the bed and rubbed his head. He felt like he'd just been run over a truck. His body was aching from the game and his hangover was the worst. Kelsey rolled over but continued snoozing. He stumbled into the hallway so he wouldn't wake her.

"Hello?" he said groggily.

"Hey, buddy. How's it going?!" Coach Thompson's enthusiastic voice replied.

"Coach? What—er, it's going good, I guess."

"Hey, if you've got an hour or so, there's something I'd like to discuss with you. In my office. Tell you what—I'll pick you up. I'm heading down South Street now. I can be there in ten minutes."

Adam rubbed the crust from his eyes. "Uh..."

"You sound a little out of it," the coach chuckled. "Probably best if I pick you up."

"Uh...I guess. I mean, no, I can come over myself."

"No, no, I insist. I'll be outside your place in ten minutes. See you then!"

Adam ended the call and stared blankly at the screen as he scratched his head. He couldn't quite make sense of things—it was too early. What had just happened? Coach Thompson was coming to pick him up...yeah, that was it...in ten minutes...

Ten minutes?

I'd better get some clothes on. I'll be back before Kelsey even wakes up...

He staggered into the bathroom, shut the door and opened the window. The cold December air was the perfect antidote for his hangover.

Adam flicked on the light and stared into the mirror. He looked like shit. His dark brown hair was pushed every which way. His eyes were red. There were a couple of odd bumps and cuts on his chest and abs. He needed to shave, too—he didn't want to meet Coach Thompson looking like a slob.

So he wanted to meet with him in his office? His heart seemed to jump with anticipation as he thought about it more and more. The day after he'd completed the season 13 – 0 and landed his team in the national championship? This had to be something good. Maybe they had just decided on the Heisman finalists, and his coach wanted to be the first to tell him?

He shaved quickly, slapped on some deodorant and snuck back into the bedroom to grab his shirt and jeans, being careful not to wake Kelsey. What if she woke to the news that they were headed to New York for the trophy presentation this weekend? He didn't want to tell her until he was absolutely sure. Yeah...he would come right back and she would be the first to know, even before his parents.

Down on the street, Randy Thompson's high-powered white pick-up cruised to a stop on the curb. Adam felt like he was climbing into a monster truck as he hopped into the passenger seat.

The coach's frame looked even bigger sitting in the two-door truck. He wore the same teal ball cap from last night's game, and his muscles bulged in the outstretched arm that guided the steering wheel.

"Have a party last night?" he asked casually as they pulled back into the street lane.

"Yeah," Adam replied, not wishing to go into details.

Thompson grinned. "I wouldn't expect anything less from you guys. Work hard, party hard, Adam...work hard, party hard, that's what I preach."

The truck's engine revved as they turned into campus and climbed a hill.

"You know, Adam, that was a really great performance you put on last night. I don't think I've praised you enough for everything you've done to get us this far. And I want you to know how very honored I am to be your coach."

"Thanks."

"I really mean that, Adam. You've really stepped it up this year. I don't think I've ever been as impressed with any of my players, in college or the NFL."

"Thanks, Coach."

"Now, were your parents at the game last night?"

"No, they couldn't make it. My grandfather had hip replacement surgery yesterday. But they'll obviously be at the national championship."

Coach Thompson seemed to lose his voice for a second as he swallowed.

"The national championship? Well...I hope they get to come down there, Adam, I really do. How are they doing these days? Doing well?"

"Yeah."

"It's a shame they couldn't be here for that performance yesterday. Boy, what a show you put on. I can only imagine how proud they are, Adam."

"Thanks."

Fifteen Minutes

They pulled into the parking lot of the football training complex, and Adam hopped down from the truck.

The head coach's office was located in a spacious corner of the main building, up a wide staircase and through two wood-paneled double doors adorned with a golden nameplate. Inside the room, mahogany bookshelves lined the walls and a glass display featured various trophies and awards from Coach Thompson's playing days. The massive desk was littered with pictures, papers and small statues—the largest frame held a photo of the coach as an offensive lineman decades ago. He was beaming with his teammates and hoisting the Lombardi trophy into the confetti-filled sky.

"So, Adam! I've been thinking," he began as he settled down in the black squishy chair behind his desk. "Have you ever thought about transferring?"

Adam almost missed the seat as he sat down.

"Have I ever—*what?* No!" he gasped, not sure if he should sound surprised, but sounding that way regardless. Did Coach think he wanted to transfer? Is that what he wanted to talk to him about? And if so, where the *hell* did he get that idea?

"Ah," Thompson said, leaning back in the chair thoughtfully. "I think you should transfer."

"What? Why? Coach, I've never wanted to transfer. I've always wanted to be a Gargoyle, I thought you knew that—"

But the head coach merely waved his oversized hand as if he didn't want to hear any of this.

"Of course you always wanted to be a Gargoyle, Adam! I'm not talking about that. I'm talking about what's best for both you *and* the team in the near future. You know, you're so good, Adam, I don't think we've even got room for you here!" he finished, chuckling lightly as if this were some kind of joke.

Adam stared.

"Let's face it. This is just a stepping stone in your career. Pretty soon, you'll be headed to bigger and better things. *That*, right there," (he pointed at the picture with the Lombardi trophy), "is your future, Adam. This place? Well…"

His voice trailed off, and the coach shifted in his seat.

"You know, my son, Danny—he's a pretty damn good quarterback, too. And I think he deserves a shot at the starting position. But you *are* the starter, Adam! And you're a hell of an athlete. So what can we do about this? I mean, can't you see my position?"

And now he chuckled again, looking more and more like a madman to Adam.

"I can't start both of you."

Fear and panic were boiling inside of him like a volcano about to explode.

"I'm not transferring."

"I think that would be the best move for everybody," Coach Thompson replied, nodding his head as if Adam had just said the exact opposite—"Sure Coach, I'll transfer!"

Words crept back into his mind from what seemed like a long time ago...

"But my dad wants—"

"You're full of it, DT. Your dad might be the head coach, but that's only going to get you so far. He's in this business to win football games, just like I'm in this business to win football games. And you're not part of the plan. That's just how it is."

His stomach curled into a knot. Had he been wrong?

"I'll tell you what we'll do, Adam. Seeing how I'm the head coach here, I think it would be best if Danny stays, and you go somewhere else. That way I can coach my son, and you can make some other coach ridiculously happy by going to their school and winning them a bunch of football games. You'll both be starters, and everybody will be content," he finished, as if this all made sense in some sick, twisted way.

"I—I'm not transferring."

Coach Thompson gazed at him intently for a few seconds, then nodded to himself and rapped his knuckles on the desktop. "Well, Adam, I guess the only question now is *where* you'll be transferring!"

Adam jumped to his feet.

"That's crazy. Absolutely crazy, Coach! You want to kick me off the team? Is that what you're saying?! You want to kick your best player off the team?!"

"Adam, of course not, of course not," Thompson said delicately, as if he were afraid his quarterback might explode and was trying to cool him down. "You're transferring. Just *transferring*."

He could see the stress in his coach's face. He wasn't acting. This wasn't a joke. He was dead serious.

"But that's the same thing!" he screamed, unable to keep his anger inside any longer. "Whether you make me transfer or not, you're still saying that you don't want me on the team anymore!!"

"Adam, it's not like that," Thompson sputtered desperately, holding out his hand.

"I JUST WENT 13 – 0 AS A SECOND-YEAR STARTER FOR ONE OF THE BEST TEAMS IN THE COUNTRY AND YOU WANT TO KICK ME OFF THE TEAM?! I TOOK OVER FOR DEREK LAST YEAR AND WENT 10 – 2, AND NOW I JUST LED YOUR TEAM TO THE NATIONAL TITLE GAME, AND YOU'RE GOING TO REWARD ME BY KICKING ME OFF THE TEAM?!"

"Now, Adam—"

"I see how it is up here, Coach!" he shouted, drowning out his feeble attempts to argue back. "Now I see why there's so many nasty rumors flying around about you! It's not just the recruiting violations, is it? *Is it?!* No, it's about cheating the players after they get here, for your own good, huh? It's about back-stabbing, lying, stealing—"

"I DO NOT CHEAT MY PLAYERS!!" Thompson screamed, thrusting himself up from his chair and slamming his hands on the desk. "I RUN A CLEAN PROGRAM, AND IT'S SELFISH LITTLE PRICKS LIKE YOU THAT GET ME IN TROUBLE!!"

His face had turned beet red. Adam had never seen him so vicious.

"Now, Adam, we can do this the easy way, or we can do this the hard way," he spat. "I am trying to protect your reputation as a college football player! That's why I want you to transfer! But if you can't cooperate, for your own good, then you are going to leave me with no choice but to ruin the reputation of this entire team! *Are you going to make me do that?!*"

They stared at each other across the wide desktop like enemies, for what seemed like minutes.

"I'm not transferring."

"Then we're doing this the hard way—"

But Adam already had his back turned and was headed out the door.

He was startled when he realized that three assistant coaches and the secretary were all eavesdropping in the hallway, but he was too pissed off to care. Offensive coordinator Tim Bauer jumped back in surprise as he flung the door open, and they made eye contact for a second before Adam hurried down the steps.

No one said anything to him as he burst into the lobby and out the door. He was angry—angrier than he'd ever been in his life. He'd just won the MVC Championship and a berth in the national title game. This couldn't be happening *now*...

He felt a strange impulse to clutch something big as he stormed back to his apartment. He wanted his friends. He wanted his girlfriend. That's what he would do—he would take off his jacket and crawl back into bed with Kelsey, pretending like he'd never woken up and nothing had happened. Then they would get naked and make out, and that would make him forget about everything else.

Kelsey was still asleep when he got back.

He could crawl into bed with her right now, just like he wanted. It was there for the taking. But that felt like a cowardly thing to do for some reason. So instead he ended up sitting on the living room couch and staring at the dirty stained carpet. Thoughts whizzed through his mind, and he felt more alone than he ever remembered feeling.

"Let him go for it...he's your starting quarterback, let him win the damn game..."

"Have you ever thought about transferring? I think you should transfer..."

"Now, Adam, we can do this the easy way or we can do this the hard way...then we're doing this the hard way...the hard way...the—"

A sudden thought hit him like lightning. He bolted to his feet, searching frantically for the remote. He flipped through the channels and found SportsNetwork. A Sunday afternoon basketball game was on—the station's news program wouldn't air for another three hours. Unless it was on SportsNetwork Plus...

He changed the channel, and two analysts stared back at him. They were discussing the pro football games airing right now. He caught his name on the news stream at the bottom of the screen, and his heart skipped a beat, but then he realized it was just his stats from last night's game. There was nothing...not yet, anyway.

No, Coach wouldn't do it. He *couldn't*. And he was overreacting about what had happened in the office. But he still felt the need to keep the TV on with the volume down as he began texting everyone he could think of.

* * *

"He did *what?!*"

It was comforting to hear Deion's mellow voice over the phone, although his receiver was just as shocked as he was.

This was the seventh teammate he'd talked to since he'd arrived back at the apartment, not to mention his parents. Kelsey was sitting on the couch and surveying the TV in case anything popped up.

"I can't believe that, Adam," Deion went on. "I mean, I sort of can, 'cause I wouldn't put it past Coach Thompson, but...wow. That's crazy, dude."

"But what do you think I should do? Just ignore him and act like nothing happened?! That's pretty much what my parents told me to do, but I don't think it's gonna work—"

"Nah, that won't work, trust me. You gotta make him see that starting DT instead of you is a bad idea. But *hell*, that shouldn't be too hard, should it?" he chuckled.

"That's what worries me! He knows how good I am! So what's the point in arguing?! He's obviously made up his mind. He'd rather have his shitty little son start instead of win national championships with me!"

"Well, I don't know, Adam. Our position coach hasn't said anything to us wide-outs about a quarterback switch, so maybe it's not a done deal or anything—"

"*What?!*"

Deion stopped short as Adam yelled at his girlfriend. She had just shouted his worst fears.

"What?!" he repeated as he stomped into the living room.

Fifteen Minutes

"It's two topics away," Kelsey continued, pointing at the lime green SportsNetwork sidebar that displayed upcoming news.

"*Turn on SportsNetwork! Turn it on right now!* There's something about me! Quick! It's coming up in a few seconds."

"Alright man, I am."

Right then, nothing existed except the two of them and the TV. The anchor's chatter seemed to drag on forever and ever. Every video clip felt like an eternity.

"Speaking of which, we have some breaking news coming in just now from Keystone State's athletic department regarding starting quarterback Adam Dorsey. SportsNetwork reporter Jeff Regata has more. Jeff?"

The screen switched to a stately man in a suit and tie.

"Thank you, Sarah. This may come as a shock to many in the college football world, but the athletic department has just released a statement announcing that Adam Dorsey has been removed from the team—"

Adam punched the wall so hard that his knuckles started bleeding.

"—for a violation of team rules. Now, Keystone State isn't saying exactly *what* the violation was, but I recently spoke to an inside source who seemed to hint that Dorsey was caught with marijuana after last night's game. He was very reluctant to get into specifics, even though I made it clear that he would remain anonymous. But all signs point towards this being about drug possession."

"Thanks, Jeff," the anchor continued. "We also have a statement that was released a few minutes ago by Keystone State's athletic director."

The broadcast switched to a fancy orange box with the athletic director's statement on the left and a picture of him on the right. The anchor read the words as they flew on and off the screen.

"*Keystone State prides itself on the integrity of its football program, and we hold all athletes accountable for any violations in team policy, regardless of their popularity or athletic ability.*

"*As such, we regret to announce that Adam Dorsey has been suspended from the team for a serious policy violation. He will not be expected to participate in the upcoming championship game, and we will review his status in the upcoming weeks and make a final decision at a later point.*

"*It's unfortunate that a model student-athlete would engage in behavior that is damaging to the team, but we hope this serves as a lesson to other players.*"

The news anchor reappeared, looking absolutely thrilled at being the first to report this exciting update. Adam wanted to smack her in the face. He suddenly realized that Deion was talking to him.

"Adam? Adam, are you still there, man?"

"Yeah, yeah."

"Well, I guess it's time to freak out," his teammate chuckled ominously.

What was he trying to do, cheer him up?

"Deion, that's complete bullshit, that whole marijuana thing," he retorted. "It's all lies! You know that, right?!"

"Of course it's made up, dude! You know most of the guys on the team wouldn't believe it for a second."

"Yeah, and what about the ten million other people that are watching TV right now? You think they know that? You think some—hold on a second—"

There was an incoming call. It was Danny Thompson.

"Hold on, I'll call you right back," he spat as he switched lines.

"Sure, man."

"This is all your fault, you little pussy! It's all your damn fault! You should have jumped off a cliff or something when you were little, you good-for-nothing, cock-sucking—"

"That's no way to treat your new starting quarterback," DT jeered through the phone.

Adam paused, only because he was searching for a nasty retort to throw back at him.

"I told you that you should have left early for the draft, Adam."

"I wouldn't have left until after the championship game anyway, so what does it matter?!"

"My dad would have probably let you play out the season if he knew you were leaving, just to save face."

"Oh, just to save face, huh? Well guess what, DT? You can tell him I'm going to fuck up his face so bad that he won't even recognize it when I'm done. You and your dad are going down. Just wait. Just you wait."

"How exactly are we going down?"

"You...you can't get away with this," Adam stuttered.

"We'll see about that."

"OK, so why did you call me? Just to have a laugh, I guess?"

"Not exactly. Just wanted to let you know that my dad's in this business to get me into the NFL, just like I'm here to get into the NFL. And, uh, *you're not part of the plan.*"

Adam hurled his phone at the wall, and it went spinning behind the couch.

"Good luck trying to get ahold of me now, you asshole!" he spat as he stormed down the hall to his bedroom. Kelsey ran after him.

"That was DT, wasn't it?" she asked cautiously after he'd collapsed on the bed.

"Yeah, and I can't decide what to make of his initials anymore. Should I call him 'Dick Turd' or 'Douchebag Tw—Terd...fuck, I don't know. What the *fuck!*"

He pounded his fist on the mattress.

"It's not his fault," Kelsey whispered. "You shouldn't blame him."

"It's *not his fault?!* Kelsey, it's *all* his fault! If the little prick hadn't been born, none of this would be happening...oh, don't you start now, too! You can't possibly think—"

But Kelsey had tears streaming from her eyes. She backed out of the room and quietly closed the door.

Adam shook his head and closed his eyes. He was losing his mind, and so was his girlfriend.

He lay there on the bed, not wanting to get up for a long, long time. Nasty thoughts chased each other through his mind as he mulled what to do next.

He could go to the team meeting planned for tomorrow. Yeah...he would go to the meeting and act like nothing had happened. Plan A. And if that didn't work he would think of something else.

Really, they weren't just going to throw him out the minute he stepped inside, were they?

This couldn't be real.

The Shoe Room
Chapter 5

"The road to Easy Street goes through the sewer."
--John Madden

"I won't let them throw you out," Joey promised as they walked into the football complex the next morning. "You're my quarterback, and you just won us the MVC Championship. As long as I'm here, they're not going to touch you."

"Thanks, Joey."

Adam had gotten ten hours of sleep since the craziness of last night, and he felt a renewed sense of confidence. His parents had helped him decide that his best option was to attend the meeting, and then talk to the other coaches—the ones who had recruited him and mentored him these past two years. Pat Peterson was at the top of that list.

They walked through the lobby and past a giant mural of the Gargoyles' game-winning touchdown in the national championship three years ago. Through the double-doors, down the spacious hallway...

Adam had that knot in his stomach again as they neared the meeting room, but before they could reach it, a door opened nearby and his quarterbacks coach stumbled out. He glanced up, saw them and froze. Adam couldn't help but freeze in return, as a dozen thoughts about what to do next invaded his mind.

"Dorsey! *You can't be here!*"

Coach Peterson looked up and down the hall frantically.

"I...Coach, I have to be here. It's a mandatory team meeting," he responded, going along with Plan A—act like nothing had happened.

They stared each other down, and Adam felt a sudden surge of power. Coach Peterson had embraced him like his own son these past two years. He would not go along with Randy Thompson's plan, he just knew it. The man had too much integrity.

"Adam, come here. Quickly!" he said decidedly, and grabbed his quarterback by the arm. Adam glanced back at his trusty center, and Joey truly looked like he wanted to say something—his mouth was half open—but he simply stood there, dumbfounded, until he disappeared from view.

They were heading towards the equipment room, and Adam suddenly found himself surrounded by washing machines and dirty laundry hampers. The little equipment manager, Brad, was leaning over the table in the middle of the room as he screwed a face mask onto a helmet.

"Oh, hey Coach!" he said as he looked up and saw them.

"Brad, I'd like to keep Dorsey in here while I attend the meeting," Peterson declared urgently as he led Adam deeper into the room. "Is that alright with you?"

"Yeah, sure!" Brad answered. "Always love company!"

Peterson wasn't even paying attention anymore—he was marching purposefully towards a small side room.

"In here...*quick!*"

Adam was nearly pushed into the room as his coach blurted out instructions over the loud hum of the laundry machines.

"Just stay here until the meeting is over, and then I'll come back for you. And make sure no one sees you! If they find out I'm helping you, my head will be next on the chopping block. Just sit tight. I'm going to close the door..."

The white door slammed in Adam's face, and he saw his coach glance around nervously through the small door window. Then he disappeared around the corner.

He turned, and realized he was inside what Brad liked to refer to as "the shoe room." It was a musty, claustrophobic space for storing extra equipment and athletic apparel. Massive teal game trunks were lined against the wall, unused helmets were piled in the corner and the shelves were stocked with orange shoeboxes.

He got restless after a few minutes and climbed onto one of the larger trunks so he could sit down. He dangled his feet over the edge and gazed around the room, as the steady buzz of the dryers and the *slosh! slosh!* of the washing machines throbbed in the distance.

Peterson returned sooner than he was expecting. He snuck back into the room, closed the door and sighed. He leaned against the wall and removed his glasses, wiping them on his Gargoyle tee.

Adam realized for the first time just how tired he looked. His lanky figure didn't seem so tall now that he was sitting high on the trunk. His hair looked grayer and thinner than ever, and he could have passed as a grandfather with the wrinkles on his forehead and fingers.

"Well, Adam, let's talk."

There was a pause. Peterson rubbed his eyes and put his glasses back on.

"Do you know why you were recruited here three years ago?" he asked softly.

Adam didn't quite know what to make of the question. "To play football for the Gargoyles."

"Yes...and no. You see, Adam, Randy has always envisioned his son playing quarterback for Keystone State, where he could personally train him and protect him from anything that might hinder his success at the collegiate level."

Adam waited. He'd assumed this much—Coach Thompson was ditching him in favor of his son.

"Danny's success here is crucial to his future," Peterson went on. "Unlike yourself, he currently lacks the fundamentals necessary to be a starter at the professional level. He has difficulty reading complex defenses. He lacks downfield accuracy. I'm sure you're quite aware of all this.

"The problem is, Danny also isn't very bright. He's a slacker, and he expects other to do the work for him. This is why his dad will be the one who gets him a job, and he'll do it through his contacts in the NFL. Coach Thompson's played on two Super Bowl-winning teams, coached three different NFL teams, led one to the Lombardi trophy, and has now brought our football program back to its elite status. You can imagine the kind of power he has, and the strings he can pull to get his son on an NFL roster."

"That's crazy," Adam scoffed. "He's not good enough to be a starter."

"Oh, no," Coach Peterson agreed. "He will never be a starter. Even someone as powerful as our head coach can't pull that off. But he can get him a place as a back-up, if he works hard enough in college. Which is *why* his success here is crucial.

"Coach Thompson is a pretty damn good coach, Adam. He knows the obstacles that must be overcome to ensure success. And if it all works out? They'll be one happy family, with Danny making a hefty sum as a back-up while his dad continues to coach. He won't be a nobody. He'll honor the family name. And this is the only way that it's possible."

"And I got in the way," Adam remarked pridefully. "I'm screwing everything up, so that's why I have to go, isn't it? DT's only a year younger than me, so—"

"—he would only have one year of eligibility remaining after you graduate," Coach Peterson finished. "And Randy knows that's not enough time. He wants three years, and he's going to get three years."

Adam stared at the concrete floor and the tips of his sneakers as they dangled from the trunk. "So why bother recruiting me in the first place?"

"Well, Adam," Peterson began, but then he paused. His long fingers were pressed against his face, and he stared at Adam with a look that seemed to evoke both admiration and pity. "You were *part* of the plan, as a matter of fact."

"I...what?"

"You were recruited to be Danny's back-up. Last season, if you recall, you were a red-shirt freshman. Danny was just a red-shirt. Derek Bridges, the senior that you filled in for last year, was supposed to go out on a high note, leaving the void for Danny to fill in his first season of eligibility. You were then supposed to be the back-up for your three remaining years.

"Well, then Bridges got hurt in the first game, and we had to put you in or throw Danny into the fire, which Coach Thompson did not want to do. He would never run the risk of embarrassing his son by starting him before he was ready.

"So you know what happened then. Ten wins as a freshman, 28 touchdown passes, nearly leading us to a BCS bowl game. And then your spectacular play in the Beach Bowl against Arizona. Randy had no choice but to name you the starter this year. How could he start his son now, with the way you were playing?"

"They'd call him biased."

"Oh, they would call him much worse than that!" Peterson replied, waving his arm in the air. "Starting his own son over the guy who saved our season last year? You can imagine the fall-out. They'd call the program corrupt, his national image would take a hit, and it would probably even hurt our recruiting! It ruined his whole plan."

"Small comfort," answered Adam, "but it's nice to know."

"The only way he could fix things," his coach continued, "was to take you out of the equation altogether. Either have you transfer, or...well, you know what he did."

There was an awkward pause, but Adam felt like things were starting to make sense.

"So why not just can me before the season started?" he asked resentfully. "Or better yet, why not just kick me off after the championship game in January? You'd think he would at least give me a chance to win the title, after everything I've done. Or is he that much of an asshole?"

He'd never called his head coach anything like that before, and now he was doing it in front of his quarterbacks coach.

"It's all part of the plan," Peterson said solemnly. "I only wish I could have stopped it."

"What plan?"

"Well, of course, if Randy had to start you this year, he would take advantage of it, wouldn't he? He would use you, Adam. Start you all 12 games and let you reach your full potential, throwing for record numbers of touchdowns and passing yardage. We couldn't be stopped. *I* even knew that, and I am a coach! It's my job to keep my players humble and cautious.

"Adam, this is the best offense I've ever coached—ever, and I've been here for 20 years. Thompson was kidding himself if he didn't think you'd lead us to the championship, and that's exactly what he was counting on."

His blue eyes fixed on Adam, and he waited, as if expecting him to solve the riddle.

"But he never intended on having me *start* in the championship? He always wanted DT to be the quarterback who won it."

"Exactly," Peterson whispered. "You see, Adam, while you deserve credit for landing us in this game, very few people will care about that now. The talk shows and sporting news are going to focus on Danny—on how an inexperienced freshman will handle being thrown to the wolves on a national stage. He will get the positive media exposure, especially if we win the game on the strength of our defense, which is what Randy's hoping for. They'll still talk about you, obviously, but the only thing they'll care about is how you managed to hide a drug habit and what a sad example you are for the rest of the college football world."

"And so if we win the game, he'll already have a national championship under his belt," Adam thought aloud. "But he never would have gotten there by himself. He never would have gotten there without me."

"He will be the new Keystone State hero—the guy who filled your shoes and finished the job that you couldn't," agreed his coach. "Nobody will care that he only threw for a hundred yards and no touchdowns."

Now there was only silence, besides the faint buzz of the machines in the adjacent room. Adam felt like a fly trapped in a spider web, carefully constructed to catch him off-guard and hold him there while the insect sucked him dry. And there was nothing he could do about it now.

"I tried saving you, Adam, I really did," Peterson went on, and now he sounded like a guilty father. "If I were a better man, I wouldn't stand for this. I'd quit. But I can't. I have a family to provide for, and a good salary here. I hope you understand."

What was he supposed to say? *"Yeah, I completely understand?"* What a lie that would be. If he were in his coach's shoes, he'd quit for sure. But maybe it wasn't that simple. So he just nodded.

"It's not my program," Peterson stressed. "I'm just a cog in the wheel—that's become very clear to me these past couple of days. Adam, if you only knew how many people are in on this—"

"The athletic director?" he guessed. "I never liked him to begin with."

"Sure," his coach nodded. "And our very own offensive coordinator, Tim Bauer. And our sports information director. I have a hunch the school president's helping him out too, although he can keep his profile nice and low since he doesn't work directly with the team. Randy's got this entire university wrapped around his finger, Adam, and the worst part about it is, I don't think anyone seems to mind."

He envisioned his offensive coordinator in a whole new light now. He hated his guts, too. He'd never disliked any of his coaches, and now he hated most of them with a passion. How long had they been in on this? Since his arrival three springs ago? Had they known all along that he would never be a four-year starter while they praised him with their fake smiles and handshakes? It made him feel sick.

"Nobody in this school's administration is man enough to go against the coach that took our football program from rags to riches," Peterson explained. "His record is 92 – 16, Adam. Nearly a hundred wins in just eight years! With a record like that, and two national championships to boot, nobody will dare question him. He's brought our schools lots of money, Adam, and in this business, money talks. And I'm so sorry this had to happen to you under my watch. I hope you can forgive me."

He nodded again, realizing for the first time that he wasn't the only one hurt by Coach Thompson's schemes.

Pat Peterson looked like he was finished lecturing. And so Adam put his anger aside and asked the question he knew he must.

"So...what do I do now?"

"You transfer to a lower division, win them the next two national titles, and show everyone where you really belong—as a starting quarterback in the NFL."

"But everyone thinks I'm smoking pot. It was all over SportsNetwork last night."

But Peterson waved his hand. "That won't stop schools from recruiting you because A, it's not true, and there's no evidence of it. B, you're just too talented. And C, you're going to tell them the real story of what happened after you leave here. Which brings me to another point."

The coach shifted uneasily against the wall.

"Until this whole thing blows over, Randy will try and keep you as far away from the media as possible. He *will* grant you a release from the team, but not for a few weeks. That way, our sports information department can control you. It's his way of making sure you keep your mouth shut."

"Which I won't," Adam stated defiantly.

"You will until you leave here," Peterson ordered. "I would strongly advise you not to try anything brash, Adam, for your own safety. Remember, as long as you're enrolled at this university, Randy and his partners have access to you, and they're powerful people with an agenda."

"So you're saying I can't just pack up and leave now? 'Cause that's really what I want to do."

"You have to finish your classes," his coach insisted. "Take your finals, get your grades. Then you can worry about transferring for the spring semester. By that time Randy will have granted you your release, because the major media outlets will have moved on to a different story."

"You don't think they'll want to update their viewers when they hear what I have to say?" Adam asked bitterly.

"But you're still outnumbered ten to one. You will be the only person telling that story, while Randy, and our athletic director, and our school president, and countless others will deny everything. And I warn you, Adam, as a friend, that you might be better off saying nothing publicly. People might think you're lying, so that other schools will offer you a scholarship. Save the real story for the dozens of coaches who I'm sure will be knocking on your door over winter break. Don't worry about the media. They're not worth it."

Yet he still felt like it *was* worth it, if only to get revenge. That was all he could think about now—revenge on Coach Thompson and the whole corrupt school. He wasn't going to a lower division, that much he was sure of. He would make the jump to the NFL, although he was kidding himself if he didn't think his draft stock had just plummeted.

Peterson glanced at his watch. "I've got to go," he said regretfully.

Adam jumped off the giant trunk and made for the door, but his coach held out his hand.

"Wait until I'm gone. I don't want to be seen with you. I'm on thin ice already, after the past few days."

He reached for the doorknob, stopped and turned. The quarterback and mentor exchanged a meaningful glance. Adam couldn't find anything to say, even though he knew this might be his last chance in person.

"Good luck at your new school," Peterson said softly. "I wish you the very, very best. I'll be watching your games when I have the chance, I promise."

Adam nodded once more, hoping that would be good enough, because there was simply no way to describe his mixed emotions.

Pat Peterson finally turned his back and walked out the door. Adam stood alone in the shoe room, absorbing everything they had just discussed. After five minutes, he calmly walked out of the building and never looked back.

An Unexpected Arrival
Chapter 6

"The measure of who we are is what we do with what we have."
                                                            --Vince Lombardi

It was over.

Everything they had worked towards, all those happy memories of late-night movies and cuddling under the sheets. All the post-game parties and the lazy summer beach trips. There wouldn't be any more of that for him. Not with Kelsey, anyway.

Adam was slumped on his bed at his parents' house in Rochester, New York, twiddling his phone between his fingers and thinking about everything that had transpired the night before.

"I just don't think it's a good idea, if you're going to be transferring to a different school," she'd insisted over the phone.

"But we can still be together! We can still hang out in the offseason and during holidays. I'll call you every week. How about that? I'll promise to call you at least once a week."

"Oh, Adam, get real. You know what college is like. I don't want a long-distance relationship right now. I want someone that I can actually see more than a few times a year. And I've had a good time with you the last two years, and I love you, hun, I really do. But I'm just not committed enough to keep it going with you off to another school. Trust me, I'm doing this because I don't want to hurt your feelings later on down the road."

"Oh, well, that makes me feel a lot better! You've had a good time with me? That's what this is all about, huh? You want a man to tote around town and take to parties, and get with in bed whenever you feel like it, and now that I won't be around, there's no reason for you to keep me? I see how it is."

"Hun, don't take it that way—"

"Don't call me 'hun!' I'm sick of your name-calling! You're a seductive little bitch is what you are!"

"Oh, that's real mature, Adam. Real mature. I feel bad for the next girl you decide to date."

"And I feel bad for you, because you're a pathetic little tramp, and that's all you'll ever be!"

And then he'd hung up, and it was over. Just like that. Coach Thompson had taken his football team from him, and now he'd taken his girlfriend, too.

He threw his smartphone into the air. The moonlight caught the tiny device as it hung suspended beside his window for a brief second before landing in his hands. Outside, there was nothing but dark shadows and their endless backyard as it stretched to the woods.

He remembered back when he was a kid. His dad used to play catch with him in that yard, teaching him the fundamentals of quarterbacking and helping him learn the tricks of the trade. During high school, they'd talk for hours about the previous night's football game—what he'd done right and what he'd screwed up. Then they would shuffle back to the house through the autumn leaves, following the delicious scent of his mom's homemade turkey.

Life was so carefree back then—hanging out with his dad or his high school friends, playing catch in the backyard and watching the trees paint a colorful picture in the sloping hills as summer changed to autumn. Everything had fallen into place exactly as he'd imagined, and maybe he'd taken that for granted. Maybe that's what made this all so hard.

The door opened, and light filled the dark bedroom.

"I'm making dinner for you," Michelle Dorsey announced as she surveyed him from the hallway.

"Don't bother," Adam groaned. "I don't have a life anymore, so why waste your time feeding me? I'll just sit up here and rot."

His mom frowned. "Honey, you really should get out of this room. Why don't you come downstairs and look over the information from these coaches—"

"I'm not going. I've already told you. I don't want to play for *any* of them."

"Oh, stop sulking. It won't do you any good. You need to decide on a school and get settled in. Then you can get out of this frame of mind you've been—"

"Go decide on a school for me then," Adam interrupted. "I really don't care. They're all the same to me."

"Sweetheart, listen to me. There's nearly been a line out our front door with all the coaches who want to recruit you. It's your responsibility to return the favor and choose the school you think is best. I can't do it for you. Now, dinner will be ready in half an hour. I'll see you downstairs."

She didn't bother to close the door behind her. Adam hated that—he really didn't want to get off the bed. Instead he stared at the ceiling fan and listened to the raindrops as they pounded against the window. It was a warm night for January, and the icy rain came down in droves.

He found the remote buried beneath his sheets and flicked on the TV. A debate show titled *The Ball's in Your Court* was running on SportsNetwork.

"—every single FCS school is out to get this kid! There hasn't been this much hype surrounding a transfer in years! Do you really think those schools would go to these lengths to recruit a troublemaker?"

Adam froze. They were talking about him.

"But Jerry, my point is, we're still talking about a guy who was good enough to win the Heisman and *still* got released by the Gargoyles," a large man countered. "I know Keystone State won't publicly state why he was kicked off. But the administrators know they have to give the media something, and I think we can all agree they've dropped breadcrumbs indicating that he was caught with marijuana. And if he was willing to break one team rule, how do I know he wasn't using steroids as well?"

"But you *don't* know, Mel, that's my point," the skinnier anchor with neatly-trimmed hair and glasses argued back. "There have been instances the past few weeks where we've heard rumors that this stuff isn't true. And let me remind you that Randy Thompson would have incentive to frame Dorsey like this, because his son is now the starter. Just yesterday, during national championship media day, a wide receiver from Keystone State said he didn't believe any of this stuff—"

"I believe the player you're referring to is Chris Cook? You can't take his word for this, Jerry, he was one of Dorsey's best friends on the team!"

"But he's not the only one," Jerry stressed. "There have been others. The bigger question, in my eyes, is whether or not Dorsey will *want* to transfer to a lower division. Because he'll lose a year if he stays at the top level."

"NCAA rules require an athlete to sit out a year, unless he transfers to a lower division," Mel explained casually while nodding his head. "And since Dorsey's already used his red-shirt, he'd only have one year of eligibility at a big school. But if he transfers down, he'd have two. I think we're in agreement that transferring down is the best option for him, Jerry, because nobody's going to spend a high draft pick on him now."

A bell rang, and the host appeared. "Well, we can agree to disagree on the subject of Adam Dorsey, but our next topic is tonight's national championship match-up," she announced. "Quite a lot to discuss here! The undefeated tilt, the Gargoyles' quarterback situation and the high-profile coaches. Mel, the ball's in your court first."

"I think I have to start with the quarterback situation," Mel chortled.

An excited butterfly awakened in Adam's chest—he'd forgotten that today was the day. The game would start in half an hour.

*　*　*

"Where's the remote?" he questioned hastily as he entered the kitchen.

"Over by the fridge," Michelle answered as she ladled chicken soup into a bowl. "I wasn't sure if you'd be interested in that," she added cautiously.

"Oh, yeah," Adam drawled. "I'd love to see them lose. Can't wait."

He grabbed a Coke from the refrigerator, took the bowl of soup, and sat down on a stool at the counter with the flip-down kitchen flat-screen straight ahead.

Sharks 7, Gargoyles 0. Perfect start.

Danny Thompson had stepped onto the field for his first snap as a starter. Adam stared at his tiny image and gleefully envisioned how nervous he must be.

A sack on the first play.

He banged his fist excitedly on the bar, causing his spoon to shiver in the bowl. It felt so good to see DT like this—on the ground, aching, and scared that he was going to lose the game for his team.

14 – 0 Sharks.

He slurped the last bit of chicken soup and watched greedily as DT threw an interception on the next possession. He wanted more and more. If only they could lose the game by 100.

Yet as he gazed at the TV with the lopsided score blaring in his eyes, he realized he'd never felt this way before. Ever. He wanted his team to get killed. He wanted to see Coach Thompson and DT stuttering in the post-game press conference, wishing to themselves that he was still on the team, because then the outcome would have been different.

But even so, a twinge of guilt flickered inside of him as he thought of Chris, Deion, Joey and all his other friends who were losing the biggest game of their lives. And he wanted that. He *wanted* them to lose. Well, he didn't, really—he wanted Coach Thompson and DT and offensive coordinator Tim Bauer to lose. He wanted Thompson to get fired, and for the new coach to reinstate him, concede that there was a big mistake, and then make everybody play the game over again with him as the quarterback. But that was impossible.

"Adam?"

"What?"

"There's somebody here to see you."

He groaned. "Who is it now? Tell them I'm not home."

"I think it's the coach from that one Catholic school. The one you talked to on the phone yesterday," his mom called as she hustled into the foyer. "He said he was going to try and stop by today."

Adam stared at his empty soup bowl, cursed under his breath and got up. *So the Catholic school coach actually made the effort to come here? I can't just brush him off. Now I have to waste more time pretending like I'm interested. Great! It just gets better and better.*

He crept down the hall and leaned against the doorframe marking the entrance into the foyer. His mom opened the door, and he saw a black man standing on the doorstep. He was soaked from head to foot, and wore a black raincoat and matching black ball cap with a green and yellow logo embroidered on the front.

"Mrs. Dorsey?"

"Come in, come in!" his mom gasped, and she hurried the man into the house.

He stepped onto the large area rug and removed his soaking-wet cap, revealing a shiny bald head. Raindrops shimmered on his neatly-trimmed beard. There were some gray hairs here and there, hinting that he was probably past 50.

The coach glanced in his direction for a second, but didn't address him.

"Mrs. Dorsey, I'll be taking my shoes off, if you don't mind. I don't want to dirty your floor any more, seeing how I will most definitely be dampening it."

"Oh, not a problem at all. And please, call me Michelle. Can I offer you a towel, or possibly some coffee, Mr...?"

"Morgan," the man replied. "Teddy Morgan."

"Mr. Morgan?" she finished as she helped him take off his jacket.

"I'd love some coffee," the coach answered. "Thank you."

"Adam, come and introduce yourself," his mom called as she hung the jacket on the coat rack.

"Hi," he said uneasily as he approached the man.

"Adam, Teddy Morgan," he replied, extending his arm for a firm handshake. "I am sorry I'm a bit late. But as I was in the area, I thought it would be prudent to make a stop today, since I'm sure you are eager to make a decision about your future. And I apologize for interrupting the championship game."

The man waited for his response, and Adam felt like he was trying to read his thoughts and figure out whether or not he even cared about the game, or who he was rooting for.

"I honestly don't care," he answered. "It's not a big deal to me. They're losing anyway. The game's pretty much over."

He'd had to catch himself there. He'd almost said, *"We're losing."* He couldn't think like that anymore.

The coach simply nodded.

"We can go in the living room," Adam suggested, and he led the way over to the sitting area near the fireplace.

He and the coach sat on opposite chairs in the dark room, with a wide coffee table between them and the only light emanating from the nearby kitchen. His mom had lit a fire for the other coaches, but she was busy preparing coffee now.

"Well, Adam, I'm sure you know why I'm here," Coach Morgan began as he leaned back in his armchair. "So let me cut to the chase and ask you what you think of becoming a St. Bruno Beaver and playing football for our school in southwestern Pennsylvania."

Wow—he'd thrown him for a loop there. He was expecting the same old campaign. *"You know, Adam, our school is one of the top competitors in the Football Championship Subdivision...Adam, we've got so many great receivers on our team, we need two different starting line-ups! Imagine what our offense would be like with you at quarterback!...Hey Adam, let me tell you about our stadium. It's the biggest in the entire conference..."*

But this coach sat down, and the first thing out of his mouth was, "What do *you* think of becoming part of our team?" It wasn't about them. It wasn't about their school. It was about him. He kind of liked that. But he had no idea what to say.

"Did you receive the information packet we mailed to you?"

Adam shook his head. He was reluctant to listen to recruiters in person, let alone something that came through the mail.

Coach Morgan seemed to read his mind. "Well, I should have expected that, with the amount of interest that you've been receiving in recent weeks," he said, waving his hand as if dismissing any notion that he was disappointed.

"As I stated yesterday, St. Bruno's Academy is a private Benedictine university near the town of Waddlesburg, Pa. We offer a quality education and superb athletic programs to students who enroll at our school. Now, you will—as I'm sure you expect—be offered a full scholarship to play for our team. The other coaches and I have researched your background, your highlights and all of that. We feel like you can contribute to our team from the get-go, with your experience and knowledge of the quarterback position. And on top of that, you will not be required to sit out a year, since you'll be transferring to a lower division."

Adam figured now would be a good time to explain his side of the story, just like Coach Peterson had told him to. He'd explained everything to all the other recruiters, but Coach Morgan simply waved his hand when he started talking.

"Forgive me for interrupting, Adam, but I don't care about any of that."

This was the first time a coach had ever told him *that*.

"You...you don't?"

"Adam, if I'm here then I obviously want you on my team. I've already heard your side of things from my colleagues. Whatever happened between you and Coach Thompson, save that for a different time. I would be glad to discuss that with you in private, if you like, but only after you become a member of our team. What I care about right now is, what do you think of our school?"

Adam paused. He fidgeted uncomfortably in the chair. His mom bought him a few extra seconds when she entered the room with a steaming cup of coffee.

"Thank you," Coach Morgan repeated, and she left for the kitchen.

What do I say? I still haven't got a clue what this school's like. I'll just tell him the truth...yeah...there's nothing else but to go for it...he doesn't seem like he'll be mad at me if I just tell the truth.

"Actually, Coach, I have to be honest with you. I don't think I can play for an FCS school. That's just not where I feel I belong. I don't want to brag or anything, but I feel like my level of play is more in line with, you know...bigger schools."

"Being in the FCS division does not mean that we can't compete with the big schools," the coach stressed. "What it means is that we play in a different league, with a playoff instead of bowl games. That's about it. Yes, most FCS schools don't make as much money from their athletic programs. We're one of those schools. Most of us do not get the national media exposure that the bowls schools get. You can count us in that category as well. But every school is different.

"At St. Bruno's, you'll find that we place greater importance on your academic life, but that we're also passionate about our football program. And while we do not invest a lot of money into athletics, our teams—especially football—have been quite successful in recent years. We're interested in making a name for ourselves by offering competitive, quality athletic programs that prepare students for life after college, and that's why our recruits choose to play for us. It's not about the fame or the glory of playing in front of a hundred thousand people. Our players come here to get a good education and play for a well-respected football team, however under-the-radar we might be."

Being in the FCS division does not mean that we can't compete with the big schools? He had a hard time believing that. That had to be PR bullshit.

"So what's your offense like?" he asked casually, just to be polite.

"We've run the option for the past couple of years now. Our starting quarterback was an exceptional ball carrier as well as an adept passer, and he's won us a lot of postseason games over the past three years. He recently graduated, so we've got big shoes to fill in that department.

"With you, we would revert back to a more traditional spread, as you've proven yourself very capable in that particular offense as a starter for Keystone State. Our wide receivers are very talented. We as a coaching staff feel like that would be the best choice moving forward, if you were to become a member of our team."

With that, Coach Morgan sat back in his chair, focusing intently on Adam.

"That...yeah, I would like that."

The coach nodded, then took a deep breath. "So, Adam, what do you think? Will you come to St. Bruno's and play for the Beavers?"

Every other coach had asked the same question, and he'd always responded the same way: *"I need some time to think about it and consider my options. Bull I'll get back to you as soon as I make my decision."* His mom had written that down for him, and he'd memorized it after the very first coach had walked out the door. He'd told that one, "I don't know. Maybe," and she had been furious.

But something felt different this time.

He really wasn't sure what made him say it. Maybe it was the heat of the moment, or the presence that Coach Morgan seemed to possess—that calm, composed, no-nonsense attitude.

"OK."

He was almost surprised when the words left his mouth. *Oh shit, what did I just do?*

Coach Morgan allowed himself to break a smile. "Well then, Adam, welcome to the team."

He sat in his chair, partly glad that this whole process was over with but more horrified at what he'd just done. He suddenly realized his expression might give away his feelings, and forced a smile.

"This coffee is delicious, by the way," the coach added, chuckling as he drained his mug. "The university cafeteria could use some lessons from your mother, Adam."

"Oh," he grinned, not knowing what else to say, but thinking that his new coach at least had a sense of humor. "I'll go and get her," he finally added, and his heart skipped a beat as he entered the kitchen.

"I just told him I'd go."

Michelle Dorsey nearly splattered coffee on the counter as she poured some into her own steaming cup. "Oh, honey..."

Before he knew it, his mom had wrapped him in a big hug. It didn't make him feel any better.

"Mrs. Dorsey," Coach Morgan said as he extended his hand in the foyer ten minutes later, "it's a real pleasure to have your son on our team."

"Thank you, thank you," his mom beamed.

"Adam, we're very excited to have you. Thank you for your time and your hospitality," he said as he turned to his new quarterback and offered another firm handshake.

There was no mistaking it—Teddy Morgan definitely had an extra bounce in his step as he prepared to leave. But he wasn't smug. He wasn't about to call up his colleagues and brag that he'd just captured the biggest prize of the offseason when they had failed, Adam was sure of it. For him, it was just another day at the office and another recruiting trip, however high the stakes were. He liked that about his new coach.

"I'll be in touch shortly, and I'll be sending you the necessary paperwork as soon as I return to my office," he added as he slipped on his black raincoat.

"In the meantime, Adam, I would like you to take a look at that packet we sent you earlier. I have already given you my number, so feel free to call if you need anything else."

Adam nodded. "Thanks."

The nervous butterflies were flying away now, and they had been replaced with a whole bag of mixed emotions. What did he feel? Relieved? Excited? Bitter? He didn't want to go to this place, but what choice did he have? It was better to just get it over with. The head coach seemed like a cool enough guy.

Teddy Morgan gave a final wave, placed his Beaver ball cap on his bald head, and turned away from the door and towards the freezing rain. He gazed uncertainly at his car in the darkness far ahead. One foot was already on the wet doorstep when he turned back.

"Mrs. Dorsey?" he asked politely. "Do you think I could get another cup of coffee for the road?"

St. Bruno's Academy
Chapter 7

"Academe, n.: An ancient school where morality and philosophy were taught. Academy, n.: A modern school where football is taught."

--Ambrose Bierce

    It was move-in day at St. Bruno's Academy, and there was a foot of snow on the ground.
    Adam Dorsey drove his 2008 Honda Civic down the highway with the music blasting. His parents' car was ten minutes behind with the rest of his luggage. They had started the drive from Rochester six hours ago, and he couldn't help but mull everything over as he sat at the wheel.
    He had felt pretty good about his decision when he went to bed the night that he'd agreed to come. But now that he was on the road, the doubts had started creeping in. He was going to a Benedictine academy—a *Catholic* school. He envisioned an old nun with a stern expression teaching his class, and slapping a cane around as she yelled at students for smiling too much. Was that where he was going? Not to mention the fact that this was an FCS team he'd be playing for. What an embarrassment.
    St. Bruno's was nestled in the rolling hills on the outskirts of the small town of Waddlesburg in southwestern Pennsylvania. The first thing that Adam noticed was the giant, red brick basilica on top of the hill. It towered over the other buildings with its two bell towers and impressive stained-glass window. The athletic fields and locker rooms were located at the bottom of the hill below the church, but right now the dirt baseball field and white yard-lines were hidden under a thick blanket of snow.
    There was a large parking lot near the entrance road and gatehouse. Hundreds of cars painted a glistening picture as the snow-covered metal colors sparkled in the sun. But that was the only clue that this place was a bustling college with thousands of students.
    He came to a light and a sign near the road that proclaimed: "Welcome to St. Bruno's Academy. Founded in 1846."
    Well, he was here. No turning back now. And so he made the turn onto campus and wound his way through the trees with the basilica flitting in and out of view. By the time he reached the gatehouse, the church loomed over him.

"Moving in?" the grandmother-like lady behind the sliding window asked.

"Yeah."

"Which building are you in?"

He groped around in his glove compartment and found the yellow orientation folder and room assignment that Coach Morgan had mailed to the house.

"Uh...I'm not sure which paper is for my apartment. Hold on a second."

He fumbled through the folder, spilling sheets of paper onto the car floor.

"You *are* living on campus, correct?"

"Yeah. I mean, is there any other option?"

"Well, you said apartment. We don't offer apartments on campus."

"It might not be an apartment, I don't know. That's what I'm used to."

"Well, if you're living on campus, we only offer dorm rooms. Is that what you meant?"

"Yeah, I meant dorm room. Sorry."

"Oh. Well, most of the new students live in Brown Hall. Are you new? I don't recognize you."

"I'm a football player, so wherever the football players stay is where I'm going."

The lady stared curiously. "We don't have special dorms for athletes. Although most of the football players live in Deifer Hall."

"That sounds familiar. I think that's it."

"Oh, Deifer is really very nice. My daughter once roomed there. It's carpeted!"

"Great!" Adam replied sarcastically.

"You know, it's got lots of history to it. It was built in the 1880s—"

"I really just want to get to my dorm room and move in, so can you bypass the history lesson, please?"

The lady's smile dropped. "Well, it's right up the hill on your left. Last one at the end of the road."

"Thanks, lady."

He put the car window up and jolted away from the gatehouse, almost accidentally running over a monk who was crossing the road. The monk looked back at him with concern. Adam avoided eye contact and continued up the street.

Coach Morgan was holding a mandatory team meeting that evening at 4:00. He'd told him it was just standard procedure, and that they always did this at the start of spring semester to go over offseason rules. But he had a nasty feeling that he was going to be at the center of attention. He was kind of dreading it, actually.

"Wow, this dorm room is really nice!" Adam sneered as he hauled his suitcase out of the clunky old elevator and down the hallway. "That lady sure was right. Look at the designs on this carpet! I feel like I'm at an antiques store or something."

"Adam, please lighten up," Michelle Dorsey begged as she followed her son down the creaky hallway with her husband. "If you're going to give this a try, you should do it with a positive attitude."

"But I don't *want* to give it a try, haven't I told you that a hundred times?" he answered as he stuffed his dorm key into the lock and shoved the door open.

His mom just gave a reproachful look.

The room couldn't have been more than 120 square feet. The white walls were cracked and peeling, and there was an old radiator below the window. His "bed" looked like an oversized cot. Oh, and to top things off, he had a roommate, judging from the stuff already in the room.

"This place looks like dog shit," he vented as he plopped down on the mattress.

Tony Dorsey entered the room with the last bit of luggage, sighed, and folded his arms. "Adam, I think it's time for another talk."

Adam groaned, and so did the mattress as it shifted under his weight.

Tony leaned against the small closet door. "I thought you said you wanted this opportunity. But the past two days, you've been acting like you're packing your bags for hell."

"Yeah, this looks like hell to me," he spat as he glanced around the room. "Right about that. I said I wanted a chance to play football again. That doesn't mean I like coming here."

"Adam, what have I told you from the day you started playing quarterback in junior high? Complaining—"

"—is for losers," he finished. "I got that. But sometimes you gotta fight back when other people try and put you down, don't you think so, Dad? My old coach is bringing this on me. Him and his bratty little son. So why should I just sit back and take it? Isn't coming here kind of like acknowledging defeat? Isn't that like admitting he won and I lost? This is what he *wants*, Dad! I'm a competitor. I can't let him do this to me."

Tony paused. "That is true," he admitted. "But on the same token, what are your other options? Staying at home and sulking in your bedroom day after day? That's no way to live your life. And it would be unwise for you to enter the draft this spring, after everything that's happened.

"So what do you do? You fight back, and this is how. Yes, this is what your old coach wants, and maybe he is selfish for wanting that. But it would be even more selfish for you to deny yourself another opportunity to play this wonderful game. You would be admitting that since you can't be the starter for one of the biggest teams in the country, then you can't be a starter at all, because you're too good for that. *That*, right there, is selfish. And if you are successful here, and it leads to a chance at the NFL and a good salary, then who will have the last laugh five years from now? Isn't that the ultimate way of fighting back? Becoming a successful NFL quarterback in spite of your old coach? That's how I want my son to respond, and I know you can do it."

Adam glared at the well-worn carpet. As much as he didn't want to admit it, his dad was making a very good point.

"I still would rather enter the draft."

"But the scouts aren't projecting you to go very high if you do," his father rebutted. "And as you know, the higher you're drafted, the more money you're guaranteed. And I want my son to have the best opportunity to succeed in the pros. Teams are less willing to part ways with high draft picks. If you are drafted in the first round, you'll have every opportunity to prove yourself and perfect your skills. If you're drafted in the sixth or seventh round, that opportunity is far from guaranteed."

"Your father still has regrets about not pursuing the pros," Michelle added matter-of-factly.

Tony nodded. "The chance was there, but I would have probably gone in the last round. I had a degree in finance and a tempting job offer on the table. And so? I took the job and entered the business world, figuring that I would never make it in the big leagues anyway.

"But here I am 30 years later, and I'm still in that same business world, Adam. You have the rest of your life to work in the 'real world' with the rest of us. My advice to you? Don't do what I did. Take the chance and see where it leads. You have a much better shot than I ever did. And I don't want that to go to waste. You need another impressive year or two to really wow the scouts, especially after recent events. Playing your hand with the cards you have now is too much of a gamble."

Adam nodded to himself. "I get what your saying. But it's still tough for me to do this."

"Sure," Tony agreed. "But you did give Coach Morgan your word that you would join the team."

"Yep," he said regretfully.

There was an awkward pause.

"Give it a chance, honey," Michelle pleaded. "You'll never know until you try it."

"Alright," he conceded. "I'll give it a try. I'll stop complaining. Let's just finish unpacking and get this day over with."

Tony checked his wristwatch. "We'd better hurry up. It's past three now, and you've got a meeting to attend at four." He ambled over to the skinny window and peered outside. "It might be a third-class dorm room, Adam, but you sure have a first-class view. You can see the whole campus from up here."

It didn't take long before 603 Deifer Hall looked like Adam's new home. Michelle Dorsey was still sweeping the dust off the floor and Tony was still packing boxes into the closet when the clock hit 3:45.

"You'd better head out," he advised. "We'll finish with the room. Good luck meeting your new teammates."

"Thanks, Dad."

They shook hands, and Adam embraced his mom in a hug. After one last wave, he was out the door and walking back down the old hallway. He pulled the yellow folder from his backpack and found the campus map as he shuffled down the stairs. There it was—a small icon next to the athletic fields told him that the Beaver locker room was located beneath the stadium stands.

He shoved the map back into his backpack, pulled on his gloves and beanie and set off through the snow, wondering how on earth he'd landed in this situation.

The Lodge
Chapter 8

"We have a lot of players in their first year. Some of them are also in their last year."
--Bill Walsh

    Loneliness and despair hit Adam hard as he made his way towards the locker room.
    His dad had made a good argument about why he should stay, and Coach Morgan seemed like a decent guy. But what other reason did he have to be here? What was he doing at a Catholic school like this, with monks and nuns crawling all over the place? There was one right now—an elderly woman in a black habit smiled as she walked past. It just wasn't right. He was sure it was only a matter of time until something catastrophic happened and he lost his mind.
    The Beavers' home field looked like a high school stadium. There was just a single structure on one side of the playing field, with room for maybe 5,000 spectators. The bleachers were built into the side of the hill below the basilica, with a gravel pathway snaking up the crest to the top level and press box. He realized that the fans entered the seats from the top row instead of the bottom.
    Adam walked up the pathway and reached a door near the press box that looked like it led underground. He stopped, took a deep breath and turned the handle.
    As he descended the staircase, a faint babble grew louder and louder. He finally turned a corner at the bottom and took his first look at the Beaver locker room.
    The space was large and bright, although the dirty yellow lockers were a far cry from the fancy wooden ones at Keystone State. The largest part of the room was rectangular with an open space in the middle, while several smaller nooks branched off into a labyrinth of lockers. A white brick wall separated the head coach's office from the rest of the area. The wall was about three feet high and supported a broad glass pane that surveyed the entire room.
    The noise only got worse when Adam turned the corner. Most of the team was already here, and they seemed to know exactly who he was.
    "Hey, it's the new quarterback!"
    "No *shit*, Tonio, who else would it be?"

"Hey, your name's Adam, right?"

"Yeah," Adam replied.

"Well, welcome to The Lodge!" the player called Tonio exclaimed. "Get it? We call our locker room 'The Lodge' because we're beavers?"

"Hey, how accurate are you? Can you hit this kid in the nuts for me? Tonio, stand up so he can try and hit you in the balls—"

"Shut up, Ferrari!"

Somebody was tapping him on the shoulder. Adam turned to see a lanky boy staring back at him. He had dreamy blue eyes, long blonde hair and clothes that didn't match at all.

"Yo, are you Adam Dorsey?" He spoke very slowly, as if he were in some kind of trance.

"Yeah."

"Dude...you're from Keystone State, right? That's like, a *really big school*, dude."

"Yeah."

"That must be *rad*, dude! There must be, like, *ten thousand fans* at the games!"

"Um...yeah, I mean, ten thousand's pretty bad. It's usually closer to a hundred thousand."

"*Whoa*, dude!"

Someone else had slapped him on the back. He whipped around. A player with wavy sand-colored hair and a strong build was smiling at him. A few freckles dotted his playful face and a silver necklace trickled beneath his white t-shirt. Bold blue sunglasses were perched on top of his head—*sunglasses*, on a cloudy winter day.

"What's up, man?! I'm Taylor Griffin. Free safety," he exclaimed. "But everyone on the team calls me 'Playboy.'"

He extended his hand, and Adam shook it half-heartedly.

"So you're from Keystone State, right?"

"Yeah."

"Alright, cool! So...you get a lot of ass up there, right?"

It wasn't a completely unnatural question between teammates, but he had to admit, it was kind of awkward when he'd just met the kid 30 seconds ago.

"Uh, I just broke up with my girlfriend."

"Aw, so you must be an expert at keeping things, you know, *on the down low*," he grinned as he made a lowering motion with his hand. "Come on, man, you must be getting a *ton* of ass up there, knowing how famous you are!"

He took a big gulp from the Gatorade bottle he was holding. Adam got the sense that the kid didn't know the difference between a locker room

Fifteen Minutes

meeting and an apartment party, and he was just making small talk while downing a keg.

"Well, uh, I don't cheat on my girlfriend."

"Nah, of course you don't, of course you don't," Taylor answered, beaming like there was no tomorrow and taking another sip of Gatorade. "So anyway, we're going to a party this weekend if you wanna come. I'm sure everyone would *love* to meet you, man! We're inviting lots of girls! Gonna give them some booze, get 'em a little banged up, know what I mean?" he winked as he nudged Adam with his elbow.

"Uh, sure."

Then something whacked him in the face. It turned out to be a paper airplane.

"Sorry, Adam! Lemme get that for you."

A large player was ambling towards them. He picked up the airplane and offered his hand.

"Z," he said as Adam shook his pudgy fingers. "Well, my real name's Michael Ziegler, but everybody calls me 'Z.'"

"Z plays defensive tackle for us," Taylor jumped in. "Oh, and where'd Max go? He's a wide receiver, so I'm sure you guys will get to know each other! He's crazy, just so you know. We don't call him 'Mad Max' for nothing!"

"Nice," Adam responded. "So, where's my locker?"

"It's right next to mine," Z answered with a friendly smile. "That's why I figured I'd come over and show you. Sorry about the airplane, by the way. That was supposed to hit my buddy Tonio over there."

It was harder to get there than Adam ever could have anticipated. They had to sidestep several plastic bottles, a spilt bag of Cheetos, and an open guitar case that was lying in the middle of the room for some odd reason. As Adam glanced around, he realized the case belonged to a taller player who was striking up some music with his guitar. He stopped playing in mid-chord when another player ran up to him furiously.

"Give me that, Mozart! I'm gonna whack his head with it if he doesn't give me back my Cheetos. *Garfield!* What did you do with my Cheetos?! I know it was you!"

"Yo, you said I could have some!" a gigantic player with curly red hair retorted as he waddled into view. His stomach and belly button bulged below his messy shirt.

"Yeah, but not the whole bag!"

Adam watched as the player who had made the balls comment when he'd arrived now came running into view. "Hey, Massey, I found them! They're over there on the floor!"

"You asshole!" the guy named Massey swore, and he scrambled over to pick up the bag. "Thanks, Ferrari."

His locker was in a far corner, halfway down one of the smaller nooks. Adam turned the handle and opened the squeaky yellow door. Yep, he definitely wasn't at Keystone State anymore. There were no fancy brass nameplates or shoe compartments here. It was just a musty hole, with a few shreds of ripped-off stickers stuck to the brown walls.

"Not the prettiest thing in the world, huh?" Z chuckled as he began rummaging around in his own locker. "But it serves its purpose."

"Guess so."

"What's up, Adam."

He shook off the disgusted look he must have been wearing and turned to see a stocky player. He had buzz-cut brown hair, a golden brown skin tone and short neck. His toned muscles made his maroon t-shirt look two sizes too small.

"I'm Anthony Campbell," he continued as he shook Adam's hand. "I play running back for the team."

"Cool," Adam answered indifferently as he sat down on the wooden bench in front of his new locker.

"I'm your roommate."

He almost blurted a swear word, but caught himself just in time. "Aw...that...that's cool."

The running back just waited patiently.

"I guess I'd rather room with another player than with a random student," Adam added when he realized his roommate was expecting something more.

"You want your own room, don't you?"

"Well, I had my own room at Keystone State, so yeah."

"Oh."

The running back was still waiting politely, and Adam got the feeling that he wasn't turned off by what he'd just said.

"Is your stuff moved in yet?" his roommate added.

"Yeah, we moved everything in already."

"Oh. I was going to offer to help, but that's cool."

He struggled for something to say in return, but just then the back doorway flung open and Coach Morgan came striding into the locker room. He was wearing the same black jacket and ball cap he'd worn to Adam's house, and was carrying a large stack of papers under his arm.

Adam thought he was going to address the team, but—

"Dorsey, follow me."

The coach didn't even look at him as he strode purposefully towards his office door. Adam reluctantly got to his feet and followed him without a glance at the running back.

Coach Morgan held the door open for him. The raucous noise from the locker room became muffled behind the large glass pane as he shut it with a *snap!*

The office was simple. A large black desk was piled with neat stacks of paper and manila folders. An inspirational poster and an academic calendar hung on the wall, and two chairs stood next to the window. That was it.

"Take a seat," Coach Morgan said plainly, and Adam edged himself onto the nearest chair, wondering what this was all about.

"As I've told you, I always hold a team meeting at the beginning of each semester," the coach began as he sat down in his own chair. "Mostly, we go over offseason rules and expectations regarding the players' academic performance. Today, in addition to all of that, I would like you to formally introduce yourself to your teammates."

His heartbeat quickened, and he could feel himself beginning to sweat. Introduce himself? To the entire team?

"We have a picnic for most new recruits in the fall," Coach Morgan continued. "But this is different. You are going to be the quarterback and, hopefully, the leader of this team for the next two years. I'd like you to say a few words before I take over and rehash the fine print of what it means to be a member of this football program."

I have to say it. I have to be honest with him.

He took a deep breath. "Coach, I don't know if this is going to work out."

"And why not?"

Coach Morgan had answered so fast that he had almost interrupted him. And now he was staring at him quizzically.

"I'm going to be honest with you, all right? That locker room's a circus. I can't fit in with these guys. I just know I can't. This isn't where I belong, and I'm never going to be able to lead this team. I'm really sorry, but I don't think this will work out."

There. I said it. Now just tell me how I can get the hell out of here. If my parents hear it from the head coach, then maybe they'll let me leave.

Coach Morgan was slow with his answer. "We've got some unique characters in there, that's true."

He paused and shifted in his seat.

Tell me I shouldn't be here if I don't think I can fit in. Then call my parents up and tell them that you made a mistake in letting me join the team. Do it. Please do it.

"Listen, Adam. Our recruits come from many diverse backgrounds and social statuses. But the one thing they have in common is football—they're all pretty damn good players. We believe in recruiting fairly, recruiting well-rounded athletes who are good students, and recruiting good people who fit our system. That's why this program has been so successful recently. And if you believe you fit into those categories, then I guarantee you that you will fit in here, and you will be respected by your teammates, despite what you may think at first glance. So my question to you is, do you?"

No, that's not fair! Don't put me on the spot like that! Fine, I'll play it your way.

"No, I don't."

Teddy Morgan raised his eyebrows.

"I'm too good to play here. Sorry, but I'm an asshole. I'm not a good person. So I guess I don't fit in here."

The head coach crossed his arms, and he seemed to stare right through him. "You don't think you're a good person?"

"I mean...OK. I don't really believe that. But I want to win, and I want to win big. And I'm not ashamed to say so. That's just my nature, I guess."

Coach Morgan shrugged. "Most of the guys in that room want to win big, too. In fact, the majority of them listed winning as one of the primary reasons why they chose St. Bruno's.

"We make no bones about who we are, Adam. You are here to get an education first and foremost. And directly below that on the priority list is helping this team win championships. We're not national news out here in Waddlesburg, Pa. But we win football games, and we're damn good at it."

He had finished with his response, leaving Adam more desperate than ever. All he wanted was an easy way out, and the man across the desk wouldn't give him one.

"I'm too good to play here."

"Did Coach Thompson tell you to say that?"

The casualness in Teddy Morgan's voice unnerved Adam even more, as if it were too easy for his coach to win the game of words.

"No, of course not. Why would he tell me to say something like that?"

"Because Coach Thompson likes to recruit players who are 'too good' to play anywhere else."

He sighed, sat back in his chair and switched to a more serious tone.

"Adam, Randy Thompson is the kind of coach who will bully his players into doing what *he* wants them to do. You could say we have extremely different coaching styles, and I do not agree with some of the tactics that he implements. Now, I have heard your side of this whole story from my colleagues, and I believe you. That is why I have allowed you to come and play football for us.

"But the fact remains: I will not tolerate players who think they are better than other people or players who put themselves above the rest of the team. If you decide to stay here, you will live in a regular dorm room, with a roommate, like every other person on this team. You will go to all of your classes, report to practices and meetings on time and follow all team rules. You will *not* get into trouble with the police, and you *will* receive good grades in your studies. If you can't do all that, then I don't want you on my team. Do I make myself clear?"

Adam wasn't sure what kind of spell he was under, but Coach Morgan had just given him the out he was looking for, and he couldn't find the courage to follow through with it.

"I...I'm not too good to play here," were the words that left his mouth, and as they did, a deflating sense of defeat overwhelmed him.

"I didn't think you were," the head coach responded. "Although I do understand that this transition will be difficult for you. Which is all the more reason to introduce yourself to your teammates and start this thing off on the right foot."

Adam nodded quietly. There was a silent moment between them.

"Coach?"

"Mm?"

"That one running back, Anthony? I'm roommates with him."

"You are."

"I was just wondering—did you set that up, or was it random?"

A hint of a smile flickered across Teddy Morgan's face. "I did, yes. There was an open room for you in Deifer Hall, and I wanted to move another player over there with you, because it's only fair. Everyone else has a roommate."

He thought that maybe he was going too far, but he had to ask. "So...why him?"

Coach Morgan was again slow with his answer. "As a coach, you have certain feelings and intuitions about things. I thought, as a gut feeling, that he would be a good match for you."

With that, he folded his hands on the desktop and stared intently at Adam, as if to signal that the conversation was over and it was time to go and speak to the team.

"OK, thanks. I, uh, guess I'd better figure out what I'm going to say to these guys then."

"Have any ideas?"

"Not really."

"Usually, when I meet someone for the first time, I tell them a little about myself. 'Hi, I'm Teddy Morgan. I'm the head coach for the St. Bruno Beavers football team in southwestern Pennsylvania.' That sort of thing. With that said, I do not intend for this to be strictly biographical. This is a chance for you to introduce yourself as a teammate and a peer to the individuals in that room."

"I think I got the hang of it," Adam lied.

Coach Morgan nodded encouragingly. "Well then, Adam. Let's get this ball rolling, shall we?" he exclaimed as he clapped his hands and sprung from the seat.

He was back in the messy locker room, with a sinking feeling that he was being led to certain and unavoidable disaster. What the hell was he going to say?

The team went silent as soon as the head coach and quarterback took their place in front of the broad office window.

"As most of you know, we have a new team member with us today," Coach Morgan announced. "This is Adam Dorsey. He was the starting quarterback for the Keystone State Gargoyles the past two seasons, and he brings an enormous amount of experience from the top level of college football. He has proven he's more than capable of not just managing a game, but leading a team to a championship. So before I begin my usual rant, he's going to say a few words. Adam?"

The coach stepped aside and left him standing alone, with dozens of strangers staring back at him quietly. He wanted to just run away, back up the steps and to his dorm room—no, to Keystone State and his good friends Chris, Deion and Joey. *They* could understand him.

"Hi everyone," he stuttered. "I'm Adam Dorsey, like Coach said, and I used to play quarterback for the Gargoyles. Uh..."

He glanced over at Coach Morgan for help, but he just stared back with his hands clasped behind his back, waiting patiently.

"I went 23 – 2 my first two years as a starter," he finally blurted out. "And I passed for 67 touchdowns and just 12 interceptions in that time span. I led our team to the national championship game this past year, but unfortunately, I didn't get to play in it. Uh...I was almost a finalist for the Heisman trophy this year, and I won an award for most outstanding conference freshman last year."

OK, OK...it's going well...just keep it up...

"So, yeah. I think I'm pretty good and everything. Plus, I heard you guys have been really good the past couple of seasons, too, so I think we'll be able to accomplish some really great stuff this year with me at quarterback."

And, that should do it...

"Oh, and I'm excited you guys are going back to the spread offense, because I'm really good at that," he added as an afterthought.

He looked at Coach Morgan, hoping he would get the message that he was finished. The head coach walked back to the front of the room, and Adam sat down at his locker with a sigh of relief.

Teddy Morgan cleared his throat. "Thank you, Adam. And I hope all of you get a chance to introduce yourselves over the next few days.

"Now, about the spring semester. We're scheduled to start practice on March 25, which is almost a full week later than last year. I have already spoken with the academic dean and informed him of my concerns—mainly, the fact that practice will now spill over into the final two weeks of the semester, and I do not like interfering with your studies for final exams..."

Fifteen Minutes

The coach's words blurred together as Adam peered around at the scene. Mozart had leaned his guitar on the bench next to him. The chubby red-haired player Garfield was stuffing down crackers, and Massey had reclaimed his Cheetos bag and tucked it inside his locker. Mad Max was quietly gazing in the opposite direction that everyone else was. Playboy still had his sunglasses atop his head.

Z nudged him in the arm, and Adam realized he was passing along the photocopied sheets that Coach Morgan had brought to the meeting. The paper was pastel green, with a cartoonish-looking beaver logo at the top and "Beaver Football Offseason Rules and Reminders" written in bold letters.

"Ninety percent of you had an excellent fall semester in terms of grades," Coach Morgan finished ten minutes later. "And I hope that continues throughout the spring. Remember, you will not be allowed to attend practices if you are failing any of your classes.

"Alright, men! We've got two long months until spring ball begins. You all have mandatory work-out sessions twice a week, but that is your only team obligation until then. Get a head start on your classwork, study hard, rest your body and don't party too much. Discipline yourself. Remember, the assistant coaches and I want you to have fun and relax during this off period, but we also want you to be responsible. I don't have to remind you all of the consequences if you are not."

With that, the head coach glanced at his watch. "Now, the dining hall opens shortly, and I hope you all take advantage of that. Good luck with your classes, and if anyone needs to see me, my office hours are posted on the handout."

In 30 seconds, the room was back to the previous noise level.

"Going to dinner, Adam?" Z asked.

"Yeah, I think so."

"Well, between you and me, here's a tip: Get there before ol' Garfield does, or he'll finish off all the strawberry pie, and you'll have to settle for peach," he grinned, motioning towards the chubby redhead.

"I'm not much for strawberries, anyway."

"Well, that's good then. Hey, feel free to sit at my table. I usually eat with my girlfriend Lindsey. And Bookworm and this guy over here usually join us," he added with a nod towards the running back Anthony. "See you there!"

"Right. See you in a bit," he said, wondering who the hell Bookworm was.

Adam was slow to get up. He glared at the beaver logo on the green sheet, hardly believing it was all real and this wasn't some dream. By the time he'd gathered his belongings and slammed his locker door, he and Anthony were the only ones left.

"By the way, I didn't tell you my nickname," his roommate said as he zipped his backpack and pulled on his gloves.

"What is it?" he growled.

"They like to call me 'Roadrunner.'"
"Oh."

Anthony shut his locker and sat back down on the bench with his jacket and backpack on. There was silence in the empty room, and Adam was just about to head for the door when he spoke.

"You don't want to be here."

He knew what the running back meant, but purposely answered as if he had misinterpreted the statement.

"Well, if this place is so bad that *you* hate it, then I definitely will."

"No, I mean that *you* don't want to be here. I can tell."

He fidgeted uncomfortably on the spot, turned, and sat back down opposite the running back.

"What do you want?" Adam asked. "If you want to talk to me some more, we're going to have plenty of time for that. We *live* together now."

His roommate just shrugged. "Are you in a hurry to get to dinner?"

"Not really."

"So then what does it matter?"

Adam paused. "OK then, I'll tell you everything you need to know about me, right now. I'm 21 years old, I grew up in Rochester, New York, I'm an only child, I want to be a starting quarterback in the NFL someday, and I just got *fucked* over by my old coach. How's that for a start?"

"OK...tell me something else."

"There isn't anything else. I should be the starting quarterback for the Gargoyles, and instead I'm here. I used to have a girlfriend and now I don't. It sucks. That's my whole life."

"Why should you?" the running back almost interrupted.

"What do you mean, why should I? Why should I what?"

"No, no," he went on, shaking his head. "Why *should* you be the starting quarterback for the Gargoyles? You're not their quarterback anymore. You're our quarterback now. So why are you saying you *should* be with them? I'm just wondering," he added politely.

Adam opened his mouth, closed it, and then stared at the ground. He was drawing a blank. Yeah. What was up with this kid?

"That's my school," he finally insisted. "That's where I'm supposed to be. I want to be there. That's where I belong."

"OK. Well, if you want to be there, then why are you here?"

"I...I don't...I'm here because I have to be," he stuttered. "Not because I want to be. You got that?"

"No, I don't. If I don't want to play here, then I'm not here. We only have players that *want* to be St. Bruno Beavers. If you don't want to play for us, then why aren't you playing somewhere else?"

"I just told you, I can't play for the Gargoyles anymore! I got kicked off the team so our head coach's jackass son could play quarterback. This is the only place that works for me now."

The running back clasped his hands together and stared at the concrete floor. There was a tense moment while he pondered what to say. "OK. I'm going to dinner so see you later."

He got up and headed for the door.

"Roadrunner," Adam called, and he was surprised that he'd subconsciously chosen that name over his roommate's real one. "I'm sorry. I'm pissed off and I'm upset. I'm not trying to be a dick. It's just that I'm a competitor and the stuff that's happened to me over the past month has been really frustrating."

Roadrunner turned around. "That can happen from time to time. But it's just like the cliché. It's 10 percent what happens to you and 90 percent how you respond. I should know."

"You should? Why? What happened?"

"Don't worry about it," the running back shrugged. "Are you coming with me or not?"

"I guess so. I got nobody else to show me how to get there, right?"

Roadrunner grinned. "See, friends are good."

"So you're saying you're my friend now?" he asked as he rose from the bench.

"Do you want me to be?"

"Hell, I don't know. I just met you."

His roommate nodded. "We'll take the long way. That way I can show you around."

And so they shuffled away in their winter gear, out the back doors and down an underground tunnel that opened onto the athletic fields. The January twilight glowed royal blue above the dark clouds, dissolving into a pale yellow and finally a brilliant shade of orange as the last flicker of light followed the sun westward. Adam zipped up his jacket as far as possible as the icy chill of winter and the darkness of night set in. Then the two of them headed off together, tramping across the snow-covered practice fields towards the cozy lights of campus in the distance.

Deifer Hall
Chapter 9

"What you are as a person is far more important than what you are as a basketball player."

--John Wooden

The dining hall at St. Bruno's was by far the best part of campus. The room was so big, Adam figured the monks could probably move all the pews and altar from the nearby basilica and have mass here if they wanted. The high ceiling featured a glass pyramid that displayed the night sky. Below that, an American flag and St. Bruno's flag sporting the school's green and yellow colors hung side-by-side. The red brick walls were so old and dirty, Adam guessed that the glass ceiling and supporting columns were part of a recent renovation.

In addition to the regular dinner line there was a salad bar, pizza oven and smoothie section where students could mix their own drinks. A dessert counter was complete with an ice cream sundae bar (Adam could see slices of strawberry and peach pies).

He'd guessed that Roadrunner wasn't much of a talker back in the locker room, but his roommate had proven him wrong in this new setting. He hadn't shut up since they'd left, talking non-stop about the college, the others players and the coaches.

"So this is the main dining hall for the whole campus," he explained as they walked through the great wooden doors and gave their ID cards to the food service employee. "The football team doesn't have their own place to eat, unlike most of the bigger schools. Me and my friends usually sit at that table over there."

He pointed through the maze of tables and chairs towards a large booth in the back. Z was already sitting there with his girlfriend.

Lindsey Clark was the exact opposite of Z—he was large and heavy, she was short and thin. Her brunette hair was wrapped in a tight bun, and the overall effect with her thick-rimmed glasses gave Adam the impression that she was very smart.

"And *you* must be the new quarterback I've been hearing so much about," she exclaimed as he sat down opposite the two of them with his tray full of food.

"That's me."

"Lindsey," she said, extending her hand. "Z has been telling me all about you."

"What can I say? I was pretty popular before I landed here."

She pursed her lips. "It must be difficult for you, transitioning from such a big school. But you're lucky you've got Roadrunner for a roommate. He's amazing," she smiled as the running back sat down next to Adam.

"Don't mention it," Roadrunner replied as he began stuffing down mashed potatoes.

"Lindsey and I have been together since we were freshmen," Z clarified. "We met in our very first class at St. Bruno's, English 001. My least favorite class of all-time, but at least I got something out of it!"

"And my favorite," Lindsey added with a sly grin. "I'm an English major, Adam. And Z here is supply chain management. Not exactly two peas in a pod, I suppose, but we've been together for three years now so *something* must be going right."

"She does my homework for me," Z chuckled, "that's why I keep her around."

Lindsey playfully slapped him on the shoulder. "I do *not!* I help him with studying whenever I'm not busy with my own work, just because two brains are better than one. I would never *do* his homework for him. That's simply ridiculous."

Adam looked around the dining hall as he bit into his roast beef. Some other players had arrived, including Mad Max, Playboy and Garfield. He recognized several more but had forgotten their names.

"So how many teammates have you met, Adam?" Lindsey queried.

"Pretty much just these two," he answered, motioning towards Roadrunner and Z. "That one Max guy came up to me, and so did sunglass boy over there."

"Oh, yes," explained Z with a knowing smile. "Playboy had a very unique childhood. You see, his parents died in a car crash when he was 12."

"That sucks," Adam said, turning around to get another look at Playboy as the safety grabbed some pizza on the other side of the hall.

"Yeah, it does. Except his parents were rich—like, loaded rich. They left him everything. The mansion, the cars, the estate…it was all his. Of course, at 12 years old, he couldn't legally own anything, so his grandparents moved into the mansion to live with him. But his grandparents weren't a very good replacement for his parents when it came to discipline. They spoiled him even more."

Adam had stopped chewing. "You're kidding?"

"No. And boy, did he make the most of it. Three different cars to drive to school. Crazy parties when his grandparents went on vacation. More hot girls than any high school kid could dream of. I wasn't there because I'm from a different city, but if half of what he's told me is true, then that place was a mad house. He still goes back there on weekends during the offseason. We've been begging him to have us overnight and throw a wild party, but he's still keeping us at bay. One of these days, though...we'll make him cave."

"And that's how we gave him the name Playboy," Lindsey added.

"That's wild," Adam remarked.

"It sucks, too," Roadrunner muttered. "I wouldn't want to be him."

"It's a dream life on one hand, but a nightmare on the other," Z acknowledged. "There's no boundaries to what he can do, but at the same time, he has no parents. He doesn't understand life like you and I do. He doesn't know what it's like to work a part-time job so you can pay the bills, or how it feels to be frustrated with your sex life."

"Or lack thereof," Roadrunner butt in.

"I wouldn't want to be in his shoes, if I had the choice," Lindsey deduced. "It makes you think about how there's a price for everything. But, you take the good with the bad."

Adam began forking down green beans and took another glance around the hall for someone else he had questions about. If he was really going to give this a shot, he wanted to know what he was dealing with.

"What about that Max kid? Playboy told me he's crazy."

Z just chuckled. "That's because he *is* crazy. Or at least we think so."

"Max is a genius, actually," Lindsey piped up. "He was a straight-A student in high school. But his mom insisted that he play sports so he could 'get in with the crowd' and make friends. She was worried about him becoming too isolated."

"Turns out he was really good at catching the football," Z added. "So he played his way to a scholarship with us. But he's such an oddball that he doesn't really socialize with the team. We don't really understand him, and he doesn't understand us. So we've reached this happy medium where he's learned to just be himself, and we've learned to tolerate him and let him do his thing."

"What's his major?" Adam asked.

"Biochemistry," Lindsey responded. "I think he'd be better off using his brains to find a cure for cancer. But first you need to foot the bill for the degree, I suppose. And his scholarship does that."

Adam surveyed the giant hall for more faces. He watched as the fat curly-headed player Garfield grabbed some cookies from the dessert counter.

"I remember him from the locker room," he pointed out. "Hope he puts all that weight to good use blocking for me."

"Garfield's an offensive tackle, and you can guess how he got that nickname," Z explained. "He usually sits with the other linemen. You'll meet them all eventually."

"Right. And that kid over there? He had a guitar at the meeting."

"Mozart," Lindsey answered. "But his real name is Shane Phillips. He plays cornerback."

"Makes sense."

Adam also recognized the heavyset player called Tonio. He looked Hispanic, with an interesting design buzzed into his hair and a stud earring.

"Does that Tonio guy play offense or defense? He looks like a lineman."

"Defense," explained Z. "He's a good friend of mine. He's from Miami, actually."

Lindsey glanced at her wristwatch and zipped her purse. "I have a meeting for the book club at 6:00. See you all later! It was nice meeting you, Adam."

"Yeah, nice to meet you."

She got up and left, leaving him with Roadrunner and Z. Not 30 seconds later, two players arrived at the table, and Adam recognized both. One was the kid who'd argued with Tonio as he'd entered the locker room. He looked Italian, with a round face and boyish features. The other was the player who had lost his Cheetos to Garfield. He had a sturdy build, with long black hair matted to his face.

"Alright, alright, I want to meet this superstar quarterback," the Italian said as he sidled into the booth.

"Well, if it isn't the dream team," Z grinned. "Brian Massey and his little sidekick Tony Ferrari. I thought you guys might show up about now."

"What do you mean?" Massey grunted.

"What I mean is that *you*," Z emphasized as he pointed his spoon at Massey, "always show up whenever *she* leaves," he finished, motioning towards the doors. "And whenever she *is* here, you're nowhere to be found. Coincidence, I guess?"

"Yeah, that must be it," Massey grumbled as he stared at his plate. "Coincidence."

"Adam, this is Brian Massey," Z went on. "He's a wide-out, so I'm sure you guys will get to know each other. And this is Ferrari. He's our field goal kicker."

"'Sup," Ferrari responded. "I gotta say, I loved your little speech back there in the locker room. Seems like you got a lot of bling on ya!"

"Yeah," Massey drawled. "Coach said you were going to introduce yourself or something, and then you just stood up there and told us a bunch of stupid statistics."

It felt like getting slapped in the face. The little bit of confidence that he had immediately evaporated.

There was an awkward silence at the table until Ferrari spoke.

"So when are we taking the newbie down to the crypt for his initiation ceremony? If he's gonna lead us to the championship, he's gotta see what we're all about." His voice was fast and choppy with a New York-style accent.

Z just laughed. "I don't think Adam's interested in that sort of thing."

Ferrari stared. "You serious? You made *me* go down there when I was a freshman!"

"He's not a freshman," Z countered simply.

"Yeah, but it's still his first semester with the team—"

"Just drop it, Ferrari."

"Where's the crypt?" Adam asked.

"Well, St. Bruno's is haunted," Z explained matter-of-factly. "This place was built by monks in the 1800s, and so it's got lots of history to it. You have to know the story to understand what we're talking about. Roadrunner's been down there before, he can tell you all about it."

Roadrunner looked less than enthusiastic. "Not my type of adventure. But go on."

"Anyway, St. Bruno's was founded in 1846 with the basilica as its centerpiece. And old Archabbot Wagner always wanted to be buried beneath it, like so many other monks who worked on the church and the surrounding buildings. But they ran out of room in the crypt before he died, so they settled for a nice mausoleum up in the cemetery instead."

"But apparently Wagner wasn't happy with it," Roadrunner interjected.

"Because now he rises from the grave every year on the day he died, and his ghost walks through campus as he makes his way to the crypt."

"And he passes through every red door at the school," continued Roadrunner. "Because the doors guarding the crypt are red, and supposedly it symbolizes how badly he wanted to be buried beneath the church with the other monks."

"Red doors are haunted—remember that," Z added.

"How many are at this place?" Adam queried.

"Not many. But I would stay away from them if I were you. You don't want to end up like those kids in the 70s. Some students back then thought it would be fun to sneak into the basilica and pry open the doors to the crypt. Bad idea. Two of the guys came to their senses and left, but as they were running back up the steps, they heard screams and saw a flash of light behind them. Then they blacked out. When they woke up, all of them were lying on the grass in the cemetery the next morning, beaten up and bloody."

"He's not lying," Massey insisted. "My dad's friends with one of those guys. He told him it was the worst experience of his life, and now I have to put up with all his warnings not to go down there."

"The running joke around here is, 'Don't offend the monks, living *or* dead,'" Ferrari commented as he munched on a cookie. "Personally I don't believe in all this hocus pocus, but that's me."

"Now, we usually take freshmen players down there and try to spook them out," Z clarified. "That's what Ferrari's talking about. But we're not making you do that—"

"Yes we are," the kicker interrupted.

"*No*, we're not," Z argued. "Adam, if anyone gives you trouble about going down there, just come straight to me. I'll settle things for you."

"Thanks," Adam replied, grinning to himself now that he knew a big defensive lineman had his back.

Ferrari looked disappointed. "I gotta go," he said suddenly, and he picked up his tray and headed off.

"Jeez, somebody's in a bad mood," Z said gleefully as he licked the ice cream off the back of his spoon.

Roadrunner nudged Adam in the side. "He's always like that," he uttered with a nod towards the kicker.

"Gotcha."

"Be right back," Roadrunner added, and he got up for the ice cream bar.

"Hey, I actually have to get going too," Z announced. "Got some errands to run. Adam?"

He extended his chubby hand, and Adam shook it yet again.

"Nice having dinner with ya. I'm real excited to have you on our team. I think you'll end up liking it here, even if you're a little uncertain at first. I was the same way. Oh, and don't worry too much about the ghosts," he added with a chuckle.

"Alright, see you later."

He left, leaving only Adam and Massey at the table.

Massey was quiet at first as he chewed on his last slice of pizza. "Got any more statistics for me?" he asked after a while.

"Why? Do you think I should have said something different?" Adam replied uneasily.

The wide receiver popped the last bit of crust into his mouth and paused. "You want to know what I think? I think you're a jackass."

With that, he rose from his chair and headed for the exit.

Adam felt like he'd been punched in the stomach this time. He just stared at his empty plate, lost in thought, and hardly noticed when Roadrunner sat back down with a cup full of strawberry ice cream.

* * *

"It sucks," he vented ten minutes later as the two of them left the booth. "Why does he have to rub that in my face the first time we meet?"

"That's why it's tough to be a quarterback. You're put in a position where, if people don't trust you, it's almost impossible to play your best. Here, want to grab a smoothie? You can get them for take-out."

They dumped their trays on the conveyor belt, and Roadrunner led him to the smoothie station, where large blenders and bowls of fruit filled the countertop. The running back opened a freezer and began scooping yogurt into one of the mixers.

"How do you know all this stuff about quarterbacking? Did you play that in high school?"

"No, but it's common sense," Roadrunner replied as he picked a few strawberries from the bowl. "You want some of this?"

"I guess. What flavor you making?"

"Strawberry banana—it's tasty stuff. Hey, can you grab me one of those bananas?"

Adam plucked a ripe one from the rack and handed it to Roadrunner. "I knew these guys were going to hate me. I tried to get out of this in Coach Morgan's office, but he made it pretty hard."

"Nobody here hates you," his roommate insisted. "I don't hate you, do I? Z doesn't hate you. Brian Massey doesn't even hate you. He takes a while to warm up to anyone, trust me!"

He pressed a button on the blender, and the smoothie mix whizzed together.

"I can't play for this team," Adam said desperately.

"What?!" Roadrunner cried over the buzz of the machine.

"I can't play for this team! I can't work with these guys!"

"You can do it! It's just a matter of how much you really want to!"

The buzz slowed to a stop, and Roadrunner tossed the cap off the blender.

"What do you mean, it's a matter of how much I want to?"

"You're Adam Dorsey," he said fiercely as he slammed two Styrofoam cups onto the counter and poured the mixture. "You can play for any college football team in the country. You have the talent. You have the brawn. So it all comes down to your effort and your desire to be successful. It's up to you."

He sloshed the last bit of smoothie into the cups and crammed the empty pitcher onto the blender.

"I can't just change my personality," he confessed.

"No," Roadrunner agreed as he handed him a cup. "But you can change your attitude, and that's way different."

Adam sipped the smoothie with a straw—it was really good, and he had to give the guy credit for making the day bearable. He followed him out of the dining hall and into the winding corridors of campus. Roadrunner went back to being his unofficial tour guide as they passed the post office, library and student resource center. He learned they could reach Deifer Hall without even going outside, since most of the old buildings at the heart of campus were connected.

"If it's warm out I'll go through the lawn," he explained, "but since it's snowy we'll take the inside route."

"Is Z as nice as he seems?" Adam asked as their footsteps echoed down a dimly-lit passageway.

"He's a nice guy, yeah. Kind of annoying once you really get to know him. But he comes from a hard-working family. His parents are pretty strict when it comes to following the rules and keeping your head down. And he had to work through some serious injuries in high school, which almost cost him his scholarship. So he knows what it's like to earn your way."

"What about those ghost stories? Are they true?"

"He's not a liar," Roadrunner said as they entered a vast hallway with creaky wooden floorboards. "As far as I know, they're true. But there is one other story you should know about…"

His voice trailed off, and Adam gulped.

"It has to do with our building, doesn't it?"

"Yeah."

They reached a landing and a staircase shaft. Adam could see the contrast between the modern stairwell addition and the centuries-old dorm building because of the ancient brick wall on one side. Roadrunner led the way up, and they climbed past door after door on their way to the sixth floor.

"A long time ago, the seventh floor housed freshmen girls," he began. "One particular student worshipped the devil and practiced dark arts in her room. Well, one day she tried to perform a satanic ritual by lighting dozens of candles and placing them along the floor. Some people say she accidentally knocked them over, and some say that the demon she summoned started it, but either way a fire broke out."

Adam thought he could tell where the story was going, and he felt a prickly feeling on the back of his neck. "Did she die?"

"We think. They got everybody out of the building except her. But here's the scary part: When the fire department arrived, they couldn't find any sign of her body. The only clue was a double-circle pentagram traced onto the wooden floorboards of her room with the remaining ashes."

"Creepy."

"The fire destroyed the whole floor, so today it's just used for storage. But every now and then, students on our floor will hear sounds coming from upstairs—really weird sounds. They always send two student advisors to check things out; one goes up this staircase and the other goes up the opposite end. They unlock the doors and walk in at the same time, so that no one can possibly escape without being caught. But they never find anything. It's empty every time."

Adam felt like something heavy had just dropped in his stomach. Was he nervous? If he was, the sight before them wasn't helping. They had passed the sixth floor and reached the seventh floor landing, and Roadrunner stopped with him to stare at the blood-red door.

"Like you saw on the way up, every other one is painted orange," he said quietly. "You can look through the window if you want."

"That's alright," Adam replied, almost shivering. "I don't think I want to."

* * *

Adam breathed a sigh of relief as they entered the sixth floor minutes later. He didn't want Roadrunner to know that he'd been freaked out by the ghost stories. He wasn't scared of 300-pound linemen, so why should he be scared of a red door?

They walked down the hallway and glanced into the rooms as they passed. Four guys were huddled on the floor around a deck of cards in one, and music was blasting from a stereo in another.

"Most of the guys up here are pretty cool," Roadrunner commented. "We're the only football players on this floor, so we'll get to see different faces at night."

They entered their own room, and Adam collapsed on the tiny bed.

"What's your major, by the way?"

"Kinesiology," replied Roadrunner as he sat down in the heavy wooden desk chair and flipped on his lamp. "I want to be a coach eventually."

Adam surveyed his roommate's half of the room and realized that Roadrunner didn't have much. A dark green comforter and striped pillows covered his bed, his schoolbag sat on the floor, and a poster of his favorite NFL team decorated the wall. That was about it.

Roadrunner turned on his laptop, and Adam noticed that his desktop background was the team photo from last year. The Beavers were sitting on the bleachers above The Lodge, squinting and smiling in the hot August sun.

"So…do you have a girlfriend?"

"Nope," the running back said casually as he sifted through his e-mail. "I had a girlfriend in high school, but that didn't last too long."

"So you've been single for most of your life? You seem like you should have girls hanging all over you."

Roadrunner turned and smiled amusingly. "You would think. But you don't get girls just because you're a football player. I know people think it must be easy for us, but there's more to it than that."

"But you seem like you've got the perfect personality for picking up girls," Adam pointed out.

"Nobody's perfect," Roadrunner warned. "And that includes me."

He went back to checking his e-mail, leaving Adam lost in thought. He'd only known him for a day, but he sensed there was something very unique and mysterious about his roommate. In many ways, he was the exact opposite of him. He wasn't cocky. He didn't demand. He didn't seem to take things for granted. And that amazed him, because he'd always forced things in his own life.

He'd always planned on being the starting quarterback for his high school team, and after that the quarterback for a really good college team. And now that he was facing the first major bump in his life's road, he didn't know how to react. Everything had been thrown off course, and maybe that's why he was so pissed. Not because things weren't fair, but because things weren't how they were *supposed* to be, and how they were *planned* to be. He'd gotten everything he'd ever wanted before now. And now Roadrunner seemed to be asking him to accept whatever came his way, as if all his hopes and dreams didn't matter. Well, of course they mattered…right?

"Where are you from?"

"Maryland. Near Hagerstown, if you know where that is."

"Not really," Adam chuckled. "But I know where Maryland is. So why did you decide to come here?"

"You always want to go where you fit in best," he answered as he typed an e-mail. "St. Bruno's is a great school. The team camaraderie is really cool, and it's only about three hours from home. Plus Coach Morgan offered me a full scholarship, which is really saying something because I didn't exactly prove my worth in high school."

"You didn't? How so?"

Roadrunner shook his head. "It's nothing. I mean, I was good on the field, but when it came to other things…maybe I was a little lacking."

"A little lacking? How so?"

"Just forget about it."

"Oh. Can I ask what your family's like?"

"It's just my mom and my little sister at home. My dad left us."

"Sorry to hear that."

"Yeah. She was pretty much forced into marriage because of me. It wasn't a healthy relationship. My dad didn't want anything to do with being a father or raising a family. It was actually better for us that he left. But by that time we had my sister, and my mom raised both of us by herself."

He said this all matter-of-factly, as if he didn't have any emotional ties to the situation.

Adam laid back on his pillow and stared at the cracks in the ceiling.

"What's your sister's name?"

"Claire."

"That's a pretty name. So she's in high school now?"

Roadrunner nodded. "She's six years younger than me. So, she's in eighth grade."

"Gotcha. Did you red-shirt last year?"

"No. So going into next season, I'll be a junior eligibility-wise."

"Oh. We're the same class then, 'cause I red-shirted. We both have two years left."

There wasn't much else going on that night. Adam unpacked his own laptop, chatted online with Chris and Deion (which lightened his mood just a bit) and took a shower in the old green-and-white-tiled bathroom up the hall. Roadrunner helped him out with everything—how to set up the wireless internet, how to create his school account name and password, and where to access his class schedule. He even tipped him off about the broken shower stall—the far left one wasn't giving any hot water (and Adam wasn't surprised in the least, considering the age of the place).

Two hours later, as he got into bed and pulled the sheets tight, he felt as though he'd known Anthony Campbell for years instead of one day. And as he lay there with the heat from the ancient steel radiator flowing over his face and snowflakes falling outside the skinny window, he decided he couldn't sleep without admitting something first.

"Hey, Roadrunner?"

"Huh?"

"You know I didn't really mean that? What I said when you first came up to me in the locker room?"

The sheets on Roadrunner's bed rustled. "What was that?"

"I said I wanted my own room. I don't want you to think that. I don't mind being your roommate. I really don't."

Roadrunner didn't say anything, and so Adam left it at that.

He couldn't see the running back's face as he glanced across the dark room. But as he rolled over and closed his eyes, he got the strange sense that his roommate was smiling.

Roster Revelations
Chapter 10

"You guys line up alphabetically by height."

--Bill Peterson

    Adam's first week at St. Bruno's could be described as nothing short of an adventure.

    The weather stayed snowy throughout January, and he quickly learned that some classrooms were colder than others. The draft in his Spanish class was so bad that he kept his winter jacket and beanie on the entire time. That room was a monstrous space on the top floor of the largest building, with high windows and holes in the roof. His management class, on the other hand, was tucked in a small cozy room underground.

    He took Roadrunner's advice and navigated the interconnected buildings whenever possible, but sometimes he couldn't avoid going outside. On the second day of classes, he got hit in the back with a snowball on his way to a distant building. He turned and recognized the person from the locker room. Linebacker Justin Brown was grinning at him, and Adam realized why most of the guys called him 'Bulldog.' He had a big flat nose, droopy chin and dark freckles that reminded him of a dog.

    He and Roadrunner would explore the campus during breaks between meals and classes. They usually met up for lunch in the dining hall and then went to a different place every day. One time they trekked through the snowy grounds to the cemetery on the hill. Another day they went walking around the Jordan Complex, which housed the basketball court and student lounge. On the first Friday, Roadrunner took him to see the basilica.

    Adam immediately felt as though he'd entered a different, more sacred world after they pulled open the high oak doors and squeezed through. They were the only ones around, and he felt a strange otherworldly presence about the place as they ventured down the main aisle. The floor was pattered with marble mosaics, and impressive chandeliers hung from the ceiling like gold spiders descending on a thread.

    "This place is so big," he whispered in awe as they walked around the altar. "I've never seen a church like this before."

    "They renovated it a few years back. It's definitely something to see. That's why I had to bring you up here."

"What's back there?" he asked, pointing towards a wooden door hidden in the shadows.

"That leads downstairs," Roadrunner whispered, as if he didn't want to disturb the spiritual presence about the place, "to the crypt."

The basilica was definitely the most dramatic place they visited on their mini-adventures, but there were others Adam grew fond of as the weeks went by. The student lounge in the Jordan Complex sported a shiny hardwood floor and black leather chairs. Two large TVs stood at either end, and he made a habit of sinking down in a cushiony seat and watching SportsNetwork during the free moments between classes...just in case. But all the drama surrounding his sudden departure from Keystone State had subsided. The hot topics now were the Super Bowl, the NBA and the occasional early offseason move of some NFL team.

Another place he loved was the snack bar at the opposite corner of the complex. He and Roadrunner would meet there from time to time and discuss football, or Adam's old girlfriend, or even a campus ghost story. His roommate had loads of them, and he soon learned that St. Bruno's was one of the most haunted colleges in America.

Meanwhile, the monks proved to be quite friendly. Adam met several brothers and quite a few fathers during that first week, and Roadrunner even introduced him to a distant relative monk they met while exploring a remote part of campus (his roommate had said he had no idea where they were going, which was a first). While trying to find their way back, they came across a red door at the end of a dark hallway. They slowly approached it after exchanging glances, but it was locked. Adam secretly breathed a sign of relief, and they hurried back the way they'd come. Roadrunner later claimed that every red door was locked, and you needed a special key that only high-ranking administration and church clergy possessed.

One other interesting fact that Adam learned—it wasn't quite a ghost story but was just as intriguing—was that a secret underground tunnel network existed below the campus.

"It's over three miles long if you add them all up," Roadrunner explained over dinner one night. "I've never been down there, and I don't think anyone else on the team has been either."

"That's pretty cool. What were they built for?"

"Well, legend has it that the monks built them to transport supplies from the lake and quarry, back when they constructed the academy. But during Prohibition they used them to secretly transport alcohol. They've just been rotting away for decades now; I don't think anybody goes down there anymore."

"Do you think they're haunted?"

"I can't think of any stories. But you never know."

Over the first couple of weeks, Adam had a chance to meet everyone on the team. He learned that Tonio's full name was Antonio Coronado, and that he had a sun-shaped tattoo on his back. Tonio would occasionally pepper Spanish terms into his dialogue, but Adam still understood everything and it was even kind of funny.

Jermaine Thomas was the team's premier tight end. He was even bigger than Tonio but hardly said a word. He would just smile at Adam whenever they bumped into each other, and then go about his own business.

Mozart always had his guitar case slung over his shoulder, and Adam and Roadrunner could even hear him striking chords from the fifth floor at times. He could play anything from 'Hollywood Nights' to 'Glory Days.' One night Adam visited his room, and the cornerback asked what his favorite song was.

"I like lots of stuff. 'Roll Up' by Wiz Khalifa—I really like that song," he added, thinking there was no way in hell a guitar enthusiast would know how to play that.

"Ah!" Mozart exclaimed. "I gotcha right here."

And he began playing a verse from the song, singing the lyrics and stomping his foot with the beat.

Garfield loved cookies, but that wasn't saying much because he loved just about anything that was edible. He sat with the other offensive linemen during meals—Jason Evans, Cody McCormack, Michael Reese and center Travis Graham. Travis' nickname was 'Graham Cracker' (apparently stemming from an incident when he was little) and Michael Reese was called 'Bigfoot' because he was so hairy.

About a week into his St. Bruno's experience, Adam knew one thing for sure—he wasn't going to get any serious pressure for the starting job. Redshirt freshman quarterback Derek Bell was a talented dual-threat guy from Virginia and the only other scholarship signal-caller. He possessed great speed and a promising skill set, but lacked any college experience and needed some training in the weight room. The biggest advantage he had over Adam was simply his knowledge of the playbook and experience with the wide-outs. Mad Max and Brian Massey were their top targets, and each had exceeded 1,000 receiving yards the previous season. But there was one receiver that he didn't meet until his second week on campus.

He was sitting alone at lunch that second Tuesday, because Roadrunner was in a meeting with his professor. A small kid with big glasses appeared, and Adam recognized him from the locker room but didn't know his name.

"Adam! I don't think we've met. I'm sorry, but I was elected president of the book club this semester and have had my hands full all week," he apologized. He had short black hair and facial features that reminded Adam of a mouse. He could hardly believe he was a player.

"I'm Book—well, I'm Trevor Hart. But everybody calls me 'Bookworm.'"

"Nice to meet you," he replied as they shook hands.

"I'm a wide receiver," Trevor explained as he set his tray down. "I really am excited to play with you. I've been following everything that happened to you at Keystone State. You should have won the Heisman, in my opinion. I can't believe you're playing for *us* now!"

"Thanks."

"Oh, and I love books. That's where I get my name from."

"Yeah, I figured."

"My dad's the head librarian in my hometown, and we even have a small library in our house. So naturally I've been reading books since I was little, and his passion for literature just rubbed off on me. Some people say I'm even worse than my dad," he grinned as he pulled several novels from his backpack. "These are all the books I'm reading now. *Moby Dick*—I've been wanting to read this one forever, but it's just so darn long. And I've got *Treasure Island* in my locker. One of my goals is to publish a book, but that's probably a long way off. I've got some ideas but haven't written any quality material."

"Cool. Just as long as you can catch the football."

"Oh, don't worry about that! I might be a book nerd, but I can catch. Just ask Roadrunner—he and I played on the same high school team. He'll vouch for me," Bookworm chuckled.

"You guys went to the same high school? He's my roommate."

"I know. He and I have been best friends since junior high."

"Really? Is that why you guys both chose this place?"

"No," Bookworm laughed. "But Teddy Bear—which is our nickname for Coach Morgan, by the way—recruited both of us. And I fell in love with this place after visiting the campus. Roadrunner coming here was kind of a bonus for me."

Adam stared into his soup bowl and stirred the broth quietly. He thought back to his conversations with Roadrunner, and his heart jumped with excitement as an idea struck him.

"What was he like?" he blurted.

"Roadrunner? You mean in high school?"

"Yeah. Was he always this humble?"

Bookworm sat back in his chair thoughtfully. "I wouldn't use that word to describe Roadrunner. But he had some good traits. He was really smart growing up. He could finish his homework in 10 minutes while the rest of us needed half an hour. And he was polite with the teachers and coaches, though that was mostly to get them on his side.

"However, he did have some flaws. He was very passionate about sports—maybe too passionate. He was determined to get his way, and if he didn't he would make people pay."

"How so?"

"Well," Bookworm replied, pausing to think, "he got into an argument with our basketball coach in junior high because he wanted more playing time. He thought he deserved it because he was better than everyone else, and truthfully, he was. But at that level it's not as competitive, and our coach wanted to play as many guys as possible."

"So what happened?"

"He quit."

Adam raised his eyebrows. "He quit just because of that?"

"Yeah, because he knew if he did, me and his other buddies would be upset, and we wouldn't have as much fun playing. And we didn't. As for our coach, he lost his best player. Basically he took his frustration out on all of us."

"And he thought that was worth it?"

"Yes, because he knew he was better than everyone else and that was his only leverage. He was greedy—I'll be honest about that. He was selfish. And that's just one example. Things really came to a head in high school."

Adam had never been so interested in someone else's past. "I thought he was hiding something from me. What happened there?"

"Well, you have to understand his home life first—"

"His dad left. He told me," Adam interrupted.

"Right. And so his mom worked two jobs to pay the bills. His sister Claire was very young at the time, and she needed someone to take care of her. Guess who the obvious choice was there?"

"Her older brother."

"Naturally. And with Roadrunner practicing football after school, he wouldn't get home until six or seven at night. His mom worked late, so that left Claire fending for herself. And when he *did* get home he had to make dinner, help her study, pack her lunch...all the stuff a mom usually does. And guess what happens when he's busy doing that?"

"He doesn't do his own schoolwork," he figured.

"Correct. And guess what that leads to?"

"Bad grades."

Adam left to get dessert, and he was so lost in thought that he didn't realize he'd selected his least favorite pie flavor. But Bookworm was just warming up.

"So he's failing his classes, but he knows he can get a scholarship for playing football. Did he even care about grades at that point?" Adam pressed on.

"I think he cared, because deep down he wants to succeed at everything," Bookworm surmised. "And some coaches look at grades just as much as talent, like Teddy Bear. But this created a huge rift with his mom. She wanted him to spend less time practicing sports, and come to an agreement with our coach. But Roadrunner would have none of that. And he had a good argument, because he knew that if he excelled at football he could earn a scholarship and a free ride in college. But you don't excel and get noticed by recruiters without lots of practice. His whole mentality was, *'This is going to pay off. I'm going to show her it was worth it.'"*

"It obviously was," Adam stated as he tasted the pie and winced. "Ugh...I hate strawberries."

"Not at first, because our coach kicked him off the team."

Adam nearly choked.

"He said he didn't think Roadrunner had the right attitude, and used his failing grades as justification."

"But did he know everything that was going on?"

"Oh, he knew, alright. And he didn't want to get caught in the middle between Roadrunner and his mom. So he took a side."

"That's...wow," was all Adam could think to say.

"Our coach was a good guy. He gave him chances before kicking him off, but Roadrunner refused to take the bait. And after that season ended, he let him back on the team—but he wasn't the same. It's amazing what one fall without football did to him. He never had another argument after that, and on the other side, his mom loosened her demands after seeing how unhappy that experience made him.

"That whole dismissal from the team was something that had to happen, I think. It cleared the air. The tension between Roadrunner, his mom and our coach just evaporated after that. And Roadrunner ran for consecutive 2,000-yard seasons his junior and senior years. That was when Teddy Bear came calling, and you know the rest of the story."

Plenty of thoughts raced through Adam's mind, but the one overriding thing was that Roadrunner had been kicked off his team in high school. He, Adam Dorsey, had been kicked off his team. Is that why Coach Morgan had put them together? And why didn't Roadrunner tell him this, when it was obvious that he needed help getting through the same situation?

"He doesn't like to talk about it," Bookworm acknowledged. "He doesn't like the person he used to be, and so he pretends it never happened."

"I gotta get to class," Adam said as he zipped his backpack. "But thanks for the story, Bookworm."

The wide receiver grinned. "Hey, I'm a reader and a writer. Stories are what I do."

"You know it. See ya later."

He dropped his tray on the conveyor belt and headed to class, wondering if he liked Roadrunner more or less. He was not as perfect as he appeared, but on the other hand, he had been through a lot.

A sense of loneliness consumed him the rest of the day, and maybe it stemmed from realizing that the person who wanted him to discover himself was also the person who was withholding the most. He had trusted

Roadrunner more than any other player. And he'd thought that was worth something—he'd thought he had a real friend. But did Roadrunner trust him back?

He didn't know anymore. And with that thought came the realization that he was still an outcast here. These guys were not Chris and Deion, or his trusty center Joey. They were Mad Max and Bookworm and Z. A hell of a lot different.

You gotta try, he told himself as he hiked back from class. *You gotta try, and just see what happens.*

Man, he couldn't wait until spring ball.

The Yellow Slip
Chapter 11

"Some people try to find things in this game that don't exist but football is only two things – blocking and tackling."

--Vince Lombardi

Practice hung over Adam like a cloud that morning.

It was March 25, and he hadn't felt this nervous in a long time. That afternoon he would walk over to The Lodge, put on his shorts and pads, and participate in a Beaver drill for the first time. His professor had been lecturing the whole class, but none of it had sunk in—he was thinking about practice, his new teammates and what it would feel like to run an offense with them.

"Eat something," Roadrunner suggested as they sat at lunch.

"I'm not hungry."

"I always fill up before practice. You'll regret it later if you don't. Practice is long."

"I'm just not hungry."

"How do you feel?"

"Nervous," he said without thinking twice.

"Why?"

"I can't really tell why. I guess it's just the new experience, you know?"

Roadrunner stuffed down the rest of his hamburger and got up for his usual bowl of ice cream. "Well the only way you can fix that is to actually experience it. So this is great!"

The snow hadn't started to clear until mid-March. But now that they were nearing a week of constant sunshine, the five-foot piles of snow had melted into small islands scattered across the grassy spaces like the tips of icebergs. Spring had come, and brought with it the warmest day yet—by 2 p.m. the temperature reached into the 60s.

A gentle breeze swept across Adam's face as he and Roadrunner walked along the gravel pathway to the locker room. He could even smell the first hint of spring in the air—a refreshing blend of wet soil and grass.

Déjà vu hit him as they descended the underground staircase; the uneasiness and doubt he had felt on that first day came rushing back. But he had Roadrunner with him, and he knew his teammates now.

He opened his squeaky locker and stared inside. His practice shell was ready alongside his green athletic shorts and white practice jersey. This was going to feel very awkward at first...

Where were his cleats? Coach Morgan had told him everything would be ready for the first practice. He checked under the bench—nothing.

"What's wrong, Adam?"

Z had appeared at his own locker.

"My cleats. They're not here. I need cleats for practice, otherwise I gotta run back to my room and get my old ones."

"Oh. We actually haven't got the shipment yet. Old Teddy Bear was telling me about it yesterday."

"Well I'm gonna have to run back then. Tell Coach where I'm going—"

"No, we'll find you a pair!" Z insisted. "All us veterans have got lots of old pairs. My shoe size will be too big, but we can find somebody that fits you...*hey, Playboy!* You got any extra cleats for Adam?"

"Sure man!" Taylor Griffin exclaimed from across the room. "I think I got some under my mags."

Adam made his way to Playboy's locker, and his mouth dropped. He'd glued magazine pictures to every inside wall, and they all showed naked (or bikini-topped) girls lying on couches or white beaches. There wasn't a single empty space left.

"That's...interesting."

"What? Oh, you like my locker?" he chuckled as he fished through the monstrous pile of magazines. "I can give you some pics if you want to spruce your own up! I've got dozens that I haven't even touched, like these!"

He turned and dumped a stack of *Maxim* issues into Adam's arms.

"Uh, thanks Playboy. But I'm not interested in any."

"No, just hold them while I search for these shoes. They're in chronological order. I don't wanna screw them up."

And he dug deeper, bending over as he threw empty deodorant cans onto the floor.

"You know, if it's too much trouble then don't worry about it."

"No, they're here somewhere. Take these," he added, dumping another foot-tall stack of magazines on top of the ones Adam was already holding.

"How many of these do you have?" he groaned.

"Lots! Probably too many. Here's some more."

Before he could protest, he found himself holding three dozen more issues, and his arms buckled under the weight. The top magazine was now inches from his face, and he couldn't ignore the scantily-clad girl smiling back at him.

Playboy looked puzzled. "Where in the heck? Maybe I threw them out with my old clothes. Don't sweat it, man, we'll get you a pair!"

Adam just answered with another groan.

The safety scanned the locker room and scratched his head. "Here, let me get those for you," he finally said, and began piling the magazines back into his locker, much to Adam's relief.

Someone was tapping him on the back. He turned to see Trevor Hart.

"Hi, Bookworm."

"I heard you need an extra pair of cleats. I've got some, if you want to try them on!"

"I don't think I'm your size, buddy."

"I've got big feet, actually," Bookworm urged. "I'd be glad to help you out, even if it's just for one practice!"

"Yeah, that's perfect!" Playboy added. "You can borrow Bookworm's. Sorry I couldn't help you, Adam, but I can offer you some deodorant if you want."

"I don't need deodorant before practice, but thanks."

"Are you sure? I always spray myself up beforehand, just in case, you know?" he grinned, with an extra wink as Bookworm pulled Adam towards his own locker.

"Yeah, makes sense."

Bookworm's locker was stuffed to the brim like Playboy's, but with books instead of magazines. He had lined most of them along the top shelf so that it resembled a bookcase. Adam spotted *Dracula, Frankenstein, A Tale of Two Cities* and *Treasure Island*—all in alphabetical order.

"Nice library. Do you have a locker in here somewhere, too?"

Bookworm just smiled. "I can't fit them all in my dorm, so I use the extra space here."

He reached behind a pile of worn novels and pulled out the cleats. Despite what he'd said about having big feet, Adam was sure they would be too small.

"Thanks," he said reluctantly.

"No problem. And just let me know if you want to borrow any books!"

"Yep."

He was right—the shoes were too small. He decided to take the laces off to ease the pressure, and consequently was the last one onto the field. A humiliating feeling overwhelmed him as he burst through the back doors and jogged to catch up. His feet hurt already.

Teddy Morgan had ditched his usual black ball cap for a pair of aviator sunglasses, and he held a stopwatch in one hand and a clipboard in the other while he waited at the 50. The whistle around his neck completed the ensemble.

"Who are we missing?" he asked as he swung his stopwatch lanyard in circles.

"Mad Max went off looking for wild blueberries again, because he says they give him an 'energy boost' before practice," Tony Ferrari snorted. "Dumbass."

Coach Morgan jotted something on the clipboard.

"Alright, men. The 2013 season officially starts now. We've got 14 good practices before the spring game, so let's start this party off right. I want two laps around the field. Then we'll go into stretches and individual drills. Let's go!"

And they were off, jogging around the edge of the field and taking their places along the yard lines for stretch. Adam glanced around under the warm sun as the strength coach barked directions, and a bead of sweat trickled down his forehead. He realized there were only two student managers instead of the 12 they had at Keystone State. There also weren't any portable water pumps—maybe that wasn't in the budget either.

"Who's that guy?" he whispered to Derek Bell, nodding towards a younger man sporting a polo and glasses.

"Stephen Hunt," the back-up quarterback answered. "He's our team doctor."

Adam sensed that Hunt was all business as he paced the sidelines, occasionally stopping to chat with players.

"What about him?" he added, pointing towards a buck-toothed man in a ball cap. A toothpick or straw of hay was sticking from his mouth—he couldn't tell which from this distance.

"Oh, that's our quarterbacks coach Bob Harris. He's a hoot."

"Really? Looks like he hasn't showered in his life."

"I don't think he has, actually."

A whistle blew. He tried to hide his discomfort as he jogged to individual drills.

Bob Harris was definitely 'a hoot.' He started calling Adam 'boss'—maybe because he was the most experienced of the three signal-callers. And he made a joke out of everything.

"You gotta play like you want it," he instructed as he critiqued their throwing techniques. "Football's gotta be yer favorite thing in the world. You can't be like me."

"What's your favorite thing?" Adam asked.

"Chugging beer! What else?" he cackled. "Football's second."

Next up were 7-on-7 drills where the quarterbacks and wide receivers went against the linebackers and secondary.

His feet were stinging with pain. All he could think about was getting out of Bookworm's shoes.

Just deal with it. You can survive until the end of practice. Coach Morgan doesn't like complainers. I'm gonna show him what I'm made of.

He was up first.

"Alright, let's go," he snarled as he checked his quarterback wristband.

It's just like Keystone State...just pretend you're back there...piece of cake...

Max barely missed his pass on the first play. Adam cursed under his breath, frustration boiling inside of him. If he could just get a better pair of cleats, he could step into his throws. This was ridiculous.

Two players were whispering behind his back—he knew they were talking about him. He gave a quick peek as he caught the football from Max. It was the wide receiver Massey and the field goal kicker Ferrari.

"Let's roll!" Coach Morgan urged as Adam squinted at his wristband. He was supposed to call the next play in the huddle, but he was really thinking about Massey and Ferrari. Those *idiots*. What were they saying? It wasn't his fault he had to wear these stupid shoes.

Maybe they'd like to try going through practice in super-small cleats. I'd like to see how they handle it.

"Next play, Adam, on to the next play," the head coach stressed. "Don't let it get to you."

"I don't know, Coach. He looks a little *tight*, if you know what I mean," Massey sniggered.

Coach Morgan shot the receiver a quick warning glance as he waited for the offense.

Adam spat out the play call. His new teammates couldn't catch the damn football, and one of the ones who actually could was standing behind him, making jokes with his stupid little friend. He hated those two players just as much as he hated DT.

"OK...hut!"

This time he tried Bookworm, but he didn't see Bulldog until it was too late. The linebacker jumped and intercepted his pass, running it all the way back just for fun as the other receivers gave him disappointed looks. It felt like everyone on the team was staring at him.

The pain in his feet was excruciating. He couldn't even think anymore. Somewhere nearby, Coach Morgan's voice called, "Alright, alright. Next play..."

No. There wasn't going to be a next play.

He pulled off his helmet and flung it at the grass. "That's it. I can't do this. This is absolutely, totally, just...this fucking *sucks*. I quit!"

Now every player and staff member was really staring at him.

Fine. Stare at me. I don't care. I'm leaving.

He stormed off in the direction of the locker room, not bothering to pick up his helmet. Coach Morgan wasn't even looking at him—he was still standing there casually with his stopwatch, his arms crossed. Were his lips curled in a small grin?

"Next man up!" he declared. "Derek, get in there."

His back-up glanced around uneasily, then jogged over to replace him.

That's right, just keep on practicing. You don't need me, and I don't need to be here, so it's all good this way. I'll just leave and nobody will even remember me come September.

He took a quick look back as he neared the doors. Roadrunner was glaring at him, though everyone else had turned their attention to the drill. He would be upset that he was leaving. What did his roommate want to say right now, if anything? What was going through his mind?

A horrible, guilty feeling pulsed through him as he pushed open the doors and dragged himself into the locker room. He kicked an empty snack bag out of the way, sat down and ripped off Bookworm's old shoes. He hurled them in the direction of the wide receiver's locker, and then leaned against his own locker door as the pressure oozed from his feet.

For about five minutes he did absolutely nothing. The Lodge seemed eerily quiet with no one around, but he liked it that way. He wanted to be alone.

Then the thoughts started.

What should I do? I guess I'll start cleaning out my locker. I'll be out of here before they get back, and then I'll clean out my room and head back to Rochester. No more Beaver football. I can forget all about this place in a few hours.

No, you can't do that, another voice said as ideas chased each other in his head. *You can't just pack up and leave. Think about what happened to Roadrunner. You think he's happy that he's still playing football? You've been here for two months and the guys are really getting to know you!*

Oh, fuck it. Who really cares about them anyway? You don't belong here. You gotta get out while you can. 'Cause if you stay, it'll be a whole spring and summer of this bullshit, and then you're stuck as their starter for the next two years. Coming here was a mistake. You gotta leave now.

He lost track of time as he mulled his options, and he still hadn't made up his mind when the back door opened and Derek Bell appeared.

The freshman quarterback glanced at him but didn't say anything. He reached his locker and started fishing for something.

"What are you back here for?" Adam growled.

"I forgot my mouthguard and Coach got mad, so he said I could go back and get it."

Coach said you could go back and get it?

For a brief moment, the idea that Coach Morgan had sent Derek in to try and reason with him crossed Adam's mind. But he shook off that notion almost immediately. If that were true, Derek would be talking to him instead of rummaging around in his own locker. No, the head coach wasn't pushing any buttons here. This was his decision, and his decision alone. He could walk away if he wanted—that option was there. And then he remembered words from what seemed like a long time ago...

"*I'm here because I have to be, not because I want to be...*"

"*We only have players that* want *to be St. Bruno Beavers...*"

Sooner or later, this moment was going to come. He had to choose.

He stared at the concrete floor, suddenly wanting to move, to do something, anything. But what exactly *did* he want? He felt as though he were underwater, and just one step forward would take three times the normal effort. Whatever he did, he might regret it for the rest of his life. And right now, there was no way to tell which choice was the right one...

But he had to choose.

Derek had found his mouthguard and was heading back out.

"So, are you leaving?"

"I don't know what I'm doing, Derek."

"Oh. I thought you'd really want to play them," he said as he rapped his knuckles on a yellow slip of paper taped to the office window.

"What? Who are you talking about?"

"*Them!*" he exclaimed, motioning back towards the window as he neared the door.

His old team crossed his mind for a second, but that was impossible. So who else could it be?

He scrambled to his feet and shuffled across the room, slipping along the floor in his socks. Team notices, special teams charts and motivational posters were taped to the window as a sort of message board. He quickly located the yellow paper that Derek had mentioned and scanned his eyes over the text excitedly.

2013 Beaver Football Schedule

Aug. 31	at Keystone State Gargoyles
Sept. 7	NEW YORK SENECA
Sept. 14	DOVER BULLDOGS
Sept. 21	at Eastern Maryland Crabs
Sept. 28	at Hartford Nutmegs*
Oct. 5	DELAWARE BAY PATRIOTS*
Oct. 12	at North Virginia Colonials*
Oct. 19	WILLIAMSBURG PILGRIMS*
Oct. 26	ALBANY MOUNTAINEERS*
Nov. 9	at Providence Islanders*
Nov. 16	ALTOONA LOCOMOTORS*
Nov. 23	at Fredericksburg Rebels*

* denotes Coastal Valley Conference game

His stomach seemed to jump into his throat, as if he were on a free-fall ride.

"Derek!" he yelled, and the quarterback poked his head back into the room. "Derek, get back in here!"

He could not take his eyes off the text beside August 31st.

"Derek, it says we're playing Keystone State on this schedule," he stated emphatically. "Are you sure that's right?"

"Yeah, man. We're playing your old team!"

"But I didn't think we'd be in their league."

Derek just chuckled. "We always play a powerhouse school on the first weekend. They make money from the ticket sales, we make money from the deal!"

Adam pressed his hand up against the glass for support. He felt lightheaded. There had only been a few times in his life when he'd felt like he was dreaming, and this was definitely one of them.

"Alright, let's go."

"Are you coming back to practice?"

"Yeah, yeah," he uttered as he slid back across the room and scooped up Bookworm's shoes. "Fuck the shoes. I can survive another hour. I'm gonna beat Keystone State."

Derek raised his eyebrows, even though he was smiling. "Oh, alright man. I sure hope we do."

"Kill 'em," he added as he shoved the shoes back on. "I can see it now—50 – 0. That's gonna be the final score. OK, 50 – 7…that's more realistic. I've at least gotta give them a touchdown. They've got like 20 draft picks on that roster!"

He could beat Coach Thompson in his own house. *I can beat that son of a bitch and ruin his whole season. Fantastic!*

He burst out of the tunnel and jogged back to practice with Derek ten steps behind. By the time he reached the sideline, half the team was staring at him. He was sure Coach Morgan had noticed him, but he was busy barking instructions to the active players and wasn't paying any attention.

"Look who's back!" Z exclaimed with a boyish grin as the linemen waited nearby.

"Yeah, I'm back."

"So you were just kidding about quitting?" center Travis Graham asked skeptically.

"Yeah, I was kidding."

"That's good news, Adam!" Z continued. "You sure you didn't check our schedule and then change your mind?"

Adam realized he was joking, ironically.

"He doesn't know about that," Cody McCormack butt in.

"I know he doesn't. That's why I'm messing with him. You *didn't* see our schedule by the way, did you, Adam?"

"No," he lied. "Why, who do we play?"

"It's nothing," chuckled Z. "We just—"

"Don't *tell* him," Travis interrupted. "Coach Morgan doesn't want—"

"I know what Teddy Bear wants, Graham Cracker! That's why I'm saying it's nothing important, Adam," he finished as he turned back to the quarterback.

"We play shitty teams," Jason Evans added.

"They suck," Cody stated.

Adam stood there looking from face to face, and he wondered if they actually believed they were doing a good job of covering it up.

"Oh, alright," he answered, just to play along. "I'm not worried about it."

And they left it at that.

He participated in the conditioning drill to end practice, and not one staff member said anything to him regarding his outburst. In what seemed like an instant, Coach Morgan had called the team together for one last huddle, and practice was over.

Lots of players approached him as they made their way to The Lodge. They all had questions—What made you come back? Are you really staying for good? Were the shoes that bad?

"Not to be rude, but yeah, they really don't fit," he chuckled when Bookworm asked him.

"Sorry. But I'm glad you're here to stay, Adam. I think we can be really successful with you."

"Thanks, Bookworm."

Roadrunner caught up to him as he journeyed to the dining hall half an hour later.

"Why did you come back?"

An intense anger bubbled to the surface of Adam's emotions, and since there were no other players near, he decided to vent his frustration.

"How come you're so eager to get inside my head and know everything about me, when you don't open up yourself?"

"What do you mean?"

"I'm talking about high school, when you got kicked off your team! You think that's something I would have liked to know? I guess I'm not trustworthy enough, is that it? You want to know every little detail about me, even though you don't trust me with your own details? Am I like a guinea pig or something for you to analyze and experiment on? What's your deal, man?"

"That's not true. I trust you—"

"No, you don't! You didn't tell me any of that stuff that Bookworm said!"

They had stopped, and were standing face to face on the pathway above the athletic fields.

"Adam, please stop," Roadrunner begged as he held out his hand defensively. "Listen to me. I didn't tell you about that because I'm ashamed of it. I'll discuss it if you want to, but I really hate bringing it up. I told you I wasn't perfect. That's why I can't stand it—I'm a perfectionist, and what happened back then wasn't perfect at all."

Adam took a deep breath, but Roadrunner wasn't done pleading his case.

"If I didn't trust you, then I wouldn't have told you all that stuff about my dad leaving, right? I wouldn't have told you all about my family."

"I guess that's true. I'm just upset because I feel like you should have told me about getting kicked off the team, since I'm going through the same thing."

"You aren't going through the same thing. What happened to me and what's happening to you now are completely different things. What happened to you wasn't your fault, but what happened to me was entirely mine. That's why I didn't think it would help if I told you about it. You want to question me? Go ahead. I'll answer anything you want."

Adam paused, and the anger subsided. "Bookworm already told me everything, so I don't need you to."

"OK, then what else can I do so you aren't mad at me?"

"I...I'm not mad anymore, I guess," he confessed. "But what Bookworm said frustrated me, because it seems like you want me to completely open up to you."

"That's because I'm trying to help you. I don't want you to make the same mistakes I did."

Adam stared at his shoes, suddenly feeling embarrassed. "I'm sorry, Roadrunner. I need all the help I can get."

"Alright, so we're cool then?"

"Yeah."

They continued up the pathway towards dinner, and he told Roadrunner about seeing the schedule and deciding to stay so he could beat the Gargoyles.

"Just do me a favor and don't tell anyone else that's the reason I came back," he pleaded as they entered the dining hall and grabbed trays.

"I won't. But you can't hide things from your teammates forever."

The energy rush he'd felt back in The Lodge had now morphed into an uncomfortable mix of euphoria, anxiety and doubt. Brand new roadblocks popped up as he thought about preparing to play his old team. True, it was the perfect opportunity. He could beat Coach Thompson and DT, and they would only be able to blame themselves, because it never would have happened without his release from the team. Yet he couldn't gain his new teammates' trust if they all thought he was in it just to beat Keystone State. He would need to be sincere about wanting to play for the Beavers. But was he?

Luke Fetkovich

An old quote his high school coach had often used came back to him now—*"The game has changed, men."* Well, this game had changed for good. He had to stay. The new question was whether or not he could motivate this team to accomplish something nearly impossible. After all, dozens of lower-division schools play powerhouses for money at the beginning of the season. And the smaller school has only won a handful of times in thousands of tries. It was the same old story year after year, and who was he to think they would win?

But that night, Adam went to bed knowing he would remain a St. Bruno Beaver through the fall, and *that* was something refreshingly new.

A Seventh Floor Startle
Chapter 12

"You'll never get ahead of anyone as long as you try to get even with him."
--Lou Holtz

He was running.

Running down a steep spiral staircase in a shadowy stone world. What he was fleeing from, he did not know. But something was chasing him—something sinister, something evil.

The staircase ended and he leapt into a cavernous room. It looked like a dungeon at first glance, with high stone pillars reaching into darkness. An ugly marble slab resembling some ancient altar rose from the center of the room, and the pearly white structure seemed to glow eerily.

Everything would be fine if he could just find what he was looking for. He scanned the room desperately—there it was.

Within seconds he'd traversed the monument-sized hall and was standing before two blood-red doors. They were locked, confirming his worst fear.

"Open up!" he demanded as he rapped his knuckles on the painted wooden surface. There wasn't much time...they were coming for him...

He turned the knob every which way, he pried the edges with his fingertips, but the red doors would not open.

"You can't get in there, Adam," a voice said, and he whipped around to see Z standing there casually.

"I have to," he breathed desperately.

"Adam, you know all the red doors on campus are locked. *Especially* the ones to the crypt. You definitely don't want to go in there."

"I've got to get in there! My life's in there. I have to get it back!"

And he thought of Chris, Deion and Joey back at Keystone State. He thought of the little wide receiver Jaden and the national championship aspirations of his team. He could get it all back if he could just find a way inside.

Time had run out. They were here.

The creatures surrounded him, and pale skeletal hands seized his arms and legs. He clung to the doorknob, praying it would open. And Z just stood there saying the same thing over and over.

"It's locked, Adam...locked forever..."

The creatures overpowered him, and the knob slipped from his sweaty grasp. They were pulling him away from the life he wanted. He had been so close, and why it was locked he could not understand. Why wouldn't it open? It wasn't fair.

The red doors disappeared into darkness as he was dragged away, deeper underground...

Adam's eyes snapped open, and he found himself staring at the wall of his dorm room. His breathing was rapid, and he was covered in sweat. The alarm clock near his bed read 4:18 a.m.

It was a dream. Only a dream.

He laid uncomfortably on his pillow for a moment, knowing that he couldn't fall back asleep in all this sweat. Then he rolled over and squinted through the dark.

The first thing that caught his eye was Roadrunner's empty bed. His roommate was on a weekend trip back to Hagerstown to visit his family, and had said he wouldn't be back until Sunday. He, meanwhile, had spent the evening at one of Playboy's apartment parties (and met a few hot girls). But now that he was alone and uncomfortable in his tiny room, that seemed like days ago.

He was just about to get up and grab some water from the mini-fridge when he heard it.

He stopped moving. He was still in the process of draining the fear from the nightmare and re-acquainting himself with his surroundings, and thought that maybe his mind was playing tricks. So he got up on his elbows and nearly held his breath as he strained to hear anything unusual.

Five seconds...ten seconds...*thump*.

The fear that had been retreating suddenly roared back to the surface, grasping hold of him like an invisible claw. He stared at the blue numbers of his alarm clock and wished that it would stop...

Thump.

It was coming from upstairs. The ghost stories came rushing back, and they seemed to paralyze him even more.

Thump, thump, thump.

Was somebody walking across the creaky floorboards?

He tore his eyes from the clock and glanced upward. For some reason he was afraid of moving too quickly or making too much noise, even though common sense told him there was nothing to be afraid of.

More noises—different ones.

He traced his eyes over the thin crack that snaked along the ceiling, though it was barely visible in the darkness. What was on the other side of that barrier?

Fifteen Minutes

He realized he was more afraid now than he had been during his nightmare.

Thump, thump, thump, thump!

It sounded like a basketball bouncing across the floor. Now it was thumping away...it had crossed the threshold from his dorm room to the adjacent one...it was almost gone...

For a few endless seconds, Adam strained his ears. Then, so faint that it might have come from the depths of his imagination, he heard the pounding of footsteps on concrete.

It's coming down the stairs, he feared, while the sensible part of him told himself he was being ridiculous. It was just some student nosing around or playing a prank. Had to be.

He could hear the footsteps clearly now—they were definitely real.

It's just some idiot student.

The door at the end of the hallway squeaked open, and then shut with a deafening *boom!* like the lock of a jail cell sliding into place. It was walking down the hallway now, getting closer and closer...

What if it wasn't a student? What if it stopped right outside his door and tried to get in?

Stop it. You're being stupid. Why are you thinking these things?

Yet he couldn't keep his heart from pounding faster and faster. He'd started to sweat again.

The footsteps stopped outside his door.

An overwhelming sense of disbelief grasped hold of him. Had he fallen back asleep, and this was some new nightmare? He could feel the thing's presence on the other side of the door.

A key turned in the lock. The door opened and light filled the room. A silhouetted figure appeared, and after a few seconds Adam realized it was...

"Roadrunner?"

His roommate set his keys down and slung his backpack onto the floor. And then he realized it had been Roadrunner's footsteps in the hallway, and that he'd been climbing *up* the stairs instead of down.

"Sorry," the running back grunted. "Did I wake you up?"

"No," Adam half-chuckled, because the question seemed so absurd at the moment. "I thought you weren't coming back until tomorrow."

"Change of plans. Sorry I'm back so late though. I stopped to visit one of my high school buddies on the way out, and we lost track of time."

"Oh. Listen Roadrunner, I, uh...I'm glad you're back."

"Yeah, well you better be. I'm you're roommate so you're stuck with me," he joked as he plugged his phone into the charger.

"No, it's not that," Adam pressed on as he sat all the way up. "I had a really bad nightmare, and when I woke up there were all these weird noises coming from the seventh floor. It was just like you said."

Roadrunner grinned as he glanced at his phone. "Yeah, pretty freaky, huh?"

"Somehow I didn't think it would happen to me," Adam laughed.

"Welcome to the club. Mind if I turn the light on?"

"Not at all."

Adam realized just how sweaty he was when Roadrunner flicked on his desk lamp.

"I was scared before you walked in," he admitted. "I'm not scared of much, but I was scared listening to those sounds. I hate to say that, but it's the truth."

"That's alright."

His roommate threw his jacket into the closet and sat cross-legged on his bed. He looked like he was ready to have a good conversation.

"Friends are good," Adam admitted after a few seconds.

"That was my comment," Roadrunner shot back playfully.

"And you were right. I didn't know how much of a difference you would make until you walked in here."

"So I'm back on your good side?"

"Yep."

"And you won't get mad if I try and analyze your dream?"

"Nope."

"Well then, what was it about?"

Adam recounted the dream as Roadrunner listened intently.

"So you wanted your old life back but you couldn't get it?"

"That was the gist of it, yeah."

The running back thought for a moment. "You think that's how you really feel?"

"No, not really."

"You're avoiding eye contact," Roadrunner pointed out. "That means you're lying."

He hadn't said it in a way that made him feel guilty or humbled. It was just a fact. And his ability to decipher emotions in such an observational manner was what made Roadrunner's people skills so special. Adam understood that now.

"Alright, you got me. I think that *is* how I feel. But everything's so confusing right now. Part of me wishes this whole thing never happened. But another part of me wants to get back at them now, and show them what they're missing. And I need this team on board in order to do that."

Roadrunner stared.

"If you want to win, you gotta go all in," his roommate stated. "One hundred percent. And you gotta make everyone on the team go all in. That's what good leaders do. They get their teammates to buy into the goals of the whole team. You gotta make them *want* to go all in. And you can't do that if it's just about you."

"I know that's part of it," Adam remarked. "I've spent two years as a starting quarterback, I know all about that—"

"Are you sure?" Roadrunner interrupted. "Because you can't convince your teammates to be 100 percent committed if you're not 100 percent committed yourself."

Adam felt a deflating sensation as he heard those words. He knew he wasn't completely committed, and his roommate was right.

"You have to buy into the team concept," Roadrunner continued. "You have to invest in it. It's like money. When you study the playbook, go hard in practice and work on improving your weaknesses, that's like saving money, and you'll be rewarded in the end. Your team will win, and you'll get your investment back from the bank."

And that was when it hit him—maybe he hadn't done that. Maybe he hadn't gone all in at Keystone State—he'd just convinced himself that he had. Maybe he was blind.

"We put just as much time and effort into this sport as you do, Adam, and most of us aren't going to the NFL," he pointed out. "You might be, but the rest of us have to get ready for life after football. 'Cause that's really what college is all about, and Coach Morgan stresses that to us every day. In the end, it's just a game."

Adam listened, and thought about how he'd always wanted to be the best, a leader, the glue binding the team together. Had he not gone all in? If someone had asked him that question last year or in high school, he would have told them they were crazy. He was *obsessed*. But maybe being obsessed and going all in weren't the same thing after all. Maybe he was missing the point.

"Some things are more important than football," Roadrunner said after a few silent moments. "You're going to find that out sooner or later."

And with that sentence there was an air of finality in the room, as if some how, some way, his roommate had been building towards that statement ever since they'd met but could not find the right way to say it until now.

Adam stared at his sheets, feeling as if his whole world had turned upside down. He was just now seeing things in a way he never had before. Sitting here and talking with Roadrunner at five in the morning, he felt like they were far away from the normal world, and maybe that's why it was so easy to see the other side. Nothing was stirring in the quiet hours before dawn. This was the time when dreams happened, and maybe even supernatural forces awakened—he sure believed that now. And that sensation of mystery and discovery swelled inside of him, arousing his most personal thoughts...

"What should I do?"

Roadrunner knew exactly what he was getting at.

Luke Fetkovich

"I can't tell you what to do," he replied calmly. "But if I know anything, it's that you can't go halfway in. You gotta go all in, just like I said. One hundred percent. If you do that, then we've got a shot."

Adam honestly didn't know what his answer would be as he sat there for one endless moment, deeper in thought than he'd ever been in his life...

"OK. I'm in."

Cowboys & Coyotes
Chapter 13

"I don't know whether I prefer Astroturf to grass. I never smoked Astroturf."
--Joe Namath

Roadrunner was ridiculous.

There wasn't any other way to describe it. And there was suddenly no question about how he'd acquired his nickname.

During the first full-team drill of the spring, Adam shoved the ball into the running back's chest, glanced upfield, and stood there dumbfounded while he tried to figure out how Roadrunner was already running into the end zone, unscathed. It seemed like he'd blinked and *poof!*, Roadrunner was gone—transported from one end of the field to the other in a few seconds. Their offensive teammates whooped and hollered while the defense stood with their hands on their hips, panting and sweating. Coach Morgan barely took notice, but Adam guessed that he was used to it.

As the weeks went by and March blossomed into April, he learned No. 34's tricks of the trade. Roadrunner patiently waited for the hole to open, and once it did, his burst of speed carried him the rest of the way. His acceleration was so good, in fact, that by the time he hit the second level of defense, the defenders had a difficult time tackling something so fast. Sometimes they dove and were unable to hang on, and sometimes they took an angle only to be outpaced. And Roadrunner never, ever stopped churning his feet, even when defenders were hanging all over him. He was the little engine that could.

"How did you get that good?" Adam asked as they knelt on the sideline during a cloudy practice the week before Easter.

"'Good' is subjective," Roadrunner answered as he gulped down Gatorade. "There's probably plenty of other backs in this country that are better than me."

"Bullshit! You're too humble, man. You're really good. You know that."

Roadrunner grinned. "OK, fine. I'm good."

"Yeah, you're freaking ridiculous is what you are," Adam laughed. "You know, I've never seen a real roadrunner before. But I bet you could handle a coyote pretty well yourself, if one was after you."

"No way. A coyote's a lot different than a college linebacker—"

"Oh, shut up. You're being too serious. Give yourself some credit. You might not be a roadrunner, but you sure as hell look like one when you're out on that field."

Tony Ferrari jogged over excitedly.

"Hey, will you two stop making out over here and come join the conversation already?"

"What's going on?" Adam asked as he noticed several linemen crowded together.

"Get your ass up and come see," Ferrari urged. "You just got us on national TV."

They found the five starting linemen huddled in deep conversation. Adam wasn't pleased to see that Brian Massey was there too. But he *was* pleased to see Bulldog—the two of them had become friends over the spring, since Bulldog usually sat with them at dinner.

"Our game with the Gargoyles was moved to prime time," Jason Evans explained. "It's a Saturday night, 8 p.m. kickoff on SportsNetwork."

"You're kidding?" Adam asked.

But no, he knew they weren't.

"It's because of you," Ferrari insisted. "They know everybody wants to watch you play against your old team!"

"That's not the only thing, Ferrari," added the starting center Graham Cracker. "It's the revenge factor. Stories have leaked out about what really happened. SportsNetwork's all over it—I've been watching their talk shows. The networks love stuff like this. They want the big ratings."

Suddenly, Adam felt as uncomfortable as he had on his first day. He had wanted to hide the idea that this was about revenge, about him versus DT, about proving his worth to Coach Thompson—the coach who could have won national championships with him but opted for personal gain instead.

"It's not about that," he uttered instinctively. "It's not about revenge. That has nothing to do with it. They can talk it up all they want, but I just want to go up there and win a football game with this team."

The way his teammates were staring only made him feel worse.

"But you *do* want revenge?" Graham Cracker replied cautiously. "Especially after the way you were kicked off. That's why you came here, isn't it?"

And now a panicked, helpless sensation overwhelmed him. "No, I never knew we were playing them until I got here! I thought you guys knew that? You were trying to keep it a secret—"

"He's right," Bulldog interrupted. "He didn't know about this game. Trust me, I've got sources. Z told me about it."

"Well, there you go," Adam approved.

Roadrunner stayed silent.

Fifteen Minutes

"But you were going to quit," Graham Cracker pressed on. "That one day at practice, you said you were going to quit and then you changed your mind. You can't have had a change of heart that fast. What if you saw the schedule and *then* decided to come back?"

"Stop bugging him, Graham Cracker!" Bulldog insisted. "You don't know that."

Fortunately, there wasn't any time to argue. Coach Morgan had blown the whistle to begin the next drill, and the coaches were staring in their direction impatiently.

Adam felt embarrassed and defenseless as he jogged onto the field. A linebacker had stuck up for him, which he was thankful for. But it shouldn't have come to that. And even though he was beginning to feel comfortable around his new teammates, there were still people he didn't trust, and those same people didn't trust him back. Travis Graham had just made that pretty clear.

***

"You're in a unique situation," Z assured him that evening as they sat at dinner with Roadrunner, Bulldog, Bookworm and Lindsey.

Adam stared at his food, feeling like he was surrounded by his best friends on a team full of enemies.

"You arrived here under a lot of controversy and confusion," he continued. "People can't wrap their heads around why a Heisman front-runner is suddenly playing for our tiny school, and it leads to a lot of speculation and assumptions."

"Well, the next time anybody asks me, I'm going to say I'm here because my last coach was a jackass and this was the best place for me."

"And you'd be telling the truth," Z agreed as he chugged chocolate milk. "Listen, Adam. I know you feel a little dissed right now, but honestly, Graham Cracker's the one who doesn't get it."

"Thanks," Adam mumbled, wondering to himself how that statement made him feel. Relieved because it was true? Or guilty because he really *was* in it for revenge? What *did* he feel? He didn't know anymore.

"Maybe you just need to spend more time with them, Adam," Lindsey suggested.

He hadn't thought of that.

"I know Z was really close with his quarterback in high school," she went on. "Sometimes they would all go to a restaurant or party in a 'guys night out' sort of thing. Obviously they weren't old enough to drink, but you guys could easily go to a bar around here!"

Adam was sure the linemen would only agree to something like that if he offered to pay, and did he really want to spend his money on these goofs?

Aside from Graham Cracker, that list included Garfield, Bigfoot, Jason Evans and Cody McCormack. Jason and Cody weren't so bad, but the other three? Yikes.

"It sounds like a good idea," he said with some effort.

"You know, we're going to have all kinds of time this summer," Bookworm suggested. "Most of the team stays on campus to train and take classes, so we'll have loads of evenings to just hang and party!"

Z grinned. "Retone's. We have to take you there, Adam. It's the best bar in town. Totally hopping on the weekends, and there's a bunch of hot bartenders."

"Playboy'd go nuts," Roadrunner commented. "He loves that place."

"Hot girls are always nice," Adam agreed. "So, are you guys all in if I do this?"

"We're down," Z assured.

"Yeah, we can always bail you out if you need," Bulldog added.

"Me and Roadrunner aren't 21 yet," explained Bookworm, "but we'll still help you out in any way we can."

But Roadrunner looked less than enthusiastic. "If he wants to develop a good relationship with the big guys, he's not going to do it by hanging out with us all night."

Adam's lips curled into an instinctive grin, because he knew that the running back was right yet again. And with that thought, he got up and walked purposefully through the maze of tables. Once he'd pulled up a nearby chair and sat down at the linemen's table, there was no turning back.

"What's up, guys?"

All five of them—Graham Cracker, Bigfoot, Garfield, Jason and Cody—had stopped chewing and were staring at him like he was the Easter Bunny.

Graham Cracker spoke first. "You know, Adam, I'm sorry if I offended you or anything back at practice. I don't want to get off on the wrong foot, with you as our quarterback."

"No problem. But first off, I just wanted you guys to know that I'm not here for revenge, or anything that has to do with my old team..."

He was staring at their trays instead of their faces.

Don't do that! Look them in the eyes!! You're all in. You told Roadrunner that, remember?

"...and uh..."

What had he planned to say next? The thought had been wiped from his mind as soon as he'd realized he wasn't looking at them. Then he had scolded himself for it and become distracted. And now he was embarrassing himself. Great.

What was I going to say the next time anybody asks me...? Oh, I got it!

"I'm here because my old coach was a jackass, and this was the best place for me."

"Alright, fine," Graham Cracker conceded. "I believe you. I just have one question for you, though. What made you come back during that first practice?"

You asshole! You just had to ask that before we moved on, didn't you? The one question I hate, and you had to ask it!

"I was just letting it all out. I was having a bad day and my shoes were too tight. But I'm trying to be a leader, and I shouldn't have done that. Sorry."

All five of them seemed to buy it, and he secretly breathed a sigh of relief.

"Thanks," Graham Cracker replied. "I apologized, you apologized. I'd say we're cool now."

OK. Good. This is going good...

"So anyway, I was thinking that since we *don't* know each other that well, maybe you guys would like to go down to Retone's some night and hang out? It'll be my treat."

There was an awkward silence.

"You mean just the six of us?" Cody asked.

"Well, yeah. Some of the other players might come, but I'd sit with you guys."

Jason Evans chuckled. "Playboy'd go nuts! There's so many hot girls down there."

"I heard."

"So you're *paying?*" Garfield blurted.

Adam paused. "That's right. It's on me."

"Are you *serious?*" he replied emphatically. "This kid's paying for the drinks?! I am getting *hammered!* Yeah!"

And he slapped his huge hand down, nearly jumping from his chair in the process. The entire table shook.

"It's my way of thanking you guys ahead of time," Adam replied. He forced a smile, but couldn't shake the thought that his wallet might have to be fatter than Garfield if he was planning on keeping his word.

"Alright Cowboy, just give us a date and we'll be there," Cody said.

"We'll wait until classes end," suggested Adam. "Then I'll get back to you."

Garfield got up for ice cream, and muttered to himself as he waddled away, ("Getting hammered...getting *hammered!*") Adam chuckled, and sensed that it was time to head back to home base.

"Well guys, nice talk. See you at practice Monday!"

He felt much better as he left the table, but something was nagging at him...

"Hey guys, does Cody McCormack ever call people 'Cowboy?'"

Roadrunner shot Z a glance.

"Did he call you that?" his roommate asked.

"Yeah. Why, what's up?"

"That's your nickname," Z explained. "A few of the guys have been calling you that recently."

"Really? Why that?"

"Well, two weeks ago us big guys were chatting about you while we waited on the sideline," the lineman went on. "And we came to the conclusion that your story is kind of like a good western plot. You come from a big school and a big city, and now you're out here in the country. You're an outlaw to the Gargoyles, so you're taking matters into your own hands and trying to get justice."

"I don't want to win just to get revenge—"

"Save your breath, Adam. You've said that at least a hundred times now. We know. It's supposed to be funny. That's what nicknames are for. We make fun of people."

"But it's a team thing," Lindsey piped up. "They never start calling anyone a nickname until they get to know them. So it really is a good sign that Cody called you that!"

"I think it's more about accepting him than knowing him," Roadrunner commented as he licked his ice cream spoon (chocolate chip cookie dough this time).

"Well, that does sound good," Adam responded as he checked the time. "But I gotta get to class. I'll see you guys later."

"Alright Cowboy," Z chuckled.

"Hey, I never approved of any nicknames yet," Adam reminded playfully as he slung his backpack over his shoulder.

But Bulldog just laughed. "I didn't approve of mine, either."

A Night at Retone's
Chapter 14

"If God had wanted man to play soccer, he wouldn't have given us arms."
--Mike Ditka

    What is a team?
    What makes one group of athletes better than another? Is it talent? Coaching? Recruiting? All of that combined? These were the questions that Roadrunner liked to discuss when they were alone.
    "You think too much," Adam laughed as he parked his car on their way back from the store one hot summer day.
    "It's better than thinking too little."
    "Ha, I guess. You really believe we can win this game? Be honest. Don't give me any of that analytical bullshit."
    "Yes. How's that?" he said as they walked along the sidewalk to their dorm.
    "Good. You better think we can win. But it's not gonna be easy."
    "It's not supposed to be easy," Roadrunner countered. "It's a fight."
    It was mid-June. Six weeks had passed since the last day of exams, and summer was in full swing. The two of them were still roommates, but they had relocated to one of the nicer air-conditioned buildings now that most of the students had left.
    He, Roadrunner, Bulldog, Bookworm and Z had formed their own little group after final exams, and Adam found himself hanging out with those four guys almost all of the time. One Friday night, they drove to Bulldog's house 30 minutes down the highway with the windows open and the music blasting. That had probably been Adam's favorite night so far, just hanging out with the guys, meeting Bulldog's brother, drinking beer and watching movies. Another time, half the team went to see Mozart and his band perform at a bar in downtown Waddlesburg.
    Coach Morgan was keeping them busy, too, with the usual grind of football-related activities. They worked out twice a week with the strength coach and had to run a mile-long course that zigzagged through the campus and surrounding forest. Adam also made it a point to study the new playbook every day, as he still hadn't learned the entire offense.

Some of the linemen—Garfield and Graham Cracker in particular—seemed hell-bent on sneaking down into the crypt before the summer was over. But they hadn't rounded up any companions, mainly because most of the guys wanted to stay out of trouble or were simply too scared, though they wouldn't admit it. Brian Massey was the leader of that pack, but he had good reason, since his dad's friend had been involved in the infamous incident decades ago.

"Is Massey coming tonight?" Roadrunner questioned as they entered the building.

Adam had forgotten that he was supposed to take the linemen to Retone's tonight.

"Don't think so. But thanks for reminding me. I better take a shower."

"But all the linemen are coming?"

"Yeah, all five of them. Z is coming too, and obviously Playboy. And I think Tonio is planning on stopping by."

"Would you buy Massey's drinks if he did come?"

Adam grinned. "You always ask the hard questions, don't you? I don't think I would, no."

"He's a wide receiver," Roadrunner pointed out as they entered their spacious new room. "You should get to know him, too. He should be one of your top targets this year."

"He called me a jackass on the very first day."

"And you've called him plenty of names over the past few months."

"Yeah, but not to his face."

His roommate paused. "Do you still have a grudge against him?"

"Yes. But I'm not going to pick any fights. I'm trying to be the leader, remember? And back in January this wasn't my team. Right now, well…it's kind of getting to be my team. Agreed?"

"Agreed," Roadrunner nodded approvingly.

* * *

Retone's Bar & Grill sat on the outskirts of town, near the woods and gentle mountain slopes of the Alleghenies. The warm summer rays of those endless June days still baked the surroundings as Adam pulled into the gravel lot outside of the restaurant. He and Garfield hopped out of the Honda and were greeted by the crunching sound of their feet on the gray stones. Adam scanned the horizon with his sunglasses, but there were no more cars humming down the country road towards the bar.

"I'm not sure how long it'll be 'til the other guys get here," he remarked. "We can just hang out inside until they arrive."

"How about some food?" Garfield suggested. "I'm starving!"

"You're always starving."

"Yeah, well *screw* the other guys. We can drink with them later. I want some food now!"

Retone's had the feel of a dingy basement pub. It sported a dozen large round tables in addition to a wide bar set against the back wall. The tables were carved from sandy-colored wood, and the lanterns hanging from the ceiling gave the whole place an old-fashioned feel, as if the bar were immune to the passing of time and had looked this way for centuries. In fact, the two TVs in the opposite corner provided the only clue that they were still in the 21st century. Out on the patio, a country band was preparing to strike up some tunes.

"Excuse me, but are you Adam Dorsey?"

Adam looked to his right and found himself face-to-face with a tall, well-groomed man. He thought about saying "no" but realized it would be too hard to conceal his identity, considering that he was here with half the team.

"Yeah."

"Mr. Ryan Retone," the man said as he shook Adam's hand cordially. "Pleasure to meet you, Mr. Dorsey. My son goes to Keystone State, so I'm quite familiar with your story. And I assume this is a new teammate of yours?"

"Yeah, I'm taking my linemen out for the night."

"Well, please make yourselves at home. Nice meeting you!"

"Thanks," Adam grunted, and they headed to a table.

He began to feel quite cozy after they had settled down and taken a look at the menu. Z had been right—there *were* lots of sexy girls here (the bartenders in particular).

"How ya'll doing tonight?" a waitress with flaming red lipstick and curly blonde hair asked as she arrived to take orders. "My name's Lucy, and I'll be taking care of ya'll!"

"Great," Adam replied, hoping this time that she *did* realize who he was.

"What's your biggest hamburger?" Garfield blurted.

"Oh, that'll be the ol' Burnin' Barnstormer! It's real hot though, just so ya'll know."

"Sweet, I'll take two! And it's on him," he added as he pointed at Adam.

Adam just smiled painfully as Lucy jotted down the order and strolled away.

"This is the first bar I went to when I turned 21 last year," Garfield explained as he devoured his hamburgers ten minutes later. "I came here all the time last summer. I had a rough time my first two years, and after I found this place I needed to come just to get away. Lucy, she's real easy to get along with. She's from down south."

"Wouldn't ever have guessed."

"But I really like Sarah. I was hoping she'd wait on us. Maybe Playboy will know if she's working tonight."

Adam toyed with a plastic straw as he debated whether or not to ask the question he was wondering.

"Why did you have a rough time?"

Garfield glared at him over the giant burger. "If I tell you, will you promise not to tell *anybody?*"

"Yeah," Adam agreed, and he wasn't sure why he was so interested. Maybe he was so fed up with his own problems that he wanted to hear another teammate's, just to feel better about himself.

"Well, I didn't want to come here at first. I never even wanted to play college football. I wanted to stay home, because I liked my hometown and I liked my friends. Maybe some of them didn't like me, but whatever. I was happy there."

"You didn't want to come to St. Bruno's?"

"No," Garfield insisted as he stuffed French fries into his mouth. "I wanted to go to the community college. But my parents wanted me to be on my own and make new friends. They thought playing football would keep me busy and in shape. Well, can't argue with them *there*," he conceded.

"So you thought you were going to hate it here, too?"

"I didn't know anybody," he told. "I thought the classes were going to be hard, and some of them were. I thought nobody would like me, because it was hard enough fitting in at my high school. And I thought I was going to be horrible and Teddy Bear would kick me off the team!"

"Well, you're still here," Adam grinned.

"Yeah, but it was real hard. The first day of practice, I slipped and fell on my *ass!* Everybody was laughing at me! I thought I was a goner for sure," he explained through mouthfuls of burger.

Adam wasn't sure why he was so surprised. For some reason, he'd just now realized something that he probably should have realized a long time ago. Garfield wasn't that much different from himself. He played a different position and lived a different lifestyle, sure, but those difficulties of fitting in that they had both experienced transcended all of that. In the end, they had gone through the same thing.

"I get it, Garfield. I know what that's like, too. Remember the first day of spring ball, when my cleats were too small?"

Garfield chuckled as he licked the grease from his fingers. "Yeah, you almost quit!"

"Exactly. But I'm still here, even after all that. And so are you."

"That makes me feel better," he commented as he slurped his water. "I feel like I'm just as cool as you now! And just as tough, too."

"You are, Garfield. You are."

Before he had finished his second burger, the other linemen arrived and filled the remaining seats around the table. Z had tagged along with Tonio, but those two defensive guys sat at an adjacent table.

"And why does this not surprise me?" Jason laughed. "Garfield's already eaten two burgers."

They ordered three pitchers of Yuengling, and Adam was just starting to feel like the night would go well when somebody slapped him on the back.

"How's it going, Adam!"

"Hi, Playboy."

"Pretty cool place, huh? Sorry I just showed up. Who's your waitress?"

Adam nodded towards Lucy.

"Oh, gotcha. She's real easy-going. Hey, you gotta meet Val before I forget. She's usually at the bar."

And before he knew what was happening, Playboy was dragging him off his chair and across the room.

"Hey, is Valerie here?" he asked the one and only male behind the bar.

"No, she took the night off. Can I get you a drink?"

"Nah, nah. Well Adam, that's too bad man. I really wanted you to meet—*hey!*"

A woman sporting a salmon-colored tank top and jean shorts had appeared from the kitchen. Adam worried that Playboy might not be able to contain his excitement.

"Aw, here we go!" the safety whispered as he nudged his shoulder.

The woman spotted them and walked over.

"Is she Valerie?" Adam asked.

"Nah, forget about her. Sarah! How are you?"

"Hi Taylor," the woman smiled. "I thought you might stop by tonight."

"Sarah, I want you to meet Adam. I'm sure you've heard of him. He used to play quarterback for the Gargoyles. He's single!"

"Oh, I think I remember seeing you on TV!" Sarah exclaimed.

"Yeah, yeah, him!" Playboy said excitedly. "Why don't you two get to know each other. Excuse me, Adam. I'll be back in a sec. You got something to drink, right?"

"Just the Yuengling back at the table."

"Aw, I can get you something else. Tell you what? Order a drink on me. Sarah, can we get a menu?"

She handed him a draft list and left to help a new customer.

"Ever had a Blow Job before?" Playboy asked as he scanned the menu.

"What?"

"A Blow Job. It's a shot—a really good one, too."

"Oh. I thought you meant...right."

"Here, order that, and I'll show you how to down it when I get back!" he advised with a wink. Then he headed for the restroom.

Adam sat at the bar and mulled his options. The linemen were content and drinking heavily back at the table. Did they even notice that he was gone?

Sarah had returned. He couldn't resist a glance at the plunging neckline on her tank top—the cleavage was *unreal*. He half expected them to just pop right out whenever she swayed her hips.

No wonder Playboy loves her.

"Well?" she beamed. "What can I get for you, Adam?"

"Uh..."

Oh God, I must be turning red. What if she notices? Help! Somebody come help!

"Can I get a, uh...uh..."

He was speaking jibberish. Strange sounds were coming from his mouth.

Just shut up before you look like an idiot.

"Well? Come on now, don't be shy!" Sarah squealed. She shifted as she placed her palms on the counter, and her breasts jiggled beneath the tank top. "Spit it out!"

I have got to be so red right now...

"You know, I think I'm just going to wait until Playboy—I mean, until Taylor gets back."

"Oh, no problem. Are you sure you're OK, Adam? Your face is as red as a tomato."

And getting redder by the second, I'm sure.

A familiar hand slapped him on the back as Sarah turned her attention to the next customer.

"You two having a nice one-on-one, I see!"

Adam breathed a sigh of relief. Somehow, everything was less embarrassing with Taylor Griffin around. He didn't seem to know the word "embarrassing."

"Did you order a Blow Job?"

"Actually, I hadn't quite got that far," Adam invented.

Playboy grinned. "Oh, I see! Too busy chatting, huh? Good for you, man, that's real good!"

He whipped out his wallet.

"*HEY!* CAN I GET A BLOW JOB FOR THIS GUY?!" he yelled to no one in particular.

Everyone at the bar glanced in their direction, and half the people at the tables did, too.

Adam sunk lower on his stool. Playboy didn't seem to care.

Sarah returned and made the drink, which she topped with whipped cream.

"OK, Adam, here's the deal," he explained. "You can't use your hands to drink it."

"Uh...I really should be getting back to the other guys," was Adam's desperate response. "This was supposed to be a night out with them."

"Yeah, sure! As soon as you finish this," Playboy replied, beaming wider than ever.

Adam stared the shot glass down.

Man, I can't believe I'm doing this...

* * *

"Hey, Cowboy! You've still got some whipped cream on your chin!" Cody joked two hours later as they crowded together at the table.

"Good one, Cody."

He'd fallen for that already, and he wasn't going to do it again.

He had lost track of how many pitchers of Yuengling they'd ordered, but it had to be more than 10. Everyone was getting pretty tipsy, but he was still attempting to police the situation and make sure the night didn't end in disaster. The bar was absolutely hopping now, but most of the other patrons were behaving better than his table. Garfield and Graham Cracker were getting louder by the minute.

"So I hear you're all football players!" Lucy shouted as she squeezed her way through the crowd with yet another pitcher.

"Yeah, you see this guy? He fucking *sucks!*" Cody yelled as he pointed at Garfield.

Garfield just nodded proudly as he downed the rest of his glass. "I suck, and I fucking like it that way! I love being the fat loser! *YEAH!*"

And he slammed the empty glass down, almost missing the table entirely.

"We're playing his old team in August!" Jason cried as he motioned towards Adam.

"Yeah, we're gonna be on *national TV!*" Bigfoot screamed. "I've always wanted to be on national TV! It's like...Mount Everest!" he finished after struggling for a better word. "I'm getting my fifteen minutes of fame in! You hear that, guys?!"

"Bigfoot, what are you *talking* about?!" Garfield yelled.

"It's Andy Warhol!" the lineman protested. "You never heard of that? *'Everyone will be famous for fifteen minutes!'* That's us! We're gonna be famous for fifteen minutes!"

"A football game is sixty minutes, you dumb fuck!" Cody screamed as he chugged half a glass in one gulp.

"But...but..." Bigfoot stuttered, and then he just gave up and poured more beer.

"*HEY!* Hey, lady!"

It was Garfield. He was yelling at Lucy.

"*Hey lady!* Do you know Sarah? Is she here?"

"Oh, I think she just got off her shift!"

"Can you get her to come over here?! I've been wanting to see her for the longest time! Can you *please, please* get her to come over here?!"

He was absolutely hammered. Adam gulped.

Lucy just smiled. "I'll see what I can do!"

"Garfield, what are you trying to do? Pick up girls?" Tonio yelled from the adjacent table. "They don't want your fat ass!"

"Tonio, give me a break!" Garfield retorted as beer dribbled down his chin.

Adam glanced uneasily around the crowded restaurant. After a minute, his worst fears came true. Playboy was pushing his way towards them, and right behind him was Sarah.

"Excuse me, buddy. Whoa, watch your beer there! Coming through. Hey, Adam! Look who I brought along!"

"Hi, Playboy," Adam replied weakly.

"I was just over at the bar, and Lucy came by and said you all wanted to see Sarah!"

"I guess so."

"She didn't want to come at first, because she thought you were all drunk! But I convinced her to tag along!"

"Uh, I think we're drunk, yeah," he confessed to Sarah.

The bartender gave him the kind of look that said, *"I know you're all drunk, but I'm putting up with it anyway."*

"Nah, you guys aren't drunk," Playboy insisted as he waved his hand carelessly. "Just buzzed, man. Just a little buzzed, right? Nothing wrong with that!"

"HEY!"

Adam groaned.

"Hey! Sarah, can you come sit on my lap?!"

Everyone at the table was laughing their guts out.

"That's our left tackle, Garfield," Playboy explained. "He's really funny! Here, want to take a seat?"

"Oh, I don't think I should," Sarah admitted. "I really should be going."

"Oh, well if you're sure!" Playboy replied as she waved goodbye.

"WAIT! *Don't go!*" Garfield screamed as he jumped from his chair. Beer splashed over the rim of his glass and soaked his shirt.

Adam attempted to think fast, but to no avail.

Save face...save face...

"Uh..."

But that was as far as he got.

"SARAH, COME BACK, HONEY!! YOU LOOK SWEET AS A CUPCAKE, AND I JUST WANTED TO ASK IF YOU WANTED A CREAM FILLING!!"

The next three minutes were complete mayhem.

Adam was on his feet and putting all his effort into containing Garfield. The lineman was flailing his arms desperately, and Sarah had become lost in the crowd. Z had come over to help the cause.

He vaguely became aware of someone tapping him on the shoulder.

"Excuse me?"

It was Lucy.

"I'm sorry," he confessed as Garfield gave up the fight. "I didn't think he was going to get this drunk—"

But he stopped in mid-sentence when he realized *why* Garfield had stopped struggling. The expression on his face told him exactly what was coming...

Adam threw himself out of the way just in time as the lineman heaved up a bunch of chunky vomit. Unfortunately, that cleared the way for some to land right on Lucy's tank top.

Shrieks and cackles erupted from the crowd. People pointed at them and doubled-over with laughter. Mr. Retone's tall figure was striding towards them...

"Sorry, honey, that was my bad," Playboy chuckled casually as he sipped his beer. "He's *definitely* drunk!"

Adam and Z exchanged glances.

"Bathroom?"

"Right!" Z replied. "Back near the bar. You take his left side, I'll get his right!"

And they were off, stumbling through the tavern with a 350-pound, vomit-covered Brian Hall between them. Adam got the guilty feeling that they were just trying to run in the *opposite* direction of Mr. Retone, and for some reason the men's bathroom was a safe haven. It wasn't hard getting there, because the crowd gladly cleared the way.

It turned out to be a cramped single stall. A second after he'd pushed the door open, Adam realized there wouldn't be enough room for the three of them. He looked back at the table, where Mr. Retone was talking with the other linemen.

"Alright, how about this? You go back and do the apologizing, and I'll do the cleaning."

"Ugh," Z answered. "I'm not sure which one is worse. It's a deal."

"Take as many other guys back with you as you can. Playboy can drive the rest."

"Alright. Thanks, Adam."

He shuffled into the tiny bathroom with Garfield leaning against his shoulder. The sink was old and rusty, and there was a live fly caught in the overhead light, judging from the tiny buzzing shadow. A screen window high on the back wall provided some fresh air.

"Aw, *FUCK!*" Garfield shouted, and he stumbled over to the toilet and threw up again.

Adam partly wanted to scold the lineman, and tell him that he wasn't getting back in his car until his shirt was clean and there was no more vomit coming. But he knew it was pointless.

"Here, give me your shirt."

"Yeah, yeah, I suck!"

"Just help me get this thing off. My car will smell like throw-up for weeks if you smear this on the seats."

"DON'T YELL AT ME!" he yelled, and then collapsed against the tiled wall outside of the stall.

Adam managed to pull his shirt off by tugging at his sleeves, and ran the whole thing under hot water. Garfield rested his head against the wall and closed his eyes.

"Just relax. I'll get you back to campus and you're gonna wake up in your bed tomorrow and everything will be fine."

He turned the faucet off and attempted to pull the soaking-wet shirt over Garfield's head.

"Come on, now, help me put this on. It's OK. Just help me get you out of here. I'm your friend. I know what it's like to need a friend. Just as Roadrunner. I was scared as hell one night until he walked in."

He pulled the shirt over Garfield's bulging belly and got him to his feet.

"You're not going to throw up again, are you?"

He just shook his head, and Adam had to steady him as he swayed on the spot.

"Good. I'll keep the window open for you just in case."

* * *

They were halfway back to St. Bruno's, with Garfield passed out in the passenger seat, when Adam's phone buzzed on the dashboard.

"Yeah?"

"Hey."

"What's up, Z?"

"How's it going with you guys?"

"It's going good," he replied as he steered the Honda down the winding country road. "He's out cold right now. I don't know if he's going to wake up when we get back, so you might have to help me carry him."

Z laughed. "Yeah, just call me when you get here and I'll be down."

There were a few seconds of silence.

"Hey, Adam? That was pretty good, what you did tonight."

Adam knew he was talking about what had just transpired, not the invitation for a free night out.

"The guys really appreciate you taking care of Garfield like this. They might be too drunk to show it now, but they do. 'Cause if you hadn't been there, then I don't know what would have happened."

"You're helping out just as much as I am," Adam pointed out, wondering to himself why he was trying to downplay the significance of it. Back at Keystone State, he would have been all over his teammates if they'd forced him into a similar situation. But now, it was almost like he *didn't* want to draw attention to himself. What the hell had happened?

"Yeah, but I wasn't dealing with somebody twice my size," Z chuckled. "See, what I'm trying to say is, they owe you one now. They won't forget this."

"Yeah," he replied, only because he couldn't think of a better way to say, *"I understand."* And he knew what Z was getting it—the "T" word. That thing that nobody ever seemed to talk about, but everybody wanted and everybody needed. Trust.

"OK, I'll call you when we get there."

"Alright, Cowboy."

Adam smiled as he set his phone down. Z had a habit of calling him that, probably because he knew it pissed him off.

The last ten minutes of the drive were quiet, but he didn't mind. It was nice to slow down and watch the tall shadows of pine trees fly by under the starry sky. And it was then that he decided it had been a successful night. It hadn't turned out the way he'd planned, but what ever did in life?

Yeah, in some ways, it had been a *damn* successful evening...

But he didn't think he ever wanted to spend another night at Retone's.

Fifteen Minutes
Chapter 15

"No one has ever drowned in sweat."

--Lou Holtz

June and July melted into August as the hot summer days wore on, and preseason camp came upon them all too fast. Before Adam knew it, he and Roadrunner were setting their alarm for 6 a.m. and that first early practice.

It was a perfect summer morning. There were no clouds, and a blanket of fog had enveloped the campus. The gravel pathway leading to the athletic fields gave them a stunning view of the basilica, which rose majestically from the fog like a castle in the sky. The air was so clear that they could see every street and house of Waddlesburg in the distance. It was still cool and comfortable, but Adam knew all too well that in four hours he would be wishing he were in Antarctica.

Inside The Lodge, the team seated themselves around the yellow lockers as Coach Morgan stood in front of his office window. It was too early for any conversation, and no one even wanted to turn the bright recessed lights on, instead opting for the dim glow from the office and the emergency lights.

Teddy Morgan turned towards the dry erase board mounted next to the window, took a marker and drew a vertical line.

"OK, those of you veterans. What's this?"

Brian Massey spoke first. "The camp barrier."

"Correct. What's on this side?"

"That's summer," Bookworm stated.

"Right. What's on this side?"

"That's preseason camp," Massey replied.

"Good. And right now, we've just crossed that line. On that side, you can sleep in, have fun and concentrate on other things. On this side, it's all football. Every day we're going to get up early, have practice, eat lunch, have practice again once two-a-days start, and then it's off to dinner and bed. And the process repeats itself. That doesn't mean you guys can't relax at night, but I don't want anyone leaving campus on the weekdays.

"Now, most of you know what Beaver preseason camps are like, and for those of you who are new, you've done it in high school. Taking care of your body is essential—that means drinking enough fluids and getting the proper amount of sleep. If you've got a significant other, I'd advise taking some time to explain that you won't be able to communicate much during camp.

"It's three weeks, men. Three weeks, and then we can switch gears into our normal fall routine. I know you can all last without girlfriends and parties for three weeks. And I know so because Taylor's done it twice already..."

There were chuckles from the team as Playboy grinned from ear to ear.

"...and if he can do it, then everyone in this room can."

The head coach tossed the marker down.

"Now, there's going to be a lot of publicity around this team for the next few weeks—probably more than the championship game, for those of you who were here for that. We're playing in a nationally televised game at the biggest stadium in college football. The publicity comes with the territory, if you will. That's just the nature of the situation that we're in, but we will *not* let the cameras become a distraction for us," he ordered, and he seemed to stare every player down at once.

"I won't let this training camp become a reality TV show. We're here to prepare ourselves for the season. We are not here to answer questions from the media and certainly not here to get on TV. You guys know that. And the sports information director and I have specific guidelines in place so that they stay out of our way. Any concerns?"

There were none. And in those few seconds of silence, Adam could sense the anticipation in his teammates. Even though they were half-asleep and lacking energy, there was a quiet sense of purpose within the room. They were all itching to get it done, itching for success...

"OK, men. Let's do it."

The Lodge filled with the quiet hustling of cleats on concrete. Adam followed his teammates out the back door and down the underground tunnel, feeling much different than he had during that first spring practice.

* * *

Camp was hot and sticky—all day, every day.

The morning practices ended around 9:30, so they escaped the extreme heat for a while. But once two-a-days started it was a different story. During those second practices, the sun beat down on them so powerfully that Adam got the nasty feeling he was inside a giant oven.

Spring ball had been a joke compared to this. Teddy Morgan was now hard on the young guys, and even harder on the seniors and star players. That meant that Adam got plenty of criticism as the days wore on—not that he needed talking to. He knew the team they were about to face. It was his job to get the message across to everyone else.

"That's *bullshit*, Bookworm!" he screamed on Thursday morning as the little receiver just missed Derek Bell's overthrown ball in the end zone. "You need to cut faster than that! You *get* to that football!"

"Sorry," he apologized as he panted over after the drill. "I tried. I almost had it."

"Yeah, that was Derek's fault," Adam agreed. "But that's not an excuse, as far as I'm concerned. We've gotta be clicking at 100 percent by the end of camp, to be ready for the Gargoyles. Because I know what that team's like, and I can guarantee you that running crisp routes and making clean catches becomes a hell of a lot harder when you've got Lukas Bowser breathing down your neck, ready to cream you at every opportunity."

"Who's that?"

"You don't want to know."

"Did you say *Bowser*?" Tony Ferrari yelled during the water break a few minutes later. "Isn't that the giant turtle from Nintendo?"

"Might as well be, yeah," Adam spat. "I mean, they're pretty much the same thing. You could ask me which one I'd rather have on the field, and I'd say go flip a coin, because there's not much difference."

"Nintendo Bowser breathes fire," Ferrari pointed out.

"Yeah, and I never said this guy *doesn't*," he shot back.

Ferrari chuckled, and Adam got a laugh out of Bulldog later in practice.

"Did you say someone on their team breathes fire?"

"What?" he asked before realizing where he was coming from. "Oh, yeah. Lukas Bowser breathes fire."

"You know, if I tell that to Mad Max, he'll believe me."

Adam couldn't help but grin, and little did he know that the fire-breathing Bowser would become the inside joke of camp.

There were some moments when the improbability of it all crossed his mind—the *impossibility* of it, really. The chance to play his old team and get back at the coach who started this whole mess? On national TV? The St. Bruno Beavers never played on national TV. Now they were doing it in his very first game.

"*Catch the football!*" he screamed in frustration when Brian Massey dropped his perfectly-thrown pass. It was the second Friday of camp, and the urgency was beginning to build. Time was running out—time that was crucial if they hoped to have any chance against Keystone State.

"You always screw something up," he vented after the drill. "Either you're cutting too late or you're not getting open or you're dropping the ball, and it's going to cost us!"

"Sorry, Coach Dorsey," Massey growled. "I didn't know you were the one in charge here."

"I'm not in charge, but I'm your quarterback and I know what it's gonna take to beat this team. So you better get your act together right now."

Massey looked like he wanted to say something, but just turned and walked away.

Adam felt slightly embarrassed when he realized that Coach Morgan had been listening. He had his aviators on but was staring in their direction.

He tried to forget about it as he jogged to the next drill. He *had* to forget about it. There was a game plan to focus on. But he couldn't dodge the fact that he and Massey still hadn't made any progress in their relationship. If it had been Bookworm, or Mad Max, would he have done the same thing? Sure, he was yelling at those guys too. But that had felt more like a fight than constructive criticism.

Forget about it.

But what if the same thing happened during the game? What if it cost them the game?

Just forget about it.

* * *

Camp only got harder as the days wore on.

If you're a football player, you wake up in the morning and still feel sore from yesterday's practice. Your arms ache when you lift them up. Your thigh muscles feel like jelly. And it almost feels counter-productive when you stretch for the next practice, because you're sore and it hurts, but you have to. Then the 85-degree heat sucks the energy from you, and the shoulder pads weigh you down. But that's what camp is all about. It's about conditioning.

"Bookworm, you should write a book about this," Adam joked as they walked around the Jordan Complex with Roadrunner and Derek Bell. They had just showered and were waiting for dinner to open. It was Adam's favorite time of day—practice was over and they could look forward to food, free time and sleep.

"Yeah, so the rest of the world knows what we go through to give them entertaining football games," Derek added.

"And maybe they'll think twice the next time a student complains that I'm spoiled and have everything I could ever ask for," chuckled Adam.

"You *were* spoiled," Roadrunner pointed out.

"Thanks for the reality check, Mr. Honest," he grumbled. "You're right. I was spoiled. But I'm different now."

"I always imagined my first book as a fiction novel," Bookworm acknowledged. "People always ask if they can star in it, but I really just want to create my own story, you know? I just need a good idea."

They entered the lounge with the leather chairs and big TVs. The latest episode of the debate show *The Ball's in Your Court* was airing on SportsNetwork. They sat down in the chairs and talked casually while Derek went to the vending machines to grab a drink.

Adam couldn't help but glance at the upcoming topics of discussion, but Roadrunner saw it before he did.

"They're going to talk about us," he pointed out. "Three topics away. It says 'Gargoyles vs. Beavers.'"

"We have to wait," Adam decided. "I have to hear this."

"What's so interesting?" Derek asked as he returned.

"We're on TV," Roadrunner commented.

"It's still a few topics away, though," added Bookworm. "So we'll have to wait fifteen minutes or so."

And that got Adam thinking. He'd been wanting to ask Roadrunner a certain question ever since that night at Retone's, but had kept forgetting about it.

"Roadrunner, who's Andy Warhol?"

"He was a really famous artist. Where'd you hear about him?"

"That night at Retone's," he answered slowly as he jogged his memory. "Bigfoot said something about getting his 'fifteen minutes of fame,' and it had something to do with Andy Warhol."

Roadrunner paused to collect his thoughts. "Andy Warhol was kind of the leader of the pop art movement back in the 1950s and 60s. He's from Pittsburgh, which isn't too far from here. That's why a lot of the guys on the team know his name."

"So he's an artist?"

"An artist and filmmaker. He did both."

"So where did the 'fifteen minutes' idea come from?"

"Well, he coined the term 'fifteen minutes of fame.' His idea was that with advances in technology, everyone could be famous in the future, but not for very long. So he was predicting YouTube and reality TV shows—stuff that we take for granted today."

"Oh, I get it."

"At the bar, Bigfoot was probably talking about how we're playing on national television. We don't usually play on TV, so this is that 'fifteen minutes' opportunity for us. The whole country's going to be watching this thing."

During Roadrunner's pause, they overheard the host's voice as she announced the topic change, and all four of them fixed their gaze on the screen.

"Alright, Mel. Let's talk about the prime time match-up between Keystone State and their former Heisman-worthy quarterback, because that's what this game's really about," insisted the skinnier anchor with glasses. "It's not about the Beavers. It's not about the coaches. It's about Adam Dorsey. Period."

"No, no, no," the round-faced Mel argued as he shook his head. "It's about Adam Dorsey to the media, Jerry. *To the media.* But on the field, this is going to be another blowout by a superior team."

The host chimed in to announce the official start of the timed debate. "Jerry, the ball's in your court first. Do the Beavers have a shot in two weeks?"

"Of course they have a shot," Jerry began, "because they've got Adam Dorsey! Mel, he won't *let* this be a rout. He's too good, he's got too much passion, and he wants revenge for the way he was pushed out at Keystone State.

"Let's face it. We were all shocked when the news broke last December. But now that some time has passed, most of us in the media believe that Dorsey was framed so that Thompson's son could become the starter. And he *clearly* has a chip on his shoulder here, whatever you believe. Not to mention that he probably would have won the Heisman last year, had he not been released. We're talking about an elite quarterback, maybe the best we've seen in years.

"Which brings me to my next point—the other team's quarterback. Know who's under center for the Gargoyles? Danny Thompson. And we all saw his performance in the national championship last year. I'd be surprised if this game *wasn't* close."

A funky-sounding bell rang, and the camera turned to Mel.

"The Beavers are not going to beat the Gargoyles because one player does not make a team," he contended. "The last time I checked, football was 11 vs. 11, not one-on-one. Sure, Adam Dorsey plays for the Beavers. Sure, he's very good. Who do the Gargoyles have? Oh, let me see. Wide receivers Chris Cook, Deion Carter and Jaden Hall—those are three accomplished young men right there. A beast at running back named Jamal Harris. A top NFL prospect in linebacker Lukas Bowser. A stand-out defensive lineman who's coming off a 12-sack season in Terrence Porter. An all-conference center in Joey Callahan. Need I go on?"

"Adam Dorsey is better at his position than all of them," Jerry argued.

"That may be true, but let me finish. You mentioned that Danny Thompson is an inexperienced quarterback. Well, let me remind you that his *dad* was an offensive genius in the NFL and knows a thing or two about the position. This guy has an impressive history of molding successful quarterbacks. You think his son's going to turn out any different? Oh, and I didn't even mention the fact that this man has won 85 percent of his games at college football's highest level. You think he's gonna blow this one to the *Beavers* in prime time? *I don't think so.*"

"If you want to talk coaches, then Teddy Morgan's résumé is just as impressive as Thompson's," countered Jerry. "You cannot overlook what he's done at St. Bruno's. He's taken a low-budget, low-profile academy and transformed it into an FCS superpower. He's won two national titles already, with a good shot at his third this year. And he snatched up Adam Dorsey when no other coach could. Say what you want, but Teddy Morgan is one of the most underrated coaches out there. And the Beavers are no pushover, Mel. This team has been competitive against top-tier programs."

The bell rang again.

"So what are your predictions for the game?" the host asked.

"38 – 10 Gargoyles," Mel said simply.

Jerry massaged his chin with his fingers. "The Gargoyles won't win this one by four touchdowns. But I can't pick against them. They have too much talent. 28 – 20 Gargoyles."

"That was my whole argument!" chortled Mel.

"I didn't argue against that. I argued that it would be close," Jerry defended.

Adam sat there as the show switched topics, not knowing how to describe his emotions—but the feeling was not good.

He picked against us, too. After all he said, he picked against us...what a moron...

It felt like he'd been served a reality check, and part of him wanted to surrender to that reality while the other part wanted to resist. He had expected Jerry to pick them, and he hadn't. Were they really that outnumbered?

"It's just one point," he stated defiantly as he rose from the chair.

Roadrunner, Derek and Bookworm exchanged glances. They knew their quarterback well enough by now, and understood that talking back would only infuriate him more. In Adam's eyes, they were going to win no matter what. And what teammate could argue with that mentality?

"We just need one more point than they do, that's it. Doesn't matter how we get there. Style points don't matter. You guys coming to dinner, or what?"

"Yeah," Roadrunner replied as they followed him.

"Well, come on, let's go. We're trying to get ready for the season, not worrying about what some jackass on TV is saying."

The Crypt
Chapter 16

"There's no substitute for guts."

--Paul "Bear" Bryant

That last week seemed to pass faster than the rest.

Maybe they were in such a routine that the days blurred together. Or maybe they were concentrating so hard on executing against the scout team Gargoyles that they didn't have time to think about how many practices were left. Adam wasn't sure. But here they were on Thursday, August 29, and the game was only 50 hours away.

The Beavers traditionally held an end-of-camp picnic for the team and their families after that last Thursday practice. Coach Morgan and the rest of the staff would mingle with the adults while the players went off and played volleyball or ultimate Frisbee.

The sun was low on the horizon as Adam sat on a log around an empty fire pit with several teammates and Lindsey (Z had come down with food poisoning and was resting in his dorm). They were conversing on the side of a grassy hill above campus, with the athletic fields and basilica far below. The sound of Mozart's amplified guitar drifted through the air as he played tunes at the picnic pavilion a hundred yards away. Near that, several players had started a sand volleyball game with a few of the little brothers and sisters.

Brian Massey and Tony Ferrari had ambled over, much to Adam's displeasure, and Massey was trying to light a fire with matches while the linemen gathered sticks or yelled advice. Adam, meanwhile, was hunched over the Gargoyles' scouting report with Derek Bell.

"You think you understand this stuff?" he asked after explaining his former team's defensive tendencies.

"Yeah, I think I got it."

"Hey! Study time's over!" Graham Cracker yelled. "We could use that paper to start this fire, you know."

"You're still looking at *that?*" Garfield cried. "It's two days before the game! Come *on!* They're just going to shred them anyway, so may as well put them to good use!"

Adam instinctively wanted to object, but knew that any more studying this close to kickoff would be counter-productive. He didn't want Derek to be overwhelmed as the game neared, and he was planning to give him some last-minute hints on the bus ride anyway.

"Probably right about that," he agreed, and handed the packets to Graham Cracker after yanking off the paper clips and stuffing them in his jeans pocket.

With a few small twigs and the crumpled up packets, Massey was able to get a small flame going. And in ten minutes' time they were roasting s'mores with the supplies that Lindsey had brought.

"Whatever happened to the rest of that chocolate?" she wondered aloud as the second round of roasting began.

"Wasn't me," Garfield announced immediately, and everyone glared at the dark spots around his mouth.

"Aw, that *figures!*" Massey cried. "I haven't even had one yet!"

"Hey, I deserve it!" Garfield retorted in his sarcastic way. "Teddy Bear was on my ass all camp long! You didn't do shit!"

"That's 'cause I stay in shape!"

"Well at least I'm not afraid of *ghosts!*"

He apparently had gone too far, because Massey was staring Garfield down like he wanted to fight him right there.

"I'm not afraid of ghosts!"

"You wouldn't go down there if our season depended on it!"

"Of course I would!"

"Fine! Let's go! You and me! Who's got a flashlight?" Garfield demanded as the rest of the team doubled over with laughter.

"You know, Z always said he'd take me down to the crypt, but I think he's regretting his promise," Lindsey mentioned. "He always makes excuses for why we can't go. So I guess I'll have to tag along with someone else!"

"Yeah, Lindsey can come as a witness!" exclaimed Garfield.

"I'd actually be down for an adventure," Cody McCormack added. "We've got nothing else to do, and we don't have to be up early for the trip tomorrow."

"Let's do it," Graham Cracker replied enthusiastically. "We need flashlights, though."

"Oh, I've got two in my dorm room," Lindsey announced. "How about we meet outside the church doors in, say, 20 minutes?"

"Sounds good to me!" Jason Evans remarked.

"Oh, I'm so excited! You guys are so much more fun than Z," she added as she hurried away down the hill. "See you all in a bit!"

Jason smirked at Massey as Lindsey disappeared through the pine trees. "Well, this is the perfect opportunity for you."

"What are you talking about?" Massey spat.

"Come on, don't play stupid. We all know you've got a thing for her. Z is sick in his dorm room so he's out of the picture. You're not going to get a better opportunity to be alone with her."

"It's not happening," he stated matter-of-factly. "Forget about it. I'm leaving."

He turned to go, but Jason couldn't resist.

"Boy, you really *must* be a wuss, to pass this up."

Massey stopped. "It...it's not that I'm afraid!"

"Then why aren't you coming? Z won't be there! Think about it. It's dark down in the crypt...lots of nooks and spaces for you guys to sneak into, and nobody will ever know..."

"Alright, I'll go."

The linemen chuckled.

"But it's not because of that. I'm going so you guys can't hold this against me," he insisted, but Adam could tell that he was struggling with his emotions.

"How about you, Cowboy?"

This time it was Graham Cracker. And for a brief moment Adam didn't know what he wanted to do. He glanced at Roadrunner, but his dark silhouette was already walking down the hill towards campus. No, he wasn't going to risk trouble on the night before they left for Sunset Vale and Keystone State—not after what he'd been through in high school, and what his football career meant to him now.

Yet even without his closest friend, a sense of excitement and recklessness overtook him as the dusk settled in and the shadows grew taller. He'd been on good terms with these guys ever since the night at Retone's, and he couldn't ruin that now.

"OK, I'm in."

Everyone at the fire whooped and hollered.

"Hoho, there's the fearless leader in our quarterback!" shouted Ferrari.

"We'll handle those ghosts no problem now that we've got Cowboy!" Jason added.

"Wait, somebody needs to hold Massey's hand! Who wants to volunteer?" Graham Cracker teased.

Massey just gave him a disgusted look and led the way.

It was a long 20 minutes. The towering figures of pine trees surrounded them as they trekked down a secluded pathway through the woods—they couldn't pass the pavilion without having to explain where they were going to the parents and coaches. Adam stuffed down the last few marshmallows as they scrunched through the underbrush, and he couldn't help but feel a bit apprehensive.

They weren't at the church doors for long before Lindsey appeared. She gave one flashlight to Cody and kept the other for herself.

"I can't wait to see the look on Z's face when I tell him about this," she giggled.

Adam hadn't been inside the basilica since Roadrunner had taken him months ago. It was just as impressive as he remembered, but slightly spookier now with the lights off and nobody in sight. He could barely see the high ceiling in the darkness, and as they tip-toed down the center aisle, it was easy to imagine this place as a mysterious lost city far away from the comforts of a college campus.

"Well, last chance to wimp out!" Cody joked as they reached the ornately-carved door at one of the side transepts. He opened it, and the creaky sound it produced could have come straight from a horror movie. Beyond the door there was no light—only a stony staircase that twisted out of sight.

"Which one of you guys has been down here before?" the lineman asked as he shined the light ahead.

"Me and Jason have," Graham Cracker divulged. "But I think Massey should go first."

"Not unless I have a flashlight—"

"Alright, then Garfield."

"Yo, I shouldn't have to go first! I don't know where the hell I'm going."

"How about we all just stand here arguing for ten minutes," Massey grumbled hopefully. "Then we can turn around and head right back outside after we can't come to an agreement."

"Oh, shut up, all of you," Lindsey scolded, and she brushed by them and plunged into the darkness.

Adam immediately felt the temperature drop as he descended the staircase, and Z's words from so long ago echoed through his thoughts as his footsteps pattered down the cold stairs...

"St. Bruno's is haunted...Wagner rises from the grave every year on the day he died, and his ghost walks through campus as he makes his way to the crypt...red doors are haunted—remember that..."

The staircase opened into a cavernous chamber. It was tough to envision how it might look with the lights on, but thick columns supported the main floor of the basilica like tree trunks, and grotesque Gargoyles were sculpted into their detailed designs.

"We gonna get whacked, we gonna get whacked," Ferrari whispered nervously.

"We're not going to get whacked," Adam reassured. "It's just the basement of the church, that's all."

"The crypt's back there," Graham Cracker pointed out, and the rest of them followed his lead.

A moment later, they had arrived.

Two red wooden doors rose ominously from the basement floor, their color especially striking against the gray stone columns and walls. The black doorknobs matched the spiky-looking metal hinges. As they approached, Adam realized they were much larger than normal doors—maybe nine or ten feet.

Graham Cracker waltzed right up to one and rattled the doorknob. "They're locked."

"I wonder if there's any way we could pry them open," Cody remarked.

"You're not going to get in there," Massey stated. "This is it. We came all the way down here for this."

"Shut up, Massey," Graham Cracker snarled. "I wanna see if there's some way..."

His voice trailed off as he began prying his fingers around the edges and peering through the keyhole.

"Well, *this* is lame!" Garfield complained as the rest of them stood there watching. "Do you think there's any food in there? I'm getting kind of hungry—"

But he was cut short when Graham Cracker started banging loudly on the door.

"Stop that," Massey ordered.

"Massey, stop being a chicken—"

"No, I'm serious. *Don't do that!*"

"I think he's right. We really shouldn't try and vandalize anything," Lindsey remarked.

"Well what else do you expect me to do?" Graham Cracker argued.

"That's it," demanded Massey. "We're done. Let's go. This is stupid—absolutely stupid."

"You *are* chicken," the center replied.

"I'm not arguing with you anymore! If I have to drag you back up those steps, I will!"

Graham Cracker crossed his arms defiantly. "I'm not leaving."

"I'm serious! You don't want to mess around down here, trust me. It's just that...we just need to go, right now."

"Chicken," the center repeated, and he resumed banging on the door and rattling the knob.

"You're in over your heads and none of you know it," Massey finally blurted, and he walked away. But he wasn't going in the right direction—the stairs were the other way.

And then Adam understood.

He can't leave. It's pride. But he doesn't want to be anywhere near these doors, with what they're doing...

His conscience began nagging at him.

You should go with him. He doesn't have a flashlight.

Nah, he'll be alright. What do I owe him?

You want to be the leader of the team, right? You gotta make sure nothing bad happens down here!

Yes. He was going.

"Cowboy, where you going?" Jason yelled as he scampered away.

"Just gotta make sure Massey doesn't get lost!" he shouted over his shoulder, and within seconds he'd caught up to the wide receiver.

"What're you doing?"

"Just making sure you're alright, that's all," Adam replied in what he hoped was a friendly voice.

"*You're* coming to make sure *I'm* alright?"

"You don't have a flashlight, and it's dark."

"I know my way around this place. I'll be OK."

Adam was glad to hear that. He'd done his good Samaritan duty, and now he had an excuse to leave. After all, what could they possibly talk about? How much of an under-achieving receiver he was?

"OK," he replied. "I'm gonna head back—"

But he never finished the sentence.

A blood-curdling scream had erupted nearby. From the corner of his eye, Adam saw lights twirling in the darkness near the entrance to the crypt—whether they were the flashlights, he did not know. Fear paralyzed him for one endless moment. And before he could think what to do, Graham Cracker was running towards them with his arms flailing and a look of horror on his face. He blew past them like his pants were on fire and there was a lake somewhere down the hall. Cody, Jason, Garfield, Ferrari and Lindsey were right behind, looking just as terrified.

After a quick glance, he and Massey bolted with them.

Looking back on it, Adam didn't think he'd ever been as scared as he was right then. He didn't know what the others were running from, but he did *not* want to be the last one in line—for some reason that was very important. Garfield, Jason and Massey were still behind him...he was safe for now...

Somebody ahead still had a flashlight, and Adam saw the beam whiz in every direction as the person ran. It was enough to see what was ahead, but barely. They had entered some kind of corridor with centuries-old stone walls. The floor had turned to dirt. Every now and then, he caught a quick glimpse of an archway above them as the beam zoomed past. Were they entering a different corridor? Were the archways built into the walls? He didn't know. All that mattered was that they keep running...

It probably wasn't five minutes, but it must have been close by the time Adam stopped. As he ran, it had seemed like they'd lost some people, until he only heard one set of footsteps trailing him. And as he glanced around now, he realized he was alone.

Or so it seemed...

Don't think like that, he told himself firmly. But it was hard not to think of the worst possible scenario, with no one to talk to and no clue how to reach fresh air. He'd lost sight of the beam hundreds of yards ago and had been stumbling in the dark. Was he in a room? Another crypt?

"Adam."

He whipped around, and a small flame flickered to life ten yards away. The sharp features of Brian Massey hovered above the match in the darkness.

"Congratulations, we're lost," the receiver spat.

He was amazed that the sight of Massey could make him feel so good.

"Where are the others?" he wheezed.

"There's an intersection with another passageway back there. I think they went that way."

"So it was *your* footsteps I've been hearing the past couple of minutes. I could have sworn somebody else was behind me."

"Yeah, that's because I followed you."

"You did?"

"I've got you covered," Massey replied simply. "You didn't realize the others had turned, so I ran after you. You don't know where you're going. You would have been lost for days."

Adam felt a powerful sense of both gratitude and embarrassment. "Thanks."

"I'm not doing it for you. Our bus is leaving for Sunset Vale at 10 a.m. tomorrow, and if you're not on it, our chances of winning this game drop significantly."

Valid point, he reasoned. "So you know your way around this place?"

"I've been down here three times, so yeah."

"Really? I never would have guessed that. What for?"

"Well, let me see. The first time I was a freshman, and the older players were trying to scare me. The other times I had to come down and save some teammates' asses because they were *fucking* around just like you guys are tonight! Maybe you'll learn your lesson now. You see why I don't like this place? You see what happens? I don't know what it is, but something bad always happens when we come down here."

"What happened to get them so scared?"

"I don't know."

"Was it...?"

He didn't have to finish the question.

"I don't know."

"Well, can you get us out of here?"

Massey paused. "I probably can. I've got no idea where we are, but there are several routes leading back out. If I can find some markers, I'll know which way to go."

He struck up another match and they started walking.

"You're lucky I had these in my pocket from the campfire," he added. "We'd really be screwed without them. The rest of them have the flashlights."

"We could use a little luck over the next couple of days," Adam acknowledged. "I didn't know this place was so huge."

"We're not in the church anymore," corrected Massey. "Are you kidding me? No church basement is this big."

And then it hit him.

"It's over three miles long if you add them all up...legend has it that the monks built them to transport supplies from the lake and quarry...during Prohibition, they used them to secretly transport alcohol..."

They were in the underground tunnel network.

Five minutes and three matches later, Massey stopped.

"Well, we're completely lost," he confessed.

Adam swore under his breath. "I wish Roadrunner was here," he whispered, but he regretted it the second the words left his mouth.

Massey glared. "You wish Roadrunner was here? What, I'm not good enough? It has to be him?"

"I...I didn't mean it like that."

"You know, there's 60 other guys on this team. Who cares about Roadrunner right now? Roadrunner's not here. I'm here. So you better deal with it or find your own way out."

He didn't want to fight, he really didn't. This couldn't happen *now*, when they were so close to the game. They couldn't get stuck down here and not be found until the game was over. They just couldn't.

"I'm going to keep heading in this direction and see what happens," Massey explained. "If you don't want to come, then scram. But I don't know what you're going to do for light, 'cause I sure as hell am not giving you any of these matches."

"Well, I guess I'm coming then."

"Do you trust me?"

It seemed like a mandate that he answer the question, and the match was burning. But Adam was ashamed to realize he couldn't look Massey in the face.

"Yes," he breathed. "I trust you. So let's get moving and find a way out of here."

It had felt like I lie, but what choice did he have? He couldn't say "no."

Massey looked skeptical. "OK, let's go."

It felt like miles before any new sight appeared in their tiny sphere of light. But just when Adam was beginning to lose hope, the receiver jogged towards a dark object up ahead.

"What is it?"

"The barrels," Massey exclaimed. "They're old-fashioned kegs from the 1920s."

Sure enough, the passageway opened into a large chamber, with a small collection of barrels stacked against the wall. Two other passageways branched off from the room.

"Hold this," he ordered as he knelt to examine the find. He passed the flame to Adam and then used his own hands to dust off a lid.

It read *Retone's Famous Keystone Lager* in fancy cursive.

"This is it," he declared. "I've been here before. I remember this stack from the first time I got lost."

He rose and scanned the surrounding chamber.

"I think I went that way. And I eventually reached a door, but it was locked. That's probably a way out."

"Well, if it's locked then it won't do us much good."

"No, but can you think of a better option right now? We have to try it. Come on, give me some light!"

And they were off again, ducking under spider webs and mysterious stone archways. Massey seemed to know exactly where he was going as he charged full-speed into the darkness.

They reached the place sooner than Adam was expecting. But as the candlelight flooded the area and illuminated the next few yards, his heart sank. He had been fearing a locked door, but what they got was even worse...

"You didn't tell me it was red," he whispered.

"Aw, *fuck* the red! You guys and your damn ghost stories. The only doors I won't touch are the ones in the crypt, for obvious reasons. The rest are all harmless."

He strode forward fearlessly and rattled the doorknob, but it was locked just like every other one. And they were probably locked for a reason, Adam couldn't help but think. A good reason.

"I need my lock-picking set," Massey spat in frustration.

"You know how to pick locks?"

"Yeah, I used to do it all the time when I was little. I went some places I wasn't supposed to go and did some bad things, but the point is, I don't have my set so we're *screwed!*"

Adam instinctively reached into his pockets with his free hand, simply to reassure Massey that he wasn't carrying anything helpful. But as he did so, his fingers touched something small and wiry...

"Paper clips! I've got two paper clips from the scouting reports!"

"Let me see."

Massey examined them closely under the candlelight while Adam held his breath.

"These'll work. But it's gonna be hard. It might take me a while."

"That's fine," Adam breathed as his hopes lifted. "As long as we get out of here, I don't care."

He was right—it took a while for the receiver to work the metal into the correct shapes. Adam had to strike the third-to-last match.

"*Fuck,*" the receiver swore as that match neared its end. "My fingers are too big. I need some pliers or something."

"I don't think we'll be able to find those down here—"

"No *shit!*" he barked, and Adam shut his mouth.

"OK," Massey said a minute later. "I'm ready. How many matches we got left?"

"Two. I'll make them last as long as I can."

"Yeah, you better. Now, I want you to hold the flame as close to the lock as you can, but don't burn my fingers. And be completely quiet. I need to hear these pins. You got me?"

"Yeah."

Adam lit the second-to-last match, and they began.

"This...is called a pin tumbler lock," Massey explained in spurts as he concentrated on the task. "All the locks on campus are pin tumblers. I know because I've picked a few before. Now, all you have to do...is work each pin...until it aligns with the shear line between the housing and the plug...and the tension wrench...which is this L-shaped paper clip...keeps the pins from falling back into place after you've aligned them."

Adam didn't understand how to pick locks, but he didn't care. Massey sounded like he knew what he was doing, and that was all that mattered.

It felt like waiting for a trial verdict. There was complete silence except for the *click! click!* of the homemade rake and their heavy breathing.

The match had reached its end.

"This is the last one," Adam whispered.

"I know. Just hold it close like you've been doing. I'm on the last pin."

The red door loomed over them menacingly, as if to signal their impending doom. Instinct told Adam to run—to get as far away from it as possible. But here he was leaning against it and praying that nothing bad was on the other side...

A final, more profound *click!* sounded.

"That's it," Massey declared with a hint of both irritation and triumph, and they made eye contact as he reached for the handle.

"You're sure about this?"

Massey shrugged. "Only one way to find out."

He pushed the door open with a squeaky thud. Adam stared at the dirt floor as his teammate poked his head through, afraid of what he might see if he looked up...

"This is it."

He glanced up, the dread inside of him extinguishing and the relief surging in one glorious second. Beyond the door was a short hallway that led to an ascending staircase. And the moonlight spattered across the stairs signaled the end of the tunnels.

They didn't exactly run, but there was an extra jump in their step as they scrambled up the staircase. They emerged from the shadow of the old storage tower on the outskirts of campus and onto a grass field.

Adam collapsed onto the cool grass and stared at the starry sky. The feel of the breeze against his face had never felt so good. He was so happy, he wished the game were starting now. He was so full of positive energy that they would win for sure.

As he tilted his head, he saw Massey standing a few feet away and staring at him with his hands on his hips.

"Are you OK?"

"Never felt better!"

The wide-out just shook his head and grinned.

"You owe me one. I just saved our asses, big time."

"I'm throwing you a touchdown pass in the game!" was Adam's giddy reply. Hell, he could have three touchdowns. The more the better!

It wasn't until the euphoria wore off a little that he hoisted himself up and brushed the grass from his knees.

Massey glanced at the surroundings and scratched his head. "I didn't know that staircase led to the tunnels," he commented casually as he stared at the storage tower. "I always thought that just led to a basement or something."

"Well, I say we go and see if the other guys made it out," Adam remarked.

"They had two flashlights and six people! They should have made it out, no problem," the receiver answered as they headed onto the dirt path leading towards campus.

Adam knew he had to say something before they reunited with the others.

"Massey, thanks. I really mean it. You saved my life."

"Yeah, like I said, you owe me one. Thanks for acknowledging that."

Adam grinned. It was, more or less, Massey's was of saying, *"I'll accept the thanks."* And to be quite honest, he didn't even feel bad about sucking up to his least-favorite teammate. He deserved every single word of it. He deserved even more than that. Yeah...

He deserved his trust, Adam finally decided. Not that he hadn't made an attempt at it over the summer. But maybe he'd done so half-heartedly. After all, you can't just fabricate something like that. It has to be genuine, otherwise it can't possibly work its magic.

"You're getting a touchdown pass on Saturday," he repeated, only this time he was dead serious.

"I'm holding you to that."

Luke Fetkovich

"Please do," he chuckled. "But don't act like I need any extra motivation for this one!"

The Homecoming
Chapter 17

"On this team, we're all united in a common goal: to keep my job."
--Lou Holtz

    Adam was so relieved to get out of the tunnels and back to his cozy dorm room that he almost forgot how close the game was. The details of their trip down to the crypt, and the mad dash getting lost, and how Brian Massey had bailed him out, all dominated his thoughts as he recounted the adventure to Roadrunner that night.
    It wasn't until they locked the door behind them the following morning that it really sunk in. He felt like a kid waiting and waiting for an exciting vacation, and now, as they packed their bags and headed for the busses, the moment was finally here. The nerves would come later, when they were suiting up in the visiting locker room.
    After half a year at St. Bruno's, it probably shouldn't have come as a surprise when Adam saw two yellow school busses parked in the vacant lot—one for offense and one for defense.
    "Classy," Adam joked as he and Roadrunner hopped up the stairs and into the offensive bus.
    "We've got so much class ourselves that there wasn't any left for the material things," replied the running back.
    Adam grinned. "That's pretty good. Who came up with that?"
    "Me."
    "Doesn't surprise me."
    There was enough space for each player to get his own seat, and so they sat across from each other near the back. Cody McCormack was right behind him, and Adam figured now would be the perfect time to ask the question he'd been wondering. The rest of the guys had found their way out of the tunnels safely, but still...
    "What happened to make you guys freak out like that?"
    Cody just grinned and shook his head. "Don't ask. All I know is, I'm never going down there again!"
    "Don't offend the monks, living *or* dead," Ferrari repeated from the seat ahead. "Whoever came up with that is a real wise guy, lemme tell ya!"

The conversation ended there, as Coach Morgan had just climbed into the bus sporting his aviators.

"OK, men! It's a six hour bus ride from here to Sunset Vale, so I hope you can all last that long without a bathroom break."

There were chuckles from the team, who knew him so well that they didn't fall for the joke.

"No, you guys are smarter than that. I should know. We'll be stopping for a lunch break around noon," he continued as he patted the humongous blue and red coolers stacked in the first row. "Compliments of the school cafeteria. I also shouldn't have to remind you about dropping your equipment bag at the truck, so we can get those to the stadium tonight. You should have all done that, and if not then you've got about two minutes until we leave. Now, let's get this party on the road!"

In a few moments they were heading for the turnpike, with the cars of the coaches and team doctor Stephen Hunt leading the way. Adam felt like he was back in high school, riding school busses through the green forests and rolling hills of upper New York on his way to an early September game.

"Hold your breath!" Garfield yelled an hour later as they entered a tunnel through the Appalachians. The rest of the offense laughed as the lineman's face went red, and he gave up halfway through.

Bookworm passed the hours reading *A Tale of Two Cities*. Tight end Jermaine Thomas sat in the very back row, playing tunes on the guitar he'd borrowed from Mozart and taking requests. And Adam quickly got to work quizzing Derek Bell on the game plan.

"How's Charles Dickens coming?" he asked Bookworm after Derek aced every question.

"I'm almost finished," the receiver answered. "So, this is kind of like a homecoming for you, huh?"

Adam struggled for the right thing to say. "It's not about me."

Bookworm just rolled his eyes. "Yes, I know it's not about you. You've been saying that for months. I'm just wondering how you're feeling, that's all."

He paused. "I'm kind of nervous, to be honest with you."

"Really? About what?"

"That's the funny thing. I'm not exactly sure."

Bookworm grinned. "Weird, huh? I bet I'd feel nervous too, if I were you. Are you going to see any of your old friends tonight?"

Again, Adam paused. Coach Morgan was giving them each twenty dollars for dinner on their own. He would have the time.

"I'm not sure. Maybe."

Just then, his smartphone vibrated in his pocket. He pulled it out and saw a text from Joey Callahan, his old center and one of his best friends ever since that first spring with Deion and Chris.

When are u coming up

He felt a rush of mixed emotions as his fingers hovered above the screen. There were so many ways he could go with the conversation. He could make an excuse to avoid them if he wanted, or he could throw caution to the wind...

We'll be there around 5:00

Bookworm saw him texting, but decided not to ask who it was.

The phone vibrated again.

We're not going to the hotel til 8 if u want to meet up

Adam stalled, then replied with the answer that was in his heart instead of the one in his head.

Yeah I'd like that. Kinda nervous tho lol

At least he'd told the truth. Joey knew him too well, anyway.

The next text rang in.

WTF Adam we're still ur friends. I haven't seen u in months

Adam smiled to himself. That was the Joey Callahan he knew—too mature and trustworthy to cave in to the expectations of lesser people. It didn't matter that they were going against each other in 30 hours, or that Adam would love nothing more than to crush the Gargoyles' national championship hopes. Above and beyond anything else, they were friends.

Before he could respond, Joey sent a second text.

DT won't be with us lol

Adam knew he was trying to convince him to meet up, and he couldn't turn him down.

OK haha. But I better get to see Deion and Chris too

He wondered if Coach Morgan would like the idea of him hanging with the opposing team, but guessed that he would understand.

Def. You know they'll be there

They better be! Does Deion still have his dreads?

Longer than ever lol

Haha nice. Where u want to meet up?

Outside Palmer Hall, 6 ish?

See u then

He was just about to put his phone in his pocket, but then he saw Roadrunner sitting across the aisle from the corner of his eye. An idea struck him.

I'm bringing one of my teammates, that cool?

Yea who is it

His name's Anthony Campbell

OK

It felt strange typing Roadrunner's real name when he hadn't used it in ages. He figured that Joey, Chris and Deion knew exactly who he was, considering that Randy Thompson had probably put them through a rigorous film study on their opponent. Even though they were offensive players, he could just imagine linebacker Lukas Bowser or defensive lineman Terrence Porter complaining about how the coaches had hammered the running back's name into their heads.

"Hey," he called across the aisle. "You want to come and meet my old friends?"

His roommate took longer than usual to reply.

"Just me?"

"Yeah."

He thought he knew what Roadrunner was thinking—that their teammates might feel dissed if they knew their starting quarterback and running back were hanging out with the other team the night before the game.

"What do you think we should do?" Adam asked.

Roadrunner bit his lip, glanced around to make sure that no one was listening, and leaned across the aisle so that only Adam could hear.

"We won't tell anybody where we're going. We'll just sneak off after we get to the hotel."

"Whoa! Since when have you ever tried to be sneaky?" he whispered back. "Where's *that* Roadrunner been?"

The running back grinned. "Sometimes being honest is more trouble than it's worth. In this case, it's better to not draw attention to ourselves. I'm truthful, but I'm not stupid. Come on, Adam!"

"OK, I get it. Good thinking."

It wasn't long before they started seeing signs for Keystone State. 50 miles, now 20 miles…

The busses exited the turnpike and wound their way down a four-lane highway leading into the city of Sunset Vale. The noise level on the bus grew as the skyscrapers finally appeared in the distance, and some of the players began snapping pictures of the view with their phones.

Before long, Adam spotted it. Keystone Stadium towered in the center of the downtown area, its black supports and teal scoreboard standing proudly as the heart and soul of the city.

"Holy shit, I'm gonna crap my pants," Jason remarked as he pressed his face to the glass. "We're playing in *that?*"

"Yeah, just don't do that during the game," Cody advised. "I have to line up next to you."

Adam didn't want to reveal how amused he was by his teammates' reaction. They had never been exposed to a crowd this big, and he knew there would be a culture shock. But it was comforting to know that at least *he* wouldn't be awed by the situation tomorrow night. Roadrunner wouldn't be either—he was too composed for that.

Fifteen Minutes

The busses turned down College Boulevard—the road that ran directly past the stadium—and the offense suddenly grew quiet as they stared out the windows in amazement. The giant structure blocked the light from the sinking sun, so that the side nearest to them appeared darker and more imposing. Adam just sat sideways with his legs up on the seat and his back against his own window as he took it all in. He was really back here. They were really going to be on national TV. And he thought back to his days quarterbacking the Gargoyles—the good memories and the great wins he'd had in that stadium. This would be the last game he ever played there. And this last win would be the hardest to get. The last win, if he dared to dream of it, would be the absolute best.

They inched their way through the city amidst rush hour and weekend football traffic. Adam saw places that he had nearly forgotten about—the famous Gargoyle memorabilia store on the corner, the student bookstore, "Marley's" 50s-themed pizza parlor, and more. He also recognized the hotel they would be staying at, as the busses finally pulled into the lot. The Fox Motel was a small but orderly inn close to the main drag and downtown restaurants.

"OK, men, here's the deal," Coach Morgan announced as he hopped onto the bus. "Coach Harris will give each of you your room key and twenty dollars for dinner as you get off. It's 5:20 right now. You need to be back at this hotel at 9 p.m. The assistants and I will be doing room checks from that point on. This is just like any other away game. You are expected to represent St. Bruno's in an honorable fashion, and I know that most of you excel in that regard. Let's make sure I don't have to remind anyone about that."

Teddy Morgan cleared his throat and continued in a more colloquial tone.

"Listen, guys. We've got a game tomorrow at 8 p.m. We've practiced hard and practiced well all week. Don't go and ruin it all now by stuffing down a quarter-pounder and fries. Be smart. Take care of your body. We don't let you guys eat out so you can treat yourself to whatever you want. We do it to save money. There are plenty of healthy choices down there. Any questions?"

After five seconds the coach clapped his hands.

"OK! 9 p.m., men! Back here by 9:00."

Adam and Roadrunner were two of the last ones off the bus, and quarterbacks coach Bob Harris gave them a buck-toothed grin as he stuffed the room keys and money into their hands.

"Hey, Adam!"

He looked up to see Z fighting his way over as he left the defensive bus.

"Do you guys want to grab something together? That Marley's pizza place looks pretty good!" the lineman asked hopefully.

Adam shot Roadrunner a glance, but his roommate wasn't about to open his mouth—this one was all on him.

"Actually, Z, we're going to meet some of my old teammates for dinner. Sorry, but I told them it was just going to be us two."

The old Adam Dorsey would have avoided the question, or lied altogether. But the new one understood that his teammates would respect him more if he told the truth, no matter what.

"Oh, I see," Z replied, looking less hurt than Adam was expecting. "That's no problem. I'll just grab something with Tonio then."

"Cool. We'll hang out on the next away trip," Adam added. "Just do us a favor and don't tell any of the sensitive guys where we're going. You know, like Mad Max or Garfield. They might take it the wrong way."

"I got your back!" Z exclaimed, and he headed off to find Tonio.

"That went better than expected," Adam commented.

"Maybe that's because you trust each other?" Roadrunner replied as they headed for the front doors of the hotel.

"Nah," Adam joked.

They took the elevator to the second floor, dropped their bags in the room and slid their room keys into their wallets. In five minutes, they were hustling back down to the lobby and walking outside with a little extra bounce in their steps.

For the first time that day, Adam freed his mind from all thoughts about the game. As they walked towards the downtown area with the early evening sun beating warmly on their shoulders, all he thought about was seeing his old buddies and having fun like they used to. He told himself the conversation wouldn't get awkward. He *hoped* it wouldn't. Really, that was the only thing that could ruin the evening—that and the Gargoyles new starting quarterback. As long as DT didn't show up, things were going to go great...

Pizza & Poodles
Chapter 18

"It's the name on the front of the jersey that matters most, not the one on the back."
--Joe Paterno

For a few minutes, they weren't football players anymore.

They were tourists, exploring the downtown area like everyone else. A strange feeling overcame Adam as he realized he was an outcast at his old school. He couldn't remember the last time he'd walked these streets without Kelsey or another Gargoyle teammate, and even then he'd been the star of the town. Now it was the complete opposite, but it satisfied him, as odd as that was.

He wondered if people would recognize him. Of course they would. After all, it had been only nine months since he'd guided Keystone State to the national championship. And the team had only played one game since he'd been replaced.

How would they react tomorrow night? Would they boo? Clap? Would there be a standing ovation for everything he'd done? He was about to encounter so many odd situations that he didn't even want to think about it.

"Are all these people here for the game tomorrow?" Roadrunner asked as they strolled down the crowded sidewalk.

"Yeah, it's ridiculous down here during football weekends."

"Do you think it's sold-out?"

"It's always sold-out. Doesn't matter who the opponent is. Ever since Thompson took over, that's how it's been. People want to see offense; they want to see points. He's brought that here. I should know. I was the center of it all."

They veered off the sidewalk and onto a brick pathway that wound through campus. Adam led them down a few shortcuts he remembered from his time here, and within minutes they were standing outside of Palmer Hall. Joey, Chris and Deion hadn't arrived, so they sat on a nearby bench and talked casually. A few students glanced in their direction as they walked past, and Adam wondered if they'd realized who he was. He'd chosen particularly large sunglasses for a reason, after all.

Before long, he spotted the three players heading their way. Deion was in the lead with his long dreads, while Chris's tall figure looked exactly the same. Joey had gained some muscle and shed some fat over the offseason.

"What's up, Adam?" Deion beamed as the two of them clapped hands. "It's been months, man, months!"

Chris and Joey were grinning too, but Adam knew they were laughing at Deion's outgoing personality.

"It's good seeing you again," Chris remarked. "It's been weird without you here this summer."

"Yeah, we don't have anybody to play quarterback now," Joey chuckled.

"It's been weird for me, too," confessed Adam.

Joey took the initiative and introduced himself to Roadrunner.

"You're pretty fast, dude," Deion exclaimed, and Adam sensed that his old buddy was awed at how small Roadrunner was, now that they were face-to-face.

"Thanks."

"So where are we headed?" Chris asked. "We should grab some food."

"Adam? You pick. You're the one who's never here anymore," Joey suggested.

"Gee, I don't even know. We'll go with Marley's. I'm in the mood for pizza."

They headed back towards the main drag, and enjoyed some temporary shade as they journeyed down a wide pathway lined with elm trees.

"So this is your new best bud, huh?" Deion teased.

"He's been talking about you the most," Chris explained to the running back while Adam pondered how to respond. "They call you Roadrunner, right?"

"That's me."

"So you've been keeping this guy in shape down there at your school?" Joey asked playfully.

"We're roommates, so I try to."

"I never would have made it to camp without him," Adam admitted. "I would have turned right back around before even getting that far."

"You're saying we could have had Adam back here if it weren't for you?" Deion laughed. "Man, you screwed things up, kid."

Roadrunner just smiled.

"So do you guys, like, hang out all the time?" Chris prodded.

"Pretty much," replied Roadrunner.

He almost didn't want this, Adam thought as they navigated an impressive flower garden dotted with green antique street lamps. He didn't want the guys to get the wrong impression, like he'd made a bunch of new friends and had almost forgotten about them. But the problem was, that wasn't the wrong impression at all. It was the truth, as much as he didn't want to believe it.

In five minutes they had arrived at the restaurant.

"Here we are!" Deion exclaimed as he held the glass double-doors open for Roadrunner. "You're gonna love this place."

Marley's Pizza Diner was a 50s-themed pizzeria featuring retro décor—a stainless steel counter, glossy red leather booths and bar stools, and a black-and-white checkered floor. Old rock 'n roll tunes blared from the sound system, a neon clock hung above the counter and images of poodles dotted the restaurant. The centerpiece was a real 1957 Chevrolet Bel Air convertible that had been re-designed as a four-person table.

Adam hoped that none of the employees would recognize him, but knew that was probably a long shot.

"Mr. Dorsey, it's been a while," the cashier said when he stepped up to order.

"Yeah. It's good to be back though."

"All set and ready for tomorrow night?"

"I think so."

The man didn't press the issue further, and Adam ordered two New York-style slices.

They grabbed a booth across from the Bel Air, and nobody said a word as they savored the first bite of their toasty slices.

Chris broke the silence. "How bad do you want this, Adam? We've known you for three years, and I can tell without asking that you want this one bad. I just don't know how bad."

Adam thought as he took another bite of pizza. "On a scale of one to ten, it's about a ten, I'm not gonna lie. We've worked for months for this one game."

"Well, you've got the edge at quarterback!" Deion grinned.

"That kid is an embarrassment," Joey commented. "He can't throw."

"He *sucks*," Chris added.

"Thanks for the encouragement," Adam joked.

"So is this, like, a big deal for you guys?" Deion asked as he wolfed down his Hawaiian pizza. "I mean, to be playing against us at night?"

Roadrunner nodded as he chowed on his Meat Lover's slice. "We play in 5,000-seat stadiums. It would have been a big deal if Adam hadn't joined the team. It's a bigger deal now. Because now, we expect to win."

The three Gargoyles just stared. Adam laughed on the inside, because he was the only one at the table who understood Roadrunner's ability to amaze people with words.

"And that's not to say we wouldn't have tried to win if he'd never arrived," the running back continued in that matter-of-fact tone that he used so well. "We always try to win. But trying to win and expecting to win are two different things. This team would never have expected to win, on the inside, without Adam. *I* would have expected to. But that's me. Now that Adam's here, the other guys on this team expect to win. And it's all because of those extra factors that he brought with him when he joined the Beavers."

Adam was grinning now—he couldn't resist. He wished his teammates could see their own faces. He wasn't even sure they had understood what Roadrunner had said.

"Dude, you should be a coach," Deion advised. "That sounds like something a coach would say."

"Plan to, actually," responded the running back as he took another bite of pizza.

"He could be the coach if Teddy Bear suddenly disappeared tomorrow morning," Adam chuckled. "But what you guys have to understand is, this is an opportunity of a lifetime for our players. You guys play in prime time like it's nobody's business. These guys have been on national TV maybe once—*maybe*, if they were around for the championship game two years ago."

"Bigfoot says it's our fifteen minutes of fame," Roadrunner added.

"It probably is," Adam agreed. "I know it's my fifteen minutes, that's for sure. I don't think I'm ever going to feel this way again."

"And we get, like, 100 minutes, if you want to look at it that way," joked Deion. "We get ten times the amount of exposure that you guys do."

Joey looked like he was thinking hard, with his pizza slice sitting untouched on his plate. "But it's not about the actual fifteen minutes," he said suddenly.

"What do you mean?" Adam asked.

"It's about the concept," he continued. "The saying is that everyone gets fifteen minutes of fame in their lives, right? Well, this is our fifteen minutes, too. Not just for the Beavers, but for the Gargoyles. And every other team."

"Joey, you lost me, bud," Deion chortled.

"It's not about one game," Joey explained. "It's about our whole college careers. I mean, think about it. Even the guys who play for the Beavers get to play in front of thousands of fans every weekend. They've still got a whole campus following them and rooting for them. Most of the other college sports don't garner that kind of interest. They still have a following, sure, but it's not the same as football. Even basketball players don't get the crowds that we do."

"So you're telling me that we should be savoring this?" Chris asked thoughtfully.

"The whole four years," nodded Joey. "Most of us aren't going to the NFL. We're going to graduate and have careers, but we won't be famous. Thousands of people won't be watching us like they will be tomorrow night. This is *our* fifteen minutes, right now. This is the time when we get to have our names in the news and our games broadcast to the world. All those fans walking the streets out there? They came here to see *us*. And that's pretty special, if you ask me."

Adam was now the one thinking hard. "You're right," he said abruptly. "I was spoiled. Ever since grade school, I thought I was going to the NFL. I probably still am. But that doesn't mean I should take any of this for granted. That's where I screwed up—I took it all for granted. And now, fourteen of those fifteen minutes of mine are up."

"Tomorrow night's the last one?" Deion queried.

"It's probably the last prime time game I'll ever play in at this level," replied Adam. "And you know what? I'm going to make the most of that last minute. Because even though I went 23 - 2 as a starter here, I don't think I really did that during those two years. I was too selfish. I didn't give anything back. I kept it all for myself. But tomorrow will be different. Tomorrow, it's not about me. It's about the St. Bruno Beavers."

They left the conversation at that, but what they had discussed would stick with Adam—and especially Roadrunner—for the rest of their lives, though they didn't know it at the time. Roadrunner couldn't have known that he would use the fifteen minutes concept to motivate his players in the future. And Adam couldn't have realized just how much the meaning of it all would help him appreciate his life in the NFL. But that was all OK, because right then and there, Adam felt like he'd finally solved the mystery of what this game was really about. He sure as hell didn't want it to be about him versus Randy Thompson. He needed something fresh and meaningful to motivate him now, and he'd found it just in time.

"I'd better go to the bathroom before we get out of here," he said 20 minutes later as they talked casually over empty plastic plates.

He got up and headed for the small hallway leading to the restrooms, passing a giant jukebox on the way. He was so preoccupied with the colorful flashing tube lights that he didn't see the person coming in the other direction. They bumped shoulders, and he turned to apologize, thinking at first that it was an ordinary customer.

It wasn't. Danny Thompson was staring him in the face.

For a few seconds, Adam was so surprised that he didn't know what to say. Pink fluorescent lights lit the hallway, and judging from the look on DT's illuminated face, he was just as surprised to see him.

Adam waited for him to make the first move. But as the seconds wore on and he didn't say anything, he realized that DT was expecting the same from him.

"Well..." he said at last, and the pressure of finding something to say finally got to him, so much that he could only think of the one thing stuck on his mind...

"...this is awkward."

DT didn't smirk. He didn't do any of the things that Adam would have expected from the spoiled and annoying Danny Thompson he'd known in the past. Maybe the pressure of being the starting quarterback had finally taken its toll.

"What the hell are *you* doing down here?" DT blurted. "I thought the visiting team stayed at a hotel."

"Yeah, but curfew's not 'til 9:00 and we've got dinner on our own, so there you have it."

DT opened his mouth like he wanted to respond but could not think how.

"Let me ask you the same question," Adam continued. "What are *you* doing here? You were the one person I was hoping I wouldn't see."

DT looked scared out of his senses by this question, but Adam couldn't think why.

"Just hanging out with my girlfriend before the game tomorrow," he stuttered.

"You have a *girlfriend* now? Wow, I guess it comes with the territory now that you're the starter, huh?"

Again, DT was speechless.

"So how do you like my old job? Going well for you?" he added, and he didn't care one bit that there was sarcasm oozing from his voice.

DT's demeanor changed from scared to humble. "It's tough. I gotta work twice as hard as I did last year. My dad pushes me real hard. He knows we've gotta win, with the way you went out and all the whispers and stuff surrounding that."

"Really?" Adam scoffed. "Wow, why am I not surprised to hear that? Get yourself in over your head, DT? Bite off more than you can chew, did you?"

"I was wrong," DT confessed, and Adam felt the grin drop from his face.

"What?"

"You can make fun of my situation all you want, but it wasn't my idea," he said defiantly. "I wasn't the one that kicked you off the team. I never made my dad do that. But I went along with it, and I was wrong. This isn't right. You don't deserve playing for that crappy team, at that crappy school—"

"It's not a crappy team," Adam interrupted, although he still couldn't get over the shock of what DT was saying. Was he hearing things?

"You don't deserve this, and I'm sorry. There, I said it. You can make fun of me all you want, but I said it."

Adam was now the speechless one.

"No, I do deserve this," he replied after a moment.

"You *do* deserve this? Gee, what happened to the old Adam Dorsey?"

"What happened to the old Danny Thompson?"

And they stood there silently once again, waiting for the other to make the next move.

"I've got to get going," Adam said. "Got some old friends that I want to hang out with..."

He paused.

"...thanks."

"For what?"

"For what you said. But I'm going to leave you with this—if you think you're in over your head now, just wait until tomorrow night. Because when you wake up on Sunday, things are going to be a hell of a lot worse for you and your dad."

DT stared him down with a calm poise that Adam didn't think he'd ever shown before.

"I can't beat you, Adam," he replied, so quietly that it was nearly a whisper. "But my team can."

Adam looked him straight in the eyes, and the easy answer that he was expecting to find never came.

"We'll see," he answered, and disappeared through the restroom door.

* * *

He looked around as he walked back to the table, expecting to see DT sitting somewhere with a girl. He found them in a booth beneath a large poodle picture, tucked away in the back of the restaurant—that was why he'd missed them before. The two quarterbacks made eye contact as Adam went past, but the girl was sitting the other way with her back turned.

"Did you guys see who's here?" he asked as he sat down.

"I *just* realized it after you left," Joey remarked. "Sorry, Adam. Didn't think that was gonna happen."

"Yeah, kind of a bummer running into your least favorite person *and* your ex-girlfriend when you just want to relax before the big game," Deion added.

Adam stopped in mid-motion as he went to throw away his trash. "Kelsey's here too?"

Deion's face dropped, and then it hit him. He glanced back at DT's booth. The girl was Kelsey Stuart—he just hadn't seen her face.

The two of them turned their heads in his direction, and he quickly looked away and pretended he hadn't seen them.

"When the hell did that happen?" he hissed as he sat back down.

"Back in February," Chris explained. "I'm sorry, Adam. We thought you knew. We thought she would have told you."

"Yeah, well it's not like she had much of an opportunity after we broke it off," Adam growled. "I left for St. Bruno's pretty soon after that."

From the corner of his eye, he saw the two of them get up, throw their trash away and head for the exit.

Yeah, you guys don't feel too comfortable hanging out here, now that you've realized I'm 30 feet away, do you?

He had made up his mind. Why he'd gotten the sudden impulse, he wasn't sure. But he was doing it.

"You guys about ready to head out?" he asked before DT and Kelsey were even out the door.

"Better not be in too much of a hurry," Deion advised, "or they'll still be in sight out on the street."

"That's exactly my plan."

He stood purposefully, and his old teammates exchanged glances.

"Well, guess we're coming!" Chris conceded.

Adam looked both ways as he pushed through the glass doors, and spotted them walking down the sidewalk about a block away. He took off in that direction, not really knowing what he was doing.

"What's your plan?" Roadrunner asked as they pushed their way through the crowd.

"Sorry," apologized Adam. "But I just have to talk to her, one last time. She won't answer her phone if she sees me calling."

Roadrunner nodded, and for the next couple of blocks he struck up a conversation with the three Gargoyles as Adam led the way, scouring the scene ahead and trying not to lose sight of Kelsey's glossy brown hair...

It wasn't long before he got his chance. The two of them stopped walking at an intersection, and Kelsey looked like she was reassuring DT as he talked animatedly. Then they kissed, and he headed off down one street while she continued straight.

Adam smiled to himself. DT was heading to his apartment to get ready for the trip to the Gargoyle team hotel, while Kelsey was probably going to her own place. If only his luck could continue through tomorrow night!

"I'm gonna go catch her," he declared. "You guys can hang out somewhere nearby. I won't be long."

He picked up his pace, weaving his way through the crowded sidewalk. His heart skipped a beat as he emerged ten feet behind her, and he felt like a bird swooping down on its prey. Did he feel guilty approaching her like this? Nah. If she wasn't going to answer her phone, then this was what she would get.

"Long time no see."

She turned abruptly. Clearly, she hadn't seen him coming. For above five seconds she just stared with her mouth open.

Adam waited. They had stopped walking, and the other passerby were scooting around them.

She instinctively glanced in the direction that DT had gone—Adam guessed that she was wondering if he'd seen her new boyfriend, or if he'd disappeared from sight in time.

"I already know," he said curtly. "You can't hide it anymore."

"Adam," she stuttered. "It...it's nothing personal. It's not about you."

"I didn't say it was. I just thought you held the bar a little higher than that."

She blushed. "We should get off the sidewalk."

They stepped closer to the brick wall of an adjacent building, where the setting sun had cast a cool shadow.

"So that was it, huh? That's why you wanted to break up. So you could go out with him."

"Adam, it wasn't like that. Honestly, we didn't even start going out until the end of February."

"Wow, that's a *huge* amount of time! I mean, we broke up in January!"

Kelsey bit her lip. He knew that meant she didn't have an answer.

"It had to at least be part of the reason. Tell the truth. I want to know."

And then a memory came flashing back—something that he'd forgotten the minute she'd said it, because he had been so distraught at the time.

"That was DT, wasn't it?"

"Yeah, and I can't decide what to make of his initials anymore..."

"It's not his fault. You shouldn't blame him."

"It's not his fault?! Kelsey, it's all his fault! If the little prick hadn't been born, none of this would be happening..."

And what had she done? She'd started crying. He should have known then.

A tear ran down her cheek, and Adam rolled his eyes.

"OK, so that's a yes, I take it?"

It was amazing how many great times they'd had together, and how none of that mattered anymore. He just wanted to forget about it all—scribble a black line through that part of his life so he couldn't see what was there. Things had been so sweet when they were dating, and now they were just sour.

"Fine. But I'll tell you what. If I'd have known the real reason why you wanted to break up, it would have saved me a whole lot of pain and suffering. Because I wouldn't have felt bad about breaking it off if I'd have known that. Not one bit."

"He's not a bad person, Adam. I could never expect you to like him, with what happened. But he's nothing like his dad—"

"I don't *care!*" he nearly laughed as he broke an incredulous grin. "I don't care what DT's like, I really don't. That's your choice. I'm not going to listen to you if you're going to try and twist things to make me feel better. That's dumb."

"Adam, please—"

"I'm not arguing anymore! And you know why? Because I've met so many great people from this whole mess, and none of that would have happened if things hadn't gone wrong! There's a running back waiting for me nearby, and he's the coolest kid I know. That never would have happened. All my other friends on the team? Never would have even known them."

Kelsey suddenly looked at him with admiration. "You've changed, Adam. I can't say exactly how, but you're not the same person you were back here."

"That's probably a good thing."

Neither of them spoke for a few seconds.

"I've said what I wanted to. So I'm going back to my friends now. I hope you're happy with your life, because you won't be hearing from me anymore."

She looked like she wanted to say something, but either she decided against it or could not force herself to do so.

That was it. He walked away, and when he finally looked back Kelsey was nowhere to be seen.

"How'd it go?" Chris asked.

"I did what I wanted to do."

"Sounds like it went well then," Joey remarked.

"Yeah. It did."

* * *

The next hour was one of the best of Adam's life. They walked around casually, chatting about new and exciting details in each other's lives and reminiscing about old times. They went to the famous downtown ice cream parlor, and Adam ordered his usual Gargoyle Green Explosion, with a scoop of mint chocolate chip and golden vanilla to mirror the home team's colors.

"Look at this traitor!" Deion gasped as Adam tasted the dessert. "He's switched sides right before the game!"

"The Beavers' colors are green and yellow, too," he defended. "The hues are just different!"

"Liking that ice cream, kid?" Chris laughed as Roadrunner licked his strawberry cone.

"It's way better than the stuff at our dining hall," he replied.

"Yeah, you should see him at school," Adam chuckled. "He doesn't skip a single meal without this stuff."

They started towards the hotel as they finished their cones, and soon it was time to part ways, as much as Adam didn't want to.

"We should probably head back," he advised as it neared 8 o'clock.

"Yeah. It was great seeing you again," Joey said.

"You too, Joey," he grinned, and he slapped hands with his two favorite Gargoyle receivers.

"And it's been a pleasure meeting you, Anthony!" Deion added. "Keep this guy in check for us, alright?"

"Sure thing."

Adam and Roadrunner started up the hill while the Gargoyles walked in the other direction. They were about ten steps apart when Joey turned around.

"Adam!"

He looked back.

"Good luck tomorrow!"

Adam smiled one more time—Joey was good at making him do that. He didn't even have to shout back. His expression told the center everything.

Joey and the wide receivers turned back around, and their silhouettes became smaller and smaller as they faded into the dusk that had fallen upon Sunset Vale.

In an hour, the only natural light came from the moon and stars in the clear night sky. A sleepy stillness settled on the town as the streets and sidewalks emptied themselves of cars and people. The bright lights and the buzz from the downtown bars remained after the restaurants and shops had closed their doors. But as time wore on, even the noise from the pubs died down, and soon the only signs of life were the lights from the gas station and the occasional hum of a solitary car.

A few blocks away, the illuminated windows of the Fox Motel shone brightly from behind the tall trees and shrubbery surrounding the building. But they had flickered off one by one as the players went to sleep, until just a single window was left.

Teddy Morgan hadn't bothered to turn off his lamp as he sat up in bed, analyzing the video on his laptop screen. The assistant coaches in the adjacent rooms wouldn't have known he was still awake, as the only sound came from the quiet clicking of his mouse as he pressed play, pause, then play again. He was searching, questioning and looking for answers that maybe they hadn't found—that maybe, somehow, they had missed...

When it was so late that the birds were chirping, he took a pad and pencil from his briefcase, jotted something down and tucked the materials beneath his desk.

Outside, the last lighted window went out.

Where the Hash Marks End
Chapter 19

"Show class, have pride, and display character. If you do, winning takes care of itself."

--Paul "Bear" Bryant

It wasn't long before Adam realized he had no idea where he was.

He was standing alone on a hilltop. The sky was bluer than blue, and the grass was greener than green. The colors were so vibrant, he felt as though he were inside a video game or a bold painting.

After a moment he started wishing for a good place to sit. Just as the thought crossed his mind, he looked to the side and saw a bench a few yards away. He walked over and happily rested his feet, taking in the view from his new seat.

The hill was one of many. Far in the distance, other hilltops featured bizarre structures and natural wonders. Giant pine trees towered over the regular-sized trees at the top of a nearby knoll. A mysterious building sat at the crest of another, and Adam couldn't tell if it was a castle or a mansion. A beanstalk climbed into the clouds from a third hill.

He looked behind him and saw a forest of vibrant green hues stretching down the far side of his own hill. In the valley below there seemed to be some sort of circus or fair, with striped tents and fluttering flags.

As he took in the surroundings, he realized he must be dreaming. That, or he'd died and gone to heaven.

He was just starting to get bored when a voice caught him by surprise.

"What the hell is going on out there?"

He turned. A man was walking towards him from the forest. He was tall and lanky with a light brown suit. A few tufts of gray hair sprouted from beneath his top hat. He looked very familiar, and Adam raked his memory as he tried to put a name to the face.

The man approached him, beaming like a grandfather to a grandson he hadn't seen in ages.

Adam recalled the days when college coaches wore suits and ties during games. This man would have looked perfect roaming the sidelines and swearing up a storm as he motivated his players during a game from that era. In fact, maybe he *had* been back there. Maybe he was very famous...

Then his identity dawned on him, and he could hardly contain his excitement.

"Whaddaya think, Adam?"

He cleared his throat, hardly believing he was about to converse with the figure. "I...I'm sorry, sir. What did you say?"

"What the hell is going on out there?" he repeated, and now he clasped his hands together and stared kindly, as if he were willing to wait all day for his response.

Adam did not know what to say.

"Ya see, it says so little, yet so much at the same time. That's the beauty of it."

"Kind of confusing if you ask me."

The figure chuckled, sat down on the bench and drew a cigar from his suit pocket. He pulled a lighter from a different pocket and began smoking.

"Now, why do you play football, Adam?"

Again, he had no answer.

The man pulled out a pocket watch, glanced at the time and tucked it away again.

"Yer gonna quarterback a game here in fifteen minutes, and ya got a hell of a long way to go to reach the stadium," the man explained as he crossed his legs casually and exhaled the smoke. "So! Let's figure this baby out. Whaddaya say?"

"Well, I never really thought about why I play," Adam replied slowly. "I've always been pretty good, so I guess I just play to win games."

But the man shook his head. "Of course ya play to win. Everyone does that! I wanna know why you *really* play. Come on, now. Think about it. You're a smart kid. You got brains. Use 'em."

He thought hard, desperately wanting to please the figure. But no easy response came.

"I don't know, sir."

The man sighed and took another puff from his cigar. He waited a moment before responding.

"Ya got to know the *truth*, Adam."

"The truth? About what?"

And now the man glared at him like he was a child, and he was disappointed that he didn't know better by now.

"*Football*," he replied emphatically. "What, you want me to whack you silly?"

"I'm sorry, sir."

"Ya got to know the truth about football, Adam. Otherwise," he said as he shook his head reminiscently, "you'll never make it."

The man now motioned towards something in the distance. Adam turned and saw a pathway leading from the hill. But this was no ordinary path. It was shaped like a miniature football field, complete with yard lines and hash marks. On and on the numbers went, from 10 to 50 to 100 and more, as the grass pathway snaked its way down into the valley.

"What is that?"

"It's a trail, naturally."

"What am I supposed to do?"

"Ya follow it."

Now the man rose as if to wish him goodbye, but did not speak.

"Thanks," was all Adam could think to say.

The figure nodded.

Adam went to follow the path, but as soon as his feet hit the 10 he glanced back. The man was watching him with an amused smile.

"How will I know when I'm there?" he called.

The man chuckled lightly. "Oh, you'll know."

"How?"

"The hash marks," he yakked as he clutched his cigar with his teeth. "Where the hash marks end."

Adam turned back to face the football field-path, and when he looked behind him a few seconds later, the man had disappeared.

He began his journey, winding beside a little river that sparkled in the sun, then into a thick wood. Adam started to feel apprehensive as strange animal calls and shuffling leaves sounded nearby. He concentrated on the numbers—200, 250—and soon the forest ended.

He had a very bad feeling he was going to be late for the game—hadn't the man said it would start in fifteen minutes? So he picked up his pace, now jogging past colorful boulders and a little cottage. The stadium was located in the carnival down in the valley, he just knew it. And he was a long way out.

400, 500...

How much longer? Surely the game had started by now. He was practically running, begging for his teammates to wait. They couldn't play without him, otherwise they would lose...

800, 1000...

Past an oddly-shaped windmill that was tucked into the hillside, and a patch of giant yellow flowers that swayed above the pathway. The festivities in the valley were straight ahead now, and as he squinted into the distance he saw a ferris wheel and colorful towers. The smell of fresh kettle corn and sugary treats wafted through the air.

Soon he was surrounded by attractions, games and sporting events. Almost there, almost there, though he knew he was far too late.

1500, 1800...

The stadium showed itself as he crested the next hill, and the yard lines ended at 2000. He was high enough to peer inside the bowl-shaped arena

Fifteen Minutes

that was nestled below. The game was in full swing, as he had expected, and the fans were cheering loudly.

He desperately scanned the area for a scoreboard, and found it above the nearest end zone. He was expecting his team to be behind, but that wasn't the case. It was ahead. Far, far ahead.

How was this possible? He was their best player. Surely his teammates couldn't perform this well without him, especially against an opponent of this caliber? Yet here he was, watching the game as a spectator, and his team wasn't missing a beat.

Suddenly. he saw the game like never before. He did not need to be on the field for his team to win. He just thought he did.

"Not whatcha were expecting, eh?"

He turned to see the top-hatted man standing casually beside him, cigar in hand.

"I thought they'd struggle without me. That's why I ran here."

"Ah, but one man a team does not make, Adam. Ya see, the true measure of a team isn't what they accomplish when the game is easy, but rather what they accomplish when they are put to the test."

"I never thought of it like that."

The man chuckled. "Once you do, you'll never see the game the same way again."

Down on the field, the quarterback hurled the pigskin into the sky as his receiver broke free from the defender 50 yards away. Adam held his breath as the football spiraled down...

The Dream
Chapter 20

"I can't believe that God put us on this earth to be ordinary."
--Lou Holtz

The thunder of the crowd echoed in the support beams above the tiny locker room. The home team has just completed their warm-ups and was heading off the field.

Adam stuffed on his pants, pads and socks in the cramped space and couldn't shake his thoughts from last night's dream.

"Roadrunner?"

The running back was tying his cleats two lockers down.

"What're you thinking?" he replied.

"Everything seems so surreal right now. You know? Being in this locker room, in this stadium? I'm starting to wonder if the dream I had last night ever ended. That line between what's real and what's not? It's kind of blurred right now."

"Good. 'Cause I don't know about you, but I sure am ready to do some surreal things tonight."

Adam grinned. Roadrunner had lessened the tension, if only for a few moments.

Coach Morgan walked purposefully through the crowd with his clipboard in hand, pausing to check his watch before addressing the team.

"OK, men!"

Their own warm-ups had ended ten minutes ago, and the entire team now seated themselves quietly at their lockers.

The head coach paused longer than usual before beginning his speech. Maybe it was for dramatic effect; Adam wasn't sure. But as the silence in the room lasted longer, he realized that the thunder of the crowd above had died down. They had entered that short space of time between warm-ups and kickoff, and everything was so close now. He felt like they were strapped in the flight deck of a shuttle and were about to launch into space. The anticipation was at its peak.

Teddy Morgan cleared his throat and spread his hands wide. "In sports, there are dreams and there is reality. The dream is here. The reality is over here.

"Now, the dream for everyone in this room is to beat the No. 1 team in the country, on national television. We're about to find out what the reality is. But the interesting thing is what's in between. Because what's in between is what counts.

"I love coaching this schedule because every season begins with a challenge. The athletic director and I, we have a philosophy. We want you guys to experience playing a powerhouse school in a tough environment. It's not just about the money. It gives us the opportunity to showcase what we're made of."

The head coach shifted in the clearing. The digital clock on the wall counted another minute closer to kickoff.

"Now, that team out there is No. 1 for a reason. But we're Beavers. And Beaver football is about embracing that challenge.

"When all of you were little, and watched your favorite team play on TV, you probably imagined yourselves playing on that same field someday. You probably dreamt about catching a winning touchdown pass or making a game-sealing pick. And I guarantee you that you weren't dreaming about beating a mediocre opponent. You were dreaming about beating the best. You might not have realized it at the time, but that's what makes the idea so intriguing.

"After this team steps up to the challenge tonight, and plays like the champions I know you are, and that clock runs out, and we have more points than they do...I guarantee you that feeling will be far better than the one you envisioned in your daydreams. It's that much sweeter when it becomes reality. And for the rest of your life, you will remember the day you scaled that impossible mountain."

Now the coach pointed towards an invisible summit above the ceiling, and Adam saw a fiery glint in his eye. For the very first time, he sensed that Coach Morgan wanted this win as much as he did. Like a sudden flash of lightning, he remembered something he'd said on that very first day...

"Adam, Randy Thompson is the kind of coach who will bully his players into doing what he wants them to do. You could say we have extremely different coaching styles, and I do not agree with some of the tactics that he implements..."

He wanted to beat him. He wanted to beat him bad.

"It's not the reality or the dream, in the end," the coach finished. "It's what's in between. That's what we're about to do. And to mold that dream into reality, you have to look inside yourself and pull out something you always knew you had, but have never used to its full potential. What is that something? That's a question I can't answer. But now is the time when you look in the mirror and ask: 'Do I have what it takes to be a champion?' And if the answer is 'yes,' then you have to prove it. Right here. Right now. No holding back. No regrets. We leave it all out on the field tonight, gentlemen."

And with that he pulled his whistle and lanyard from his pocket, gave it a flourish, nodded ever so slightly in Adam's direction, and stepped back into the crowd with his final words...

"Let's go kick some ass."

Adam stared at the floor with his hands clasped. He felt like he was hurdling towards an ultimatum, a final battle, and there wasn't anything beyond this point. His childhood memories, his playing days in high school and his transfer to St. Bruno's had all been formalities in preparation for this game. There was no tomorrow.

He got up and walked to the center of the clearing.

"I had a dream last night. And someone asked me, 'Why do you play football?'

"Hell, I didn't know what to say. I'd never thought about it. Why *would* I play football? It's time-consuming. It's brutal on your body. And it definitely sucks when you lose. Why the hell would any of us want to do that?"

He turned on the spot, so that every teammate felt like he was talking directly to him.

"But we're not just playing for us, are we? We're fighting for our school and for our community. We're competing for our families, our coaches, our friends, our fans and our teammates. *Definitely* our teammates. So yeah, it sucks when we play our guts out and we lose, but we've still partially won. We've had the chance to go out and represent something bigger than ourselves, and have thousands of people rooting for us when *we* make a stop, when *we* catch a pass, when *we* score a touchdown. *That's* what's really special. And when we go out and play this game tonight, and actually win, that's the pinnacle of everything you could ask for in life, man.

"Go out, get beat up. That's OK. Because when we're out there fighting, we can do whatever the hell we want. If we stick together, we can do *anything*. Don't let anybody tell you we *can't* win this game. Of course that's going to fire us up. Of course we want to prove everybody wrong. You always want to prove people wrong when they doubt you."

He was pacing furiously now, conjuring up a fiery batch of emotion for his teammates.

"But that won't be enough for us tonight. You have to know, deep in here," he emphasized as he pounded his chest proudly, "that you can do it. You have to have that faith in yourself. You have to believe. Because you need to believe in yourself before you can believe in the people around you."

He switched tones and became a little more frank.

"You know, I had everything. I really did. I didn't realize how good I had it until I got kicked off that team, but you know what? I'm glad it happened.

"I was dumb. I was stupid. I thought I knew football. But I didn't know a damn thing about football. I thought I could do whatever the hell I wanted, and it would always work out, because *I* was privileged and *I* was special. I thought being a star was easy. Well, you know what? It isn't easy. And the reason it *was* so easy for me was because I wasn't really a star. I thought I was, but I wasn't. *You* were right," he proclaimed as he pointed at Brian Massey. "I *was* a jackass."

"So was I," the receiver grinned.

"Not anymore, Cowboy!" Jason cried.

"Well, maybe not. But guess what?" Adam yelled, rage spitting from his voice. "*FUCK* all that past shit! You guys know football! This team knows football! And I know that everyone in this team believes in themselves and believes in their teammates, because I've seen it the past eight months. There's no team that we can't beat, not here, not *anywhere!*"

"We'll get last year's national championship back for you, Adam!" Cody shouted.

"Undefeated again!" Bulldog added as the team clapped in approval.

But he wasn't finished.

"Now, I'll tell you what I'm sick of. I'm sick of turning on the fucking TV and seeing all this shit about this game, and about how it's all just built on hype, and you really shouldn't bother watching because it's going to be a blowout! And jeez, what the hell were they thinking, putting us in prime time, if it's going to be so lopsided?!"

The team looked ready to jump from their seats.

"I am *sick* of hearing about how this game is about me! I'm *SICK OF IT!!*"

And he kicked an empty bottle across the room, finally letting out all of the frustration that had been boiling inside of him.

"This game isn't about me! It's not about Randy Thompson! It's not about Danny Thompson! It's not about Coach Morgan or you or me or *anybody!* This game is about our team versus their team! And you know what? I really hope that everyone in the country tunes in to watch this game, and watch me play for 'revenge,' and they all realize it was worth their time. But not because of me. It was never because of me that they should have watched this game.

"No. They'll realize the real reason why they wanted to watch us—because we're gonna put on a show like *nobody in the world of football has ever seen!* We're gonna show them what a real team's made of! And it's not the one across from us on the field, it's not the No. 1 team in the rankings, it's not the school that's won more national championships than anyone. Tonight is about *us*. This game? It's about *us*. It's about showing the world who we are and why we're here. Now LET'S GO GET IT DONE!!"

The room erupted in an explosion of cheers as his teammates stormed to their feet and flooded the clearing. He felt like he was in the middle of a touchdown celebration, and they'd already won the game. But the easy part was over. The hard part was just about to start.

Through the crowd, he caught a glimpse of Coach Morgan glancing at the digital clock.

"*HEY!*" the head coach screamed. "Two minutes, men! Two minutes, and we're out of here!"

Adam instinctively felt the sides of his pants to make sure he was ready. His wristband? Check. His quarterback towel? Check. His helmet? He needed that.

He worked his way back to his locker, where his shiny yellow helmet hung from an old hook. The thunder from the support beams above the cramped room had returned, and he envisioned what was happening on the field at that very moment. The color guard was raising its teal and copper flags. The smoke was wafting from the mouth of the giant green gargoyle. The team was running onto the field with the fans going wild. He'd been there dozens of times.

Coach Morgan gave the signal to leave, and the team began filing from the room.

"Adam, are we going to win today?"

The voice came from Roadrunner.

Adam momentarily forgot that he was supposed to be walking through the doors with his teammates. His roommate hadn't thrown him for a loop like this in a long time.

"How did you find out about that?" he gasped.

"You told me, a long time ago. You just don't remember."

He didn't remember, but he must have done so. Otherwise Roadrunner would never have known about Joey Callahan and his pre-game question. He would never have known about the answer he always gave, and how he'd vowed never to lose again after that freshman season. Joey had put him to the test each and every game, and he'd passed so far. He was undefeated since the ritual began. But this team was not the Keystone State Gargoyles, and it wasn't Joey who was asking the question.

Time was up. The last few players were walking through the doors.

Roadrunner stared at him in an innocent but powerful way, as if he wanted to uphold the trust that he and Joey had enjoyed. Adam knew he had to answer. So he looked his running back in the eyes, and when the words left his mouth they were barely a whisper.

"I don't know."

Roadrunner didn't have a response, but maybe there was nothing to say. This time, there was no way to spin the answer into a positive.

Adam grabbed his helmet, stuffed it over his head, and caught up with the rest of the team with the running back at his heels.

As he exited the locker room, the sight ahead made his spine tingle. There was no covered tunnel here, but a sloping cement passageway with high walls angling down to a point at the edge of the field. There was a flurry of lights and activity in the window of space beyond the support beams and stands, far past the sea of bobbing yellow helmets. In that window, powerful stadium lights flooded the night scene as flags waved, trumpets sounded and cameras flashed.

Strangely enough, Adam didn't remember that the spectators would be focusing on him until he reached the grass. He was glad he'd forgotten until now.

He stared at his cleats, took a deep breath, raised his head and jogged onto the field.

The (End)Zone
Chapter 21

"On the road we're somebody else's guests - and we play in a way that they're not going to forget we visited them."

--Knute Rockne

"And welcome back to Sunset Vale, where we're just getting set for an exciting match-up between the Keystone State Gargoyles and the St. Bruno Beavers!" the charismatic voice of Corey Cousins exclaimed from SportsNetwork's booth.

"During the break, Corey and I were discussing how the last time we broadcast a game here, Adam Dorsey was playing for the team in teal and copper. Isn't it funny how things can change quickly in the sports world, Corey?"

"It sure is, Mike. And let's be honest, Adam Dorsey versus his former team has been the lead story of this game. But it will be interesting to see whether this Beaver *team* can hang with a championship contender from the big leagues."

"Well, one person that hasn't received the attention he probably warrants is Beaver head coach Teddy Morgan," Mike added. "There's no doubt he's been a driving force for his squad the past decade."

A sparkling profile and headshot of Coach Morgan appeared on the broadcast.

Teddy Morgan at a Glance

Born: April 15, 1954
Family: Wife Katherine, daughters Alexis (age 20) and Kailey (18), and son Cory (14)
College: Williamsburg-Penn University, Bachelor's Degree in Psychology, Master's Degree in Education

School	Position	Years	Team Record
Williamsburg-Penn University	Safety (4-year starter)	1973 - 1976	31 - 17
Williamsburg-Penn University	Graduate assistant	1977 - 1981	43 - 19
Philipsburg College	Defensive backs coach	1982 - 1994	112 - 57
Mount Washington University	Defensive coordinator and defensive backs coach	1995 - 2001	63 - 28
St. Bruno's Academy	Head coach	2002 - present	119 - 37

"There's no doubt success has followed Edward B. Morgan throughout his impressive coaching career," Cousins remarked. "He even turned down a head coaching offer from Ohio Valley so he could take the job at St. Bruno's in 2002."

"Yeah, and so it's pretty clear he's not after the biggest or most prestigious gig," Mays added. "Ohio Valley is in the MVC, so he would have recruited and coached against the likes of Randy Thompson and Paul Eberly at Michigan. But it seems he felt a calling at St. Bruno's, and he chose this academy of 5,000 undergraduates instead."

"And it's worked out better than anyone could have anticipated, Mike. Since that hire, Teddy Morgan has turned a relatively insignificant program into a perennial FCS powerhouse. He's won two national championships in his 11 years there, and what's even more impressive is the way he's done it."

"With Teddy, it's an academics-before-athletics approach," agreed Mays. "And before we move on, we should mention the success his teams have experienced against elite competition. Corey, they've played several competitive games against top-level programs during Morgan's run, and while they have yet to win one, it sure makes you wonder if this could be another nail-biter."

"Which bring us to his opponent, Randy Thompson," Cousins transitioned. "Before the commercial break, we mentioned the recruiting violations he was cited for earlier in his career. Well, aside from the rumors swirling about Adam Dorsey's departure, the new developing story is the improper benefits allegation by an unnamed source this week."

"Corey, you have to be concerned with the number of violations popping up in big-time athletics. Whatever it takes to win, I guess. That seems to be the motto in college sports these days," Mike sighed.

"But win he has," emphasized Corey. "To the tune of a 92 – 17 record in eight years. Whatever he's doing—legal or not—it's working."

"We certainly have two of the most accomplished coaches in the profession roaming the sidelines tonight. And it looks like we're ready for kickoff!"

* * *

Adam would never forget the sight as he walked to midfield for the coin toss. There was no snow or cloud cover like the last time he'd stepped foot on this grass. Instead, the humid August night created a perfect summer evening.

There had been some boos when they'd exited the tunnel, but he had expected that. In fact, he felt strangely calm now that they were finally here—he could stop thinking about the game and just play it. He was back in his element.

As he looked ahead, he saw the Gargoyle captains Joey, Deion, Lukas Bowser and Darius Frazier walking towards him and Z. The referee began talking as they met on the logo, but he barely heard the words. He'd never experienced anything like this—seeing his old teammates on the other side of the coin toss.

"Captain already with your new team?" Deion asked as they all exchanged handshakes. "Impressive, Adam!"

"Congratulations yourself," he replied. "Never expected it from you, Deion, I have to admit."

"Well, don't blame me. I didn't vote for him," Joey grinned.

Deion nudged the center in the shoulders playfully.

"No. 3, your call," the ref announced as he drew the silver coin from his pocket.

"Tails."

"Tails is the call," proclaimed the official, and the coin glinted like a gem under the floodlights as it whirled into the sky. Adam couldn't help but peer down in anticipation as it landed on the grass.

"It is tails. Would you like to kick off or receive?"

"We want the ball."

"OK then. The visiting team will receive the opening kickoff. The home team will defend the north end zone, and will get the ball to start the second half. Let's play a good clean game, men."

He jogged back to the sideline with Z, hardly believing the time had come at last. Everything they had worked towards the past eight months came down to this. Three hours.

"No. 8 Shane Phillips is back to receive for the Beavers," Mays informed. "They actually call Phillips 'Mozart' because he's such a good musician. How's that for a skill set, Corey?"

"Lots of talent on this Beaver roster."

The ball shot into the sky like a cannon, and Mozart ran forward to catch it as the white shirts and green pants of the Beavers mixed with the teal shirts and copper pants of the Gargoyles.

"And Phillips is down at the 24 yard-line," announced Mays. "So here we go, folks. Adam Dorsey is taking the field against his former team."

"Alright, let's go," Adam ordered to his offense as he jogged back onto the field.

"Dude, this is *wild!*" Mad Max exclaimed in awe as the crowd erupted with noise and boos.

The other linemen were wide-eyed, too.

"It's just a game," Adam emphasized as they reached the ball. "Just like I've been telling you. It's just like any other game, the stadium's just bigger. Don't think about the crowd. You have to block it out. Concentrate."

He surveyed the defense—the defense he'd practiced against so many times.

"Alright, we got this, we got this," he repeated confidently.

"Cowboy."

It was Jason Evans.

The play clock counted below 15. Roadrunner was running in motion behind the line...

"Hey, Cowboy."

Adam couldn't think what on earth he wanted. It wasn't exactly the best time for a conversation.

"Set..."

"Cowboy."

"*What?!*"

Jason couldn't look back or else it would be a false start and a penalty, so he talked from the side of his mouth.

"I crapped my pants."

Adam couldn't see his own expression, but it had to be something between exasperation and amusement.

"Set...*HUT!*"

Playing quarterback is like speed-reading. It's a tough skill to master, but Adam Dorsey was a pro.

"And Dorsey hits wide receiver Trevor Hart across the middle for a first down!"

"There you go, Bookworm!" Adam applauded as they jogged to the new spot.

Another play, another first down. And with every new snap they moved closer and closer to the end zone in front of the student section. Nearly every student was dressed in teal, creating the effect of a giant green monster that threatened to swallow them whole as it wrapped its arms around both sides of the field.

"Alright, let's show them what we came here to do," he spat as they lined up inside the 10.

"Dorsey takes the snap...and it's a play-action-pass! Dorsey looks downfield...waits...throws...*TOUCHDOWN!*"

Of all the things that could have happened on that first drive, maybe it was fitting that Brian Massey caught the game's first touchdown and made the statement they'd wanted to make.

Adam raced into the end zone to congratulate his receiver while Garfield, Graham Cracker and Bigfoot threw their hands into the air in celebration.

"I knew you'd come through," he smiled as he slapped Massey's shoulder pads.

Massey laughed—something he didn't do very often. He took off his sweaty helmet as they reached the sideline. "You kept your word, man."

"What?"

"Two nights ago, you told me I was getting a touchdown pass after escaping from that hellhole," he explained.

And now Adam laughed. How could he have forgotten in only two days? Maybe that's what games like this did to you. They made you forget about everything else in life, if only for a few hours.

"Hey, it's what I do."

They were back with their teammates, getting pats on the back and gulping Gatorade and water from Doctor Hunt's table. But Adam didn't want any congratulations until the game was won.

"Let's go, defense!" he yelled as Tonio, Playboy, Bulldog and Z took the field. The Gargoyles tried calming DT's nerves and running it up the gut with senior running back Jamal Harris. They reached midfield, but the stop finally came when Danny's pass fell incomplete on third down.

"Mike, possibly some nerves for Thompson on that last pass there?"

"It looked like a relatively easy completion to me. He's going to have to shake the jitters off if Keystone State wants to regain control of this game."

Back on offense, and back to the chess match. How could they gain enough yards to move the chains against a defense with Lukas Bowser, Terrence Porter and Darius Frazier? By making plays—that was how. If Roadrunner could make that one extra move. If Mad Max and Bookworm could catch every pass. And if Garfield and Graham Cracker could keep making those key blocks...

The Gargoyle secondary overpowered the small receivers, stalling the passing game. But Roadrunner picked up the slack and managed to move them into field goal range. Ferrari drilled it, taking the score to 10 – 0.

"This Beaver team is committed," Cousins remarked. "They aren't making mistakes. They're not necessarily scoring a touchdown on every drive, but they're not making mental errors and missing assignments. They're focused. You hear coaches talk about execution and how important it is. Well, this is why, right here. The coaches know that a game is not necessarily won by the biggest or fastest team, so much as who makes the least amount of errors. This Beaver team is on a mission right now."

Yellow flags flew onto the playing field. False start on the Gargoyles.

Adam watched quietly from the opposing sideline as Coach Thompson's red face spat in the referee's ear. He always knew he was in for a tight game when the head coaches screamed that hard just because of a blatant five-yard penalty. He could tell by the way their demeanor changed—they held their play card a little closer to their chest and they looked stressed instead of relaxed and in control. That's how Randy Thompson looked right now, and he was loving every second of it.

Jamal Harris burrowed his way through the defense for a touchdown as the second quarter began, bringing the score to 10 – 7.

Time slowed. Every play seemed magnified, every yard that much more precious. They just needed those small victories, and eventually they would amount to the big one.

"HUT!"

Graham Cracker snapped the football, and Adam immediately saw six defenders bearing down on him. It was a blitz, but no matter. They had planned for this.

"And there's pressure on Dorsey right away...Dorsey dumps it off to Campbell, and he's out into the open for a first down and more!"

Bowser stopped himself just in time and went stumbling into his old quarterback. But Adam hardly cared—Roadrunner was gone, running like there was no tomorrow and slicing through the last line of defense. The only guy who could stop him now was the free safety, Darius Frazier.

"Go! Go! Go! *Go! GO!!*" Adam screamed, and he lost track of how many times he yelled the word as he rushed forward.

"Campbell at the 25...the 20...Frazier comes in for the tackle...*what a move!* Oh, what an excellent move by this young running back!" Mays cried. "And he's in for the Beaver touchdown!"

He was sprinting down the field and not caring one bit about conserving his energy. He and Roadrunner high-fived in the end zone, and all of a sudden the stadium didn't seem so intimidating and the green monster didn't seem so scary.

He didn't shrug off the pats on the back and congratulations from his teammates this time around. He was already thinking about getting one last score before halftime...

"The Gargoyle defense gambled with the blitz there, Mike," Corey examined during the replay. "It's common for the running back to stay in and block on a third-and-long situation like this, but keep in mind, Campbell is a 188-pound back going against some of the biggest linebackers in the game. So Teddy Morgan sends him out on a screen, and the Gargoyles don't account for him until it's too late."

"He sure will make you pay if he gets out into the open," Mays added.

"Well, we knew this was a special running back coming in," replied the ex-coach. "But the way he's stepped up against this tough Gargoyle front seven is really something. This defense just cannot seem to stop Anthony Campbell."

Adam sat on the offensive bench, gulping more Gatorade and wondering how they were up 17 – 7. He'd had faith that they would perform well, but this was just plain crazy. They were officially "in the zone," whatever that meant.

He recalled a conversation with Coach Morgan during camp, when the head coach had explained his own theory of winning close games. Teddy believed there was a perfect medium between determination and pushing the matter too far, between playing to win and gambling too much, between trusting your instincts and sticking with the game plan. Somewhere between all that was the line you had to walk.

Well, they were tight-roping that thin line to perfection right now, aware that they were against such a colossal talent gap that any mistake would push them too far one way or the other, and they would lose. Maybe that's what being "in the zone" really meant. And why they were able to execute so perfectly right now was a mystery. Why they couldn't just flip a switch and play like this at will was too abstract of a concept for anyone to grasp.

It didn't matter, because it was working. Adam had watched enough upsets to see the common similarities in each—the pride of the underdog team, its heart, its steely resolve, its relentless attack-mode game plan. He could almost feel the energy of that same situation swimming around him in the warm August night. Whatever they had done to play like this, he never, ever, ever wanted to let it go. They had captured something special—lightning in a bottle—and he was smart enough to know that his situation had helped conjure that during these past few months, but wise enough now not to boast about it.

The Gargoyles attempted to mount a drive from their own 20, but time wasn't on their side. The scoreboard ticked to zero before Jamal Harris could carry them into field goal range.

"So time has expired here in the first half, and the St. Bruno Beavers will take a 10-point advantage into the locker room!"

Fifteen Minutes

"I think we might see some changes after halftime," Cousins surmised. "It looks like Thompson's coaching staff wanted to rattle Dorsey with a blitz-heavy game plan, but the strategy has backfired. They need to respect the speed and elusiveness of Campbell, because he will continue to take advantage of blitzing defenders. This Gargoyle secondary has done a good job covering these undersized Beaver receivers, and I'm not sure a little extra time in the pocket would make much of a difference for Dorsey."

"Folks, we've got a good one here in Sunset Vale!" Mays finished as the two commentators faced the camera. "See you in a few for the second half."

A Tale of Two Halves
Chapter 22

"Make sure when anyone tackles you, he remembers how much it hurts."
--Jim Brown

When you're out there on the road, it's so much harder.
It's harder because every mistake is magnified, and every completion or first down seems to take twice the effort it should. The crowd is so loud that you can't hear yourself think. And when the other team scores or makes a big play, the screaming is so intense that the ground seems to shake. You can get lost in it, as if there's this invisible force pulling you and your teammates further and further from victory, and it becomes harder to resist with every opponent first down, touchdown or defensive stop.
On the road, you have to combat that. You have to limit mistakes, or else the crowd will suck you into that inescapable black hole. It's a game of momentum that is tilted in your opponent's favor—it's easy for them to gain momentum and keep it, but for your team it's hard to get and even harder to keep.
"Let's go guys, let's keep it rolling," Adam urged as the offense took the field for that first second half drive.
As he surveyed the defense and glanced to his left, he noticed Coach Peterson on the sideline with his slender build and familiar glasses. He made eye contact with his old quarterbacks coach. Peterson nodded his head in acknowledgment ever so slightly, looking relaxed and composed—the exact opposite of Randy Thompson. Did he care if his team lost? Or was he just fine with his old quarterback beating his boss? Surely, a part of him wanted the Gargoyles to win. But would he be that upset if Thompson lost this one, after what he'd told him in the shoe room?
Adam chuckled to himself as he remembered their last conversation.
"I'll be watching your games when I have the chance, I promise."
No, you'll be coaching against me, actually.
"Set, go!"
He waited until the last possible second before surrendering the deep routes and throwing the screen. But as soon as the ball left his fingertips he wished he hadn't. Lukas Bowser flattened Roadrunner a split-second after he caught the ball, and Adam was reminded of a bulldozer squashing a car.

Fifteen Minutes

Guess that play wasn't going to work anymore.

"Oh, what a phenomenal play there by Bowser!" Mays cried. "He stops the screen behind the line of scrimmage."

"Great acceleration by the linebacker," Cousins added. "He saw where the play was going and ran about 15 yards to make that tackle. This Gargoyle D finally seems to be picking up on some of these new wrinkles in the Beavers' game plan, Mike."

Adam rushed over and helped Roadrunner to his feet.

"Are you OK?"

"I'll be alright," he groaned, but Adam knew that meant, *"No, I'm not. But I'm not going to complain."*

DT was back on the field, and he meant business this time around. Adam squinted at the opposing sideline and realized that Coach Peterson was no longer motioning the play calls with his hands. Randy Thompson was, and he had a dangerous look in his eyes as he held the plastic sheet over his mouth and spat instructions to offensive coordinator Tim Bauer up in the booth. He was making signals that Adam hadn't seen before, and he realized they had changed the system so that he couldn't decipher the play. And all the while Coach Peterson was standing to the side with that indifferent look on his face, like he was a mere spectator watching this madness unfold, without the authority or the desire to intervene.

"Thompson takes the snap and hands off to Harris. And Harris is up the middle for a big gain! He's at the 10…the 5…touchdown Gargoyles!"

Adam threw his empty Gatorade cup at the trash can in frustration. It bounced off the rim and onto the grass.

"So with the extra point, the Gargoyles have cut the lead to 17 – 14."

"And you know what else, Mike? They really asserted themselves on that possession. All that offensive talent is finally showing, and as a result, they delivered their most complete drive of the game."

The crowd was as loud as ever now, and it seemed like the floodwaters were about to come crashing from the dam. They had to hold that force back somehow, as tough as it was. They had to keep the volcano from blowing its top, otherwise they would never regain their footing.

Nasty feelings crept into Adam's thoughts, and the notion that their success in the first half had been the result of a bad game plan and a few lucky breaks crossed his mind.

"I can't beat you, Adam…but my team can." Those words came back to life now. He would be damned if that ended up as the truth—he didn't want to think about how he'd feel if it was. No, he wouldn't be humbled like that. They *had* to win.

"Come on, guys. Let's keep these chains moving, now!" he yelled to his offense after Roadrunner carved out five total yards on the first two downs.

"WHAT?!" Cody shouted back as the linemen got set.

"We can't hear you!" Jason explained.

Adam rolled his eyes in frustration. The play clock was winding down.

"Never mind, never mind...SET...HUT!"

In a second, Terrence Porter and Lukas Bowser were bearing down on him, looking like giants against Garfield and Graham Cracker. The motions of his receivers and the Gargoyle pass defenders played themselves out before him, and his quarterback senses indicated that he could not throw the ball, even though temptation wanted him to squeeze it past the defense...

The imaginary buzzer in his head screamed that time was up. It had been up for one, two, three seconds now, and still he held onto the ball, hoping and praying. Red lights flashed in his mind and sirens whistled, ordering him to throw the football now or surrender the play, even though he just wanted a split-second longer...

SMACK!

Bowser and Porter smashed into him, and he became wrapped in their arms. Their limbs pulled him down like the tentacles of a giant octopus dragging him underwater. Something whacked the ball loose. He tried to corral it with his legs on the way down, but it bounced away.

A sharp pain seared through his ankle. He was flat on the ground, with Terrence Porter roaring and flexing his muscles above him like he'd just delivered the knockout punch in a boxing match. The crowd must have been going wild, but his senses were zoned in on the football. Where was it?

He crawled around to see Garfield squashed on top of it nearby, cradling it in his piggy hands and fighting with two Gargoyle defenders as they tried to pry it away. They looked like oversized kids fighting over a toy. The white pants of a referee ran past his line of sight, and a whistle blew forcefully.

He tried getting to his feet, but the sharp pain rushed back as soon as he put weight on his lower right leg. He grimaced and fell back to the grass.

"Oh my, it looks like Dorsey's hurt," Mays cautioned. "He's clutching his right foot. This doesn't look good, folks."

"Yeah, his leg became entangled with Bowser's on the way down, and his right foot bent awkwardly when he hit the ground. It looks like a serious injury to me."

Lukas Bowser had appeared above him with his arm outstretched. Adam was mildly surprised, but he took it eagerly. Bowser's strong body hoisted him up without much effort.

"Thanks."

"Yup."

Stephen Hunt was jogging towards them from the sideline, but Bowser had something to say.

"We didn't mean to, Adam. I swear."

"Yeah," he panted. "I know, Bowser. It's OK."

The linebacker nodded and headed off.

"Can you walk?" were the first words out of Hunt's mouth.

"Yeah, I think so."

He did, but the doctor supported him all the way to the medical table, and he was extremely aware of all the excited stares from the fans as he limped to the sideline.

"Sit up for me, and hold your leg out," Hunt ordered as Adam sat on the squishy teal training table.

"I want to go back in," he blurted without even thinking.

Hunt just gave him a funny grin as he removed his cleats and socks. "Save your breath, Adam. It doesn't help. I might be young, but I've heard some variation of that from a hundred different athletes. Just relax and we'll see what's wrong."

Coach Morgan had arrived at the scene. "What's the word?"

"Hold on. Adam, I want you to tell me where it hurts."

He winced as the doctor applied pressure to different areas of his foot and ankle. "Right there, that hurts bad."

"What about that?"

"Not as much."

His offensive teammates had started to gather around them—Derek Bell, Bookworm and Roadrunner were the first to appear. He also noticed the sexy reporter Jennifer Rush squeezing her way towards them with a microphone.

Out on the field, the Gargoyles were on fire. DT was completing passes left and right, and gaining confidence with every first down.

Hunt sighed and looked up. "Adam, I think you have a high ankle sprain."

"So...can I go back in?"

Judging by the look that Coach Morgan and Hunt were exchanging, that meant "no."

"Adam, let me be very clear with you," the doctor began. "This is a serious injury. We really need to do a CT scan before I can verify anything. But right now there's not much I can do to treat it, except give you an oral anti-inflammatory and wrap it with ice."

He was about to interrupt, but Hunt read his mind.

"Having said that," he emphasized, "I'm not naïve, and I know what the situation is. I can give you an ankle brace and the anti-inflammatory and get you back out there if I so choose. So my answer is yes, you can go—"

Adam could see the excitement in his teammates' faces, though they remained calm.

"—*but*, you probably won't be very effective. The mobility that you had when I practically carried you to the sideline is how you'll be in the game. And that also means you won't be able to put pressure on your leg and step into your throws. It will be very painful."

Coach Morgan had been listening intently, and now he took a deep breath. For one horrible second Adam feared he might tell him to sit out, and put Derek in the game instead. But—

"Adam, it's your call. I'm not taking you out of this one."

"I'm going in."

The head coach nodded without hesitation. "Then you're back in next series. Now get off that table and get a brace on. You need to be ready to walk when we get this thing back."

Roadrunner and Bookworm helped him put his cleats back on while the reporter began interviewing Hunt. They had just finished tying the laces when the score came.

"Thompson stands in the pocket...good protection...he throws to the end zone, and it's caught by Jaden Hall for a touchdown!"

"Danny Thompson really stepped it up there, Mike, and he's got his first passing touchdown as a college quarterback. I'm sure these fans are thrilled to see him finally make some clutch throws, and this place is on fire right now!"

"So the extra point is good, and the Gargoyles take the lead, 21 – 17!"

"Speaking of quarterbacks, Mike, we've got an update on Dorsey's status from Jennifer Rush. Jennifer?"

The broadcast switched to the sideline reporter.

"Well, I've just talked with St. Bruno's team doctor Stephen Hunt, Corey. He said that Dorsey has a high ankle sprain. Usually he does not allow players with this injury to re-enter the game, but he said he's making an exception in this case. So expect to see him out there on the Beavers' next drive. I asked Hunt if we will be seeing Dorsey for the rest of the game, or if this next possession is a test to see if he can still play. He just said, 'We'll have to wait and see. But if I know Adam, he's not coming off that field until this game is over.' Back to you guys."

He was limping onto the field with the brace tied tightly around his ankle, wondering whether he could even make it to the spot of the ball.

"Set...set, HUT!"

His heart sank when he realized it would be a struggle to simply give a clean hand-off. Even if he sucked it up, he still wouldn't be able to step into his throws. His body would not allow it.

"And Dorsey's not looking good at all," observed Mays as Roadrunner took the football again on second down. "He's wincing in pain even as he hands off. Corey, I can't imagine the Beavers will throw very much with Dorsey's situation."

"They'll have to. It's third-and-long now."

The truth was sinking in, as much as Adam didn't want to believe it. He felt as though fate was pulling him from the thing he wanted most, and the harder he tried to get it, the further it would fall from his reach. Why did he have to get hurt now? Why couldn't it have happened on the first play of next week's game, or the week after that? But no, it had happened when it mattered most.

Yet they were so close...*so close*...

"Dorsey takes the snap...throws deep down the right sideline...and it's over the head of Stephen Maxwell. That one was a bit too high for the junior wide-out."

"Mike, we've covered lots of Gargoyle games over the past couple of years, and I can count the times Dorsey has overthrown a ball like that on one hand. You can't help but wonder if that ankle's causing his accuracy to be a tad off."

"It really has been a tale of two halves, Corey. This Beaver offense has done nothing since their touchdown at the end of the second quarter."

Adam limped over to Coach Morgan as the punting unit came running on. He wanted to kick something in frustration, but knew it would hurt extremely bad if he did. There wasn't much time left—the fourth quarter had begun.

"What do you think?" he asked his coach, and Teddy Morgan stared him down with his arms crossed. His expression showed that he meant business.

"Adam, do you want to stay in this game, or do you want me to take you out?"

"I want what's best for the team. I want whatever gives us the best chance to win."

"We can win this thing with Derek Bell at quarterback. I coach my players to be ready when they are called upon. So if you think we have a better chance with him, then by all means, I'll take you out."

Even though they had known each other for months, Adam was surprised to hear those words from his coach. Did he honestly think they could win with Derek?

"It's your call," Teddy Morgan said decisively. "I can't tell you how you feel out there. That's something you have to decide for yourself."

He couldn't do it. He *wouldn't* do it.

"I still think we have a better chance with me."

Coach Morgan grinned as the defense took the field again. "So do I. I just didn't want that to influence your decision. Now go get more treatment for that ankle. We're going to give you as many cracks at this thing as we can."

* * *

If the Beavers needed a miracle, they got one when the football squirted from Jamal Harris' grasp as the Gargoyles threatened to score again. Bulldog recovered it at the 15, and so they prevented Keystone State from adding to its lead. But with Adam hobbling on one leg, the offense stalled again around midfield and they were forced to punt.

That was when Adam began the most excruciating waiting game ever. Their defense *had* to make a stop and keep it within a touchdown, or it was over.

Another first down, another two minutes. And the clock drained from eight to seven to six to five to four…even if they got the ball back, there wouldn't be much time…

"Time-out!" Coach Morgan yelled to the ref. Z had just stuffed Harris for no gain with a little over three minutes left.

The defense stopped the running back again after a gain of four on second down, and the coach called their second time-out. Now it was third-and-6, and Randy Thompson opted to put the game in his son's hands.

Danny waited for what seemed like ages to Adam, then threw a dart over the middle that was batted away by Playboy.

"Wow! What a play there by Taylor Griffin to give this Beaver offense one more opportunity!"

"Just a really great desperation move by the safety," Cousins remarked. "He had to cover a lot of ground to make that play, and he got there just in time."

Even though he was hurt and the outcome was in doubt, Adam had never experienced a sigh of relief quite like that. He was free—free to go and win the game. He wanted it to be on him. This was how it should be.

One time-out, 2:54 left.

The Gargoyles punted, and the ball rolled out of the back of the end zone.

Second-and-5
Chapter 23

"The main ingredient of stardom is the rest of the team."
--John Wooden

    Months later, Adam would think back to the moment when they took the field for that last drive and marvel at how ironic life could be.
    During those lazy summer months at St. Bruno's, whenever he didn't have a morning work-out and could sleep in, he would think about this game and play out scenarios in his head. The one he thought about most often was needing to score a touchdown to win at the end. If they accomplished that, with him at the helm and throwing the final pass, there would be no doubt about who had won the Adam Dorsey/Randy Thompson grudge match. And while he no longer cared about the talking heads in the media, a large part of him wanted to experience that feeling, with his team victorious and his old coach bitter and broken.
    "Well, it's do-or-die for the Beavers!" declared Mays as the ref spotted the ball at the 25. "Cory, this is the position every quarterback dreams of, isn't it? Down four points with time running out, and needing to score a touchdown to win?"
    "It sure is, Mike. If you're a true competitor then this is what you want. After all the talk about Dorsey possibly upsetting his former team, it's really ironic that it's coming down to this. Hollywood couldn't have scripted it any better."
    The deafening crowd noise bore down on them one last time. With all the whistles and shouts, and the rumble of the stands as fans jumped up and down in anticipation, Adam could have sworn a tornado was howling above them or a hurricane was tearing the stadium apart. They could smell victory now, those Gargoyle faithful.
    "Set, HUT!"
    He hit Massey for a 12-yard gain, but the clock continued to tick as he was tackled in-bounds.
    "Alright man! Let's keep it up!" he urged as they huddled quickly. "We just need to get close enough to have a shot at the end. No pressure!"
    "Shut the *fuck* up, Adam!" Cody cried. *"No pressure?!* It's the end of the fucking game!"

He did have a point. But the way Cody flashed a quick grin reassured him that it wasn't out of spite. And really, that quote eased everyone's nerves more than anything he could have said himself.

"Alright, man. We got this," he replied, even though his ankle told him otherwise.

Coach Morgan had signaled a run, which they could afford because of the new set of downs and big gain on the last play. They had to keep the defense honest.

He saw Lukas Bowser make a little move before he snapped the ball. Was he blitzing? No matter—he would complete the hand-off in time.

"HUT!"

Bowser was barreling towards him, unblocked. It *was* a blitz.

Adam backpedaled and nearly tripped Roadrunner up as he desperately stuffed the ball into his arms, and the running back squirted past Bowser just in time. But the linebacker was so close that he didn't have time to stop, and the two of them went crashing to the ground. Bowser's massive body squashed Adam's right leg on the way down, and his eyes watered with pain.

Gasps and screams erupted from the crowd. Adam writhed about on the grass as Bowser climbed off him, and he expected to see a bone sticking from his skin or a mangled body part as he glanced down at his legs. His hurt ankle was burning, but as the seconds passed he realized there was no new injury. Bowser had just aggravated it.

He turned and looked upfield, and that was when his heart sank.

Roadrunner was lying facedown on the grass ten yards away, and he wasn't moving. His arms were sprawled at an odd angle. Doctor Hunt was already running onto the field with two graduate assistant trainers close behind.

"Wow. Campbell just took a serious hit from those two defenders, folks, and he's down and out on the field."

"Yeah, Bowser comes on a blitz and almost takes down Dorsey before he's able to give the hand-off," articulated Cousins. "But he has to guess if it's going to be a pass or a run. He guesses wrong, takes down Dorsey, and that leaves a nice hole for Campbell. But that hit he took looked brutal. I sure hope he's alright."

Adam was afraid of what he'd see as he looked up at the giant video board. The replay showed Roadrunner sprinting through the hole and gaining five yards, but then two defenders met him at the same time. The running back's head hit one Gargoyle's shoulder pad and then ricocheted like a pinball off the other's helmet.

He turned away from the screen in disgust, realizing now why he'd heard gasps from the crowd. They had been scared by Roadrunner's hit, not his. The replay alone made him feel ten times worse than he already did, even with his aching ankle.

Fifteen Minutes

He hobbled over to the small group of people kneeling around the running back, and blurted out the first thing on his mind.

"Is he gonna be OK?"

Stephen Hunt held up his hand as he conversed with the others. "In a moment, Adam. We need to figure this out for ourselves first."

One of the assistants was calling for a stretcher on her radio—that couldn't be a good sign.

"You saw that replay, didn't you?" the other assistant asked. "It's probably rotational, from what I saw."

"I think it's a rotational force head collision," Hunt replied. "We need to get his neck stabilized for the stretcher. He's still out cold."

Adam didn't understand what they were saying, but he didn't feel optimistic. New thoughts raced through his mind. What if Roadrunner wasn't OK? He didn't have any family up here for the game. What if he had to stay at the hospital? What if this was a life-threatening or paralyzing injury?

The rest of the team was kneeling in prayer, and the crowd had gone silent. A Gargoyle trainer was driving a green utility vehicle onto the field, and two EMTs were riding in the bed with special neon vests. The sight made him extremely nervous.

This wasn't the script. It was not supposed to be this way. But that was life, and he understood that now.

Hunt finally rose after securing the neck brace on Roadrunner, and Adam decided that he needed answers.

"What does that mean, 'rotational force?'"

"It means we think he has a very serious concussion."

"He's gonna be OK, right?"

Hunt sighed and looked at him soberly. "I don't know, Adam."

"Can you guess? Do *you* think he's gonna be OK?"

"If it's just a concussion then yes, he should recover. But I can't guarantee that."

And with that, he left him standing alone as the medical staff lifted Roadrunner into the vehicle.

He couldn't leave his teammates. He wouldn't have even dreamt of that before now. But an idea had come to him, and now he felt the immense pressure of time running out. He would have to act, one way or the other. There was no in-between.

If he wouldn't have hurt his ankle, the decision would have been easy. If he were at 100 percent, he would have finished the game with his teammates and won it for Roadrunner. But he was far from 100 percent. He was borderline ineffective, as much as he didn't want to acknowledge it.

"So my answer is yes, you can go...but you probably won't be very effective...and that also means you won't be able to put pressure on your leg and step into your throws..."

Those quotes replayed themselves in his mind, and he realized there was no easy way out. There was no right, no wrong, no textbook procedure to follow. Coach Morgan wasn't about to make things easy for him, either—he wasn't that kind of a leader.

He looked at the scoreboard, with the clock stopped at 1:52 and a second-and-5 to go. He glanced at the utility vehicle with Roadrunner. He gazed at his teammates kneeling in prayer on the sideline. And he knew then that he alone had to make the tough decision. He had to make the choice that no one else could make.

"Adam."

Coach Morgan's voice drifted through the air—a calm, poised, reasonable force fighting to be heard in the sea of frustration and fear that had clouded his thoughts. He glanced up, and the look in his head coach's eyes said it all. Suddenly the game didn't matter, the national spotlight irrelevant. He had saved his best coaching decision for this moment. And ironically, after a career focused on preparing young men for life after college, this decision was more about life than it was about the game on the field.

"If you want to go with him, I would respect that decision. I promise I will not judge you, whatever you decide."

Adam nodded, and there was a quiet understanding between them as they stood five yards apart in the middle of the stadium. His coach was intuitive enough that no extra words needed to be said. He had guessed what his quarterback was thinking, and he had needed to tell him that in his eyes, leaving the game now was not abandoning your team. It was not quitting. It was not a shameful thing by any means. In fact, it was the exact opposite. It was helping a friend in need. It was putting the team first. It was showing courage and character and selflessness right when his team needed a great leader the most. And strange as it might sound, those qualities would carry over into the final seconds of the game and affect his teammates, even though he would not be here to exhibit them himself.

In his eyes this was how it was, though Randy Thompson or a hundred other coaches might have disagreed, might have seen something else through their own eyes, something that maybe wasn't quite as powerful...

Adam thought about his emotions for wanting to finish the game—his desire to help his teammates, his passion for leadership, his competitive fire. And then he thought about those other emotions that had sunk below the first three during the offseason, but were still floating uncomfortably close to the surface—the revenge factor, his bitter feelings, his eagerness for proving people wrong—especially Randy Thompson.

All of that stuff now seemed less important than ever. It *wasn't* important. It was irrelevant. Those other emotions and desires that were burning inside of him? He had to let them go. And he would be at peace with himself if he did. They were a crutch—a drug. But he'd known that March morning when Roadrunner had burst into the room at 4 a.m., known during spring ball, and known throughout the summer that he couldn't keep living on that drug forever...that sooner or later, he would have to let it go...

And he would. He didn't need that stuff anymore.

He had made up his mind—made it up long ago, it seemed, before this injury had happened and before they'd taken the field three hours ago. Somewhere between the time he arrived at St. Bruno's and the minute he woke up this morning, he had decided this, though he hadn't known when or how to show it until now.

"I'm going," he said quietly.

Teddy Morgan nodded, a somber but proud expression on his face and a glimmer of hope in his eyes. Then, as if following orders from some higher power, Adam began jogging towards the EMTs without even thinking about what he was doing or what he was giving up.

"Excuse me?"

One of the EMTs shot him a quick glance as she helped secure Roadrunner's stretcher.

"I'm Adam Dorsey. He's my best friend. I'd like to come with you."

"He won't be able to make it on his own," Hunt interjected. "He's got an ankle sprain. Adam, you'll have to ride with us if you want to come."

He was about to hop on when he suddenly realized he was forgetting something. The rest of the team was staring at him from the sideline.

"I have to talk with someone first," he explained. "I'll be right back!"

"We can't wait for you, Adam," warned the doctor. "Hurry up, because we're almost ready."

"Right!"

He struggled to the edge of the field, where most of the team eagerly surrounded him.

"What's going on, Adam?"

"Is he gonna be OK?"

"We thought you were actually going with Roadrunner—"

Adam held up his hand to stop the onslaught of questions. "Whoa, guys. Everyone just shut up and listen for a minute! I don't have much time."

The babble ceased immediately.

"Good. Now, Roadrunner's going to the hospital, and I'm going with him. They think he has a serious concussion. That's all I can tell you right now. For the rest of you guys, we've got a job to finish. There's almost two minutes left in this game, and we *are* going to win this game. Everyone got that?"

His teammates nodded quietly.

"Now, where's Derek? I need to talk to him."

"I think he's talking with Coach, Adam," Z advised.

He glanced around the area and spotted the two of them in deep conversation just outside the huddle of players. He and the back-up quarterback made eye contact. Coach Morgan saw him too, and immediately stopped talking.

"Excuse me, Playboy...don't worry about my foot, I can walk on my own," Adam said as he and Derek worked towards each other, finally meeting at the edge of the huddle.

"Cowboy, Teddy Bear says I'm going in."

Adam got the feeling he was expecting him to say, "Nah, he's joking, Derek."

"You are. You gotta finish the game," Adam instructed. "Remember everything I taught you in camp? Now you gotta go out and do it. Don't be nervous. I'm rooting for you more than anybody, so just go out there and do your thing! You got this, alright?"

Derek just nodded.

"Cowboy, you really have to leave us?"

It was Bulldog, who was standing nearest to them in the huddle.

"Yes," he stated, and now he addressed the entire team. "Don't you guys get it? Roadrunner's got nobody but Doctor Hunt to go with him! He has no family up here! I'm his best friend, and I have to look out for him. There's nothing else I can do to help us win this game! I know you guys think I can lead you down the field and win this thing, and I'm really humbled by that. But I can't do it on this foot! I can hardly walk! You saw my crappy passes after I got hurt! It's up to you guys now!"

He looked at Brian Massey, Bookworm, Garfield and Graham Cracker—everybody had a look of sadness that their leader couldn't be there at the end...the very end...

"Listen, I know this team, and I know that we can win. We've come so far since the winter, and this is when it all pays off! You leave it all out there these last two minutes!"

And now he pointed his finger at the ground emphatically.

"Don't give up! Whatever happens out there, don't you dare give up! And I'll be with you guys the whole way. Maybe not on the field, or even in the stadium, but I'm with you right here!"

He pumped his chest with his fist, right over his heart, and the buzz of the utility vehicle engine revved in the distance.

"I gotta go," he announced. "Derek!"

The freshman quarterback looked up.

"You good?"

"I'm good, Adam. I ain't giving up."

He gave Derek a thumbs-up, and a second later the vehicle rolled past.

"Adam! We're leaving!" Hunt called.

"I'm coming," he replied, and hobbled onto the back bed of the car.

Past the Gatorade coolers, past the training table, past the thousands of fans who were sarcastically cheering or pointing as he was carried away. A

Fifteen Minutes

few people yelled nasty things at him, but as he stole a quick glance at the crowd, he realized there were just as many disappointed fans. Some of them even looked like they felt bad for him.

Past the end zone, onto the concrete ramp, underneath the support beams...

Why was he so content to leave this place, when the game still hung in the balance? Maybe he was feeling so many emotions that he'd gone numb. Maybe all of this was too much to bear, and so everything cancelled out and he felt nothing? The pre-game speech back in the locker room seemed like ages ago, with the way things had gone. It felt like a dream again, like this wasn't real, what was happening.

The ambulance came into view straight ahead. The car rolled to a stop at the back doors, and Adam hopped inside as the EMTs lifted Roadrunner's stretcher into the back of the vehicle.

He heard the crowd begin to thunder back inside the stadium, and he couldn't help but think about what was happening on the field at that very moment...

The EMTs closed the back doors with a *snap!*, and that was it. The dark shadow of the stadium was gone. No more game. No more football. No more Randy Thompson or DT or nasty fans.

It was over.

The ambulance pulled away from the stadium, and the little room lurched from the momentum.

Adam sat down in a small padded seat that was anchored to the wall, and the finality of it all sunk in. He would not get to throw the winning touchdown pass to beat his old team. He would never experience that thrill. It had been right there for the taking, exactly how he'd wanted. And yet he knew he had made the right decision.

Wow.

He didn't realize how sore his ankle was until he had sat for a few minutes. The pain he'd felt out on the field was just as agonizing now, even as he rested. He knew it had been a bad idea to try and play. But it didn't matter now. He was where he needed to be.

One of the EMTs stuck an IV in Roadrunner' arm and was now reading his blood pressure. Adam hated needles, so he chose to look towards Doctor Hunt instead, who was bracing himself against a white cabinet in the opposite corner.

Objects whizzed by outside the small black windows—trees, cars, traffic lights and illuminated signs.

His throat was dry and his stomach hurt, and he was sure it had nothing to do with the game and everything to do with Roadrunner's situation. It felt like he'd swallowed a rock, and now it was just sitting there and causing a painful stomachache.

"Hey there, big guy," he heard an EMT say.

Roadrunner had woken up and was frantically glancing around the room with just his eyes, because of the neck brace.

"What happened? Where am I?" were the first words out of his mouth, and the rock in Adam's stomach disappeared. His best friend was back, talking and acting just like his normal self.

"You got knocked out," the paramedic answered. "You're in an ambulance. We're taking you to Blue Ridge Hospital."

"What happened to me? What's on my neck? I can't move my head."

Adam got to his feet so that Roadrunner could see him. "Hey, chill out buddy. I'm here."

And that look on his face, when he realized who was with him? That made everything worth it, right there.

Despite the state he was in, Roadrunner found the strength to crack a friendly joke. "OK, so the game must be over, otherwise you wouldn't be here."

Adam smiled and glanced across the stretcher at Hunt. But the doctor gave no indication one way or the other, so he decided to withhold the specifics for now.

"Don't you worry about the game, Roadrunner. We gotta get you fixed up first."

The running back tried to lift his head, but realized that he couldn't.

"Adam, what's on my neck? This thing is freaking me out."

"I think we gotta keep it on there until we get to the hospital," he reassured. "Come on, I'm here so that you won't freak out. Don't go all goofy on me now."

Roadrunner nodded as best he could. "Adam?"

"Yeah?"

"Hold my hand. I'm scared."

He grabbed his hand and held it tight. "All better now?"

Roadrunner gave another little nod. "Yeah. I think I'll be OK now."

"Good, buddy. That's what I'm here for."

"Can you hold it all the way there?"

"All the way."

And they did, without any other words needing to be said, until the ambulance rolled to a stop outside of the emergency center.

The Waiting Room
Chapter 24

"The only place you can win a football game is on the field, the only place you can lose it is in your hearts."

--Darrell Royal

They say that history only remembers the winners.

They say that the losers, or the teams that gave it their best but couldn't quite reach the top, are destined to be forgotten.

Adam knew, as he limped into that hospital alongside the medical staff and Roadrunner's stretcher, that in the future he would have to come to terms with that concept. People would ask him questions and second-guess his motives. *"Don't you really think you could have won the game if you had stayed in?...But you couldn't have been hurt that bad, I saw you playing on the drive right before that!...I think that last hit by Bowser finally did you in...You must have put money on the game, otherwise you'd never have left."*

Those questions would come eventually, but right now he didn't care about them, and wasn't sure he'd ever care. He was used to criticism by now. In high school he'd been criticized for being too reckless or holding onto the ball for too long, even as he racked up win after win. Now they would shake their heads because *they* think he could have won the game, even when he knew he'd made the right decision.

Well, screw them. Those people were just a bunch of hypocrites, and he didn't need them anyway. He wouldn't have won the game nor lost it, despite what they'd say on the morning talk shows. No, the team did that. Not any one individual.

They wheeled Roadrunner into a spacious section of the emergency center, where long curtains divided the private bed spaces. The two EMTs lifted him onto an empty bed and carefully removed his neck brace. A physician's assistant had joined their party at the hospital entrance, and Doctor Hunt brought up the rear.

The EMTs pulled the pale yellow curtains halfway closed, then left to go park the ambulance. Adam sat down in a simple chair near the bed. Hunt remained standing with his arms folded across his chest.

It wasn't long before the doctor on duty entered the makeshift room.

"Doctor Crawford," she said to Hunt, and they shook hands. She was middle-aged, with curvy features and jet-black hair that flowed gracefully over her white coat and shoulders.

"Stephen Hunt. I'm the team doctor for the Beavers."

"Nice to meet you, Mr. Hunt. And you are...?"

"Adam Dorsey," he replied, and quickly stood up while trying to hide the pain in his ankle. "I'm the quarterback for our team," he added as he shook the doctor's hand.

"And are you here for treatment as well?"

"Uh, no, I'm just here for Roadrun—er, Anthony. It was an away game for us. He doesn't have any family up here."

The doctor pursed her lips. "But you *are* hurt?"

"Um...yeah, how did you...?"

"I am a doctor," Crawford said matter-of-factly. "I saw you wince when you got up. And you're favoring your left leg right now."

Adam grinned sheepishly.

"I think he's more concerned about his friend," Hunt interjected. "I was planning on ordering tests when we get back to the university. It's a high ankle sprain. Right now he'll be fine with some ice and rest."

"Well then, I'll have Amy get you some ice," she answered, nodding towards the physician's assistant before turning her attention to Roadrunner.

"My name is Doctor Crawford," she repeated. "Can you tell me what your name is?"

"Anthony Campbell," muttered Roadrunner. "Am I going to have to answer all those questions now?"

"Just a few," Crawford replied, and she began taking notes on her clipboard as she asked him all sorts of things—his birthday, the date, the names of his parents, why he was here, and what city they were in.

"Now," she said after she'd finished scribbling, "how do you feel right now?"

"Like I got laid out by Garfield after he stuffed himself at Burger Canyon."

Adam chuckled to himself.

"Do you feel dizzy at all? Lightheaded?"

"Yeah. I feel like there's a hundred-pound weight on my head. It really hurts. I don't think I can even get up by myself. I just feel really scared, like I might not wake up if I fall asleep—I don't know if that stuff's true or not. And there were flashing lights in my eyes back in the ambulance, but they went away a little bit since then."

More scribbling on the clipboard.

"Anthony, you most definitely have a concussion of some sort," Crawford continued. "From here, we'll get a blood sample and another blood pressure reading. I am going to order CAT and MRI scans as well, so we can see exactly what is going on. Mr. Hunt, would you have any additional recommendations at this point?"

"That all sounds good," he replied. "But I'd like to talk with you a little more and make sure we're on the same page."

The two doctors made their way outside the room and disappeared behind the curtain. Adam was left alone with only Roadrunner and the physician's assistant, who promptly began taking a blood pressure reading. There was silence for a few moments as she pumped the monitor full with air, let it sit and jotted down the numbers.

"So you just came to make sure your friend was alright?" she asked suddenly.

Adam shifted uncomfortably in his seat. "Yeah. That's in my job description, you could say."

The assistant began leafing through the stack of medical forms on her own clipboard. "Well, that was awfully nice of you, I must say!"

Adam wasn't sure he liked her as much as Doctor Crawford. She was wearing one of those fake smiles right now.

"And did you boys win the game?"

He gulped. His throat had gone dry.

"I don't know. We left before it was over."

The lady stopped in mid-motion as she flicked through the pages, and now she peered at him over the clipboard. Adam stared right back.

"Are you sure you don't need any treatment for that foot?"

"Nah, Doc will take care of me. I would kinda rather get back home first. We're probably gonna be here until dawn anyway."

"I have a hard time believing you left the game early, if you were still able to play," she continued sternly. "I know how you football players are."

Adam bit his lip. But after a quick glance at Roadrunner, he wasn't afraid to say what he was thinking.

"A long time ago, somebody told me that some things are more important than football, and I would find that out sooner or later," he answered quietly. "Well, it turned out to be sooner."

And now the assistant smiled, as if she had seen it all and was immune to the emotions surging through him. She didn't understand, but how could she? Having to miss the end of the game and then not knowing whether Roadrunner would be OK had been so hard, but that part was over now. Done. Finished. There was no going back...

It was over.

He and Roadrunner sat there quietly as the lady left to help another patient. He was glad that his smartphone was still at the stadium—there might be a text, or a missed call, or a voicemail from his parents, letting him know how sad they were that they'd lost the game but that they were thinking of him. He didn't want that stuff right now. It was too much to take.

There were no TVs in the area, and the ones in the nearby waiting room were probably turned on to some soap opera that sure as hell wasn't going to give him the final score of a football game. And he liked it that way. Yes, he would sit here and wait. He didn't want to see it anyway, didn't want to see that final score flashing all over the web. He'd never been so afraid of the numbers 21 and 17...

They waited. And waited. And finally Doctor Crawford poked her head through the curtains, announcing that they were ready for the CAT scan. She and the assistant lifted Roadrunner into a wheelchair (with lots of help from Adam), and they went off down the bright hallway, leaving him alone in the room.

He sat silently for a few minutes, with the faint babble of doctors and hospital personnel coming from beyond the curtains. Doctor Crawford hadn't pulled them completely shut when they'd left, and so he glanced out into the hallway and saw other patients rolling by in wheelchairs, a surgeon in a teal outfit and latex gloves—and Teddy Morgan, walking right towards him with his signature black ball cap and matching Beaver polo. He pulled the curtains back, took one glance around the tiny space and smiled.

"What did they do, Adam? Make you save the room while they're administering the tests?"

Adam grinned. "I guess you came at the right time. I'm bored to death. I just want to know what the diagnosis is and get the hell out of here."

"Hospitals can be like that," his coach said as he ventured over to the empty bed and sat down. "So where are we at with Roadrunner?"

"They're taking him to get tests now."

"He is conscious?"

"Yeah."

"Did he remember anything that happened?"

"He did really good, actually. Remembered mostly everything."

"Well, that's a promising start."

There was a short pause, and Adam realized he couldn't wait any longer.

"Did we win?"

Coach Morgan gave him an inquisitive look, and it reminded him of that first day in his office.

"And what if we didn't? What would you say?"

Adam lowered his head and thought.

"People remember the winners," he finally said. "If we lost, then I would say maybe we're not going to be front page news across the country, but we still gave it all we had. We played them close, in their house. That's a pretty encouraging way to start the season. But in the end, a loss is a loss. Nobody remembers the losers."

"Really?" his coach asked with raised eyebrows. "Nobody remembers the losers? And why do you believe that? Nobody remembers them, because they lost? It's that simple? Black and white?"

Adam was having a hard time putting his emotions into words. He was afraid he'd start crying.

"Maybe not," he muttered weakly. "But stuff isn't going to be the same as if we won, you know? It's different."

Teddy Morgan took a deep breath. "When you have been in this business for as long as I have, you see all the small things that make coaching this sport so great. You see the little nuances—the shades that tint winning or losing, and make it better or worse. There are so many shades, Adam. It's not black and white."

He paused, and there was silence except for the gentle chatter from outside the curtains.

"It's not the final result, Adam, but how you got there. It's just like life. It's about the journey."

Adam sensed that his coach was preparing to tell him the news he was hoping would never come, and his heart dropped.

"Yeah, I get all that. But winning, to me, is what always made it worth it. I liked playing football in high school because we won games. I liked it with the Gargoyles because we won games. That's what it was always about with me."

He paused to collect his thoughts.

"I think I was wrong," he continued. "There's so much more to it than that, and I realize that now. But sometimes I wonder if it's worth it—even when you lose the biggest of games."

Coach Morgan stroked his beard with his fingers. "In football, like many other sports, you have to be a true team to win. It cannot be a one-man show. And with true teams, the players must make a greater sacrifice if they want to achieve their goal. But sometimes that goal never comes. So is the sacrifice all for nothing? It is worth it if you don't win the ultimate prize?"

"I guess it is. I still enjoyed my three years in high school that we *didn't* win the state championship. It was still worth it, so yeah."

His coach nodded. "It is, but there's even more to it than that. I would say it's worth it because of the change you create within the team, and within the players around you. You will always be remembered for the things you did, Adam, even if you didn't win every game. Players like Roadrunner make sacrifices because they understand this. They understand that being great isn't just about being fundamentally sound, but respecting the intangibles and the responsibility that comes with a leadership role. They understand that being great isn't all just skill. You know he roomed with Bookworm last fall, but switched rooms so that he could be with you?"

Adam stared. He had not known this.

"I can't believe he never told me that."

"Before your arrival, I met with him in my office and asked him to be your roommate. I knew you would need some sort of guidance, with the transition that you were about to undertake," Coach Morgan explained. "And he was more than willing to jump in and help, even though he and Bookworm are very close friends. That, right there, is a sacrifice."

Adam shook his head, feeling humbled. People had gambled on him. They'd done things to help him succeed, and he only realized that now. Were there other things his teammates had given up so that they could be a better team with him at quarterback? Things like what Roadrunner had done, only on a smaller scale? He was sure there were, even though he'd never noticed them.

These guys had invested their lives in him, these past few months. If he would have quit, or turned into a bust, then what did all those grueling practices amount to? What was the point of them learning a new playbook just for him? What did that crazy adventure down in the crypt really mean?

Nothing. All of that would have meant nothing.

They had thrown their two cents into the pot, all of them. Now it was his turn. And he'd returned the favor by letting them finish the game themselves.

"Are you glad I took myself out?"

Teddy Morgan chuckled. "I'm glad you made the decision you thought was best for the team, Adam. You know, we've got back-ups for a reason. Wasn't exactly how we drew it up, no. Usually the starter's the guy on the stretcher instead of the one riding with him. And usually you've still got your starting running back to rely on. But hey, same idea."

"So I guess it's worth it even if you lose," he decided.

"I would agree with that assessment, yes," Coach Morgan nodded. "You see, Adam, you can slice up the decision you made tonight in lots of different ways, but to me, you chose the team. And in my book, the team wins. The team always wins. Maybe not on the scoreboard, but they win in life. And that's what matters most. That's what makes the losing worth it."

That thought made Adam feel so content, he almost didn't want to ruin it by hearing the final score. But there was no escape from the anticipation. He had to know.

"So anyway..."

"Ah, yes. I believe you were asking me what happened after you left the stadium, and that's how we got sidetracked in the first place?"

"Will you tell me everything?"

"Yes. Are you absolutely sure you *want* to hear everything?"

Adam couldn't resist a little grin at the situation he was in.

"You know, I think we all want that happy ending. But I guess in life, you get all kinds of endings, and so you just have to take what you get and make the most of it. So yeah, I'm absolutely sure I want to hear everything."

"OK, then. Now I'll tell you what happened."

The Final Minute
Chapter 25

"Believe, deep down in your heart, that you're destined to do great things."
--Joe Paterno

It turned out that Derek Bell wasn't quite loud enough in the huddle.

The floodlights of Keystone Stadium illuminated the field for the entire nation as the Beaver offense gathered at their own 42 with 1:52 left. Derek cautiously glanced towards the sideline, where Coach Morgan was bent over earnestly with his hands on his knees.

"Right squirm Texas 34!" he repeated.

"That's better," Massey exclaimed as all eleven players huddled together.

"Alright guys," Cody stated. "We've worked our asses off all summer for this game. And nobody's worked harder than the two guys who just left with injuries. Let's win this one for them."

"You remember what Adam just told us!" Jason reminded. "Nobody here is giving up until that last second ticks off the clock! I don't care if it's fourth-and-forever! Let's give it all we got! Now let's fucking *do* this!!"

The Beaver offense clapped their hands and strode purposefully to the spot of the ball. Derek peered uncertainly over the heads of his linemen, and all three Gargoyle linebackers took several quick steps forward, as if they were blitzing.

"They're faking it, they're faking it," Jason muttered from the side of his mouth, but he didn't hear.

"Set..."

The linebackers were bouncing on their heels, seemingly ready to pounce.

"No, they're faking it!"

Derek threw his hands into the air and signaled for a time-out. The whistle blew.

"Oh, that's not good," Mays sighed as the Beaver linemen groaned and stood up. Derek was running back towards his coach, who was already 20 feet onto the field.

"The Gargoyle defense is toying with the young quarterback here," analyzed Cousins. "I don't think Randy Thompson would leave the entire middle of the field exposed on a split-wide receiver set like this. This is similar to causing the defense to flinch on fourth-and-short. Only here, they tempted Bell to burn the Beavers' last time-out, and he took the bait."

"So now St. Bruno's will have to drive the length of the field with no way to stop the clock and conserve time. A tough situation for a freshman quarterback, for sure."

Cousins chuckled. "That's an understatement. This is a ridiculously challenging environment, even for an experienced QB. Let's face it, this Beaver offense has done nothing since that touchdown run at the end of the first half. They've scored zero points and managed just 48 total yards since that score, Mike. That's horrendous."

"And now they'll have to get a touchdown without two of their best offensive players."

Down on the field, Teddy Morgan held out his hand gently. "Relax. You've got first-year jitters right now," he advised as Derek stood there with his hands on his hips and his head drooping in frustration. "If they blitz, then you know that Massey's open over the middle. Sometimes taking a deep breath and clearing your thoughts is the best way to concentrate. That's what I want you to do right now."

Derek nodded. "OK."

"Alright, now get out there and show us what you've got."

"OK."

He slapped Derek on the back as they parted ways. The referee placed the ball back where his teammates were standing restlessly.

"Let's kick some ass, Derek."

"It's not all on you, bud. All eleven of us gotta do our jobs too, and keep you upright."

"Set, HUT!"

Jason had been right—it wasn't a blitz.

"Bell stands in the pocket, he's got time...throws a deep ball downfield...and it's almost intercepted! Oh, what a close call there! That would have ended the game."

"I thought he had that one," Cousins remarked as free safety Darius Frazier covered his face with his hands in shame.

The video board showed a replay, and the crowd let out a collective "awww" as they watched the football slip from his grasp.

Bookworm, Massey and Mad Max lined themselves up once more. Tight end Jermaine Thomas flanked the left side.

"Short memory, short memory," Cody emphasized before he got set.

"Right," Derek nodded.

A short pass to Massey turned into a big play after he managed to break a tackle. The receiver was finally pulled down at the Keystone State 34.

"Brian Massey with a nice move, and the Gargoyle faithful have got to be worried now, don't you think, Corey?"

"Yeah, but that clock's still ticking. The Beavers need to hurry."

Derek threw a screen pass to Mad Max on the next play. Max was able to gain eight yards before getting pushed out by the defender. The clock stopped with 40 seconds left.

"Nice play call there," exclaimed Cousins. "It's a bubble screen, designed for the wide receiver to step out of bounds after gaining as many yards as possible. That will give the Beavers some time to catch their breaths."

"HUT!!"

Derek scanned the field hopefully, but there were Gargoyles blanketing every receiver. He scrambled out of the pocket as Lukas Bowser broke free and chased after him, finally hurling the football out of bounds.

"There was absolutely nothing open that time. A good choice to get out of the tackle box and throw that one away," Cousins remarked.

"The Beavers only have 31 seconds to work with, Corey."

"Yeah, and the Gargoyles have done a tremendous job with this prevent defense. Their strategy is to give the Beavers the easy underneath throws, and force them to dink and dunk their way to the goal line. Of course, time will run out before they get there, which is why this strategy is usually successful. If it weren't for that missed tackle on Brian Massey, the Beavers wouldn't be anywhere close to the end zone."

Coach Morgan signaled the next play.

"You got that, Derek? Horseshoe 27X double dig!" he yelled excitedly. "You know where to go with it!"

They were two plays away from the game being lost, and yet they were two plays away from winning it all. And still they were chasing...chasing that happy ending...

"Set...HUT!"

Derek didn't wait long to make his decision. Mad Max had slipped past the cornerback and was sprinting towards the end zone with only the free safety nearby.

"Bell throws a bomb to the right corner of the end zone! And it's out of bounds. I think that was intended for Stephen Maxwell."

"I don't know if that would have been a completion anyway, Mike. The safety was closing in pretty fast and might have knocked that ball away even if it had been a perfect pass. It's obvious that Bell is lacking a bit with his downfield accuracy, although he's done well with these short to intermediate routes."

"So now it's fourth down. This is it, folks."

Teddy Morgan hollered his last-gasp play.

"You got this," Cody whispered as he got set, and his quarterback could only rub the sweat from his forehead and size up the defense in response, using every precious second of that play clock...

"HUT!!"

The three receivers dashed forward in a mad race as they weaved through the imposing Gargoyle secondary. Instinct told him to heave it towards the end zone again, this time towards Bookworm and the left side of the field. And so he lifted the football into the air with the game on the line.

"Bell throws to the end zone! Trevor Hart reaches for it, and it's over his head and incomplete. So that should do it...but there's a flag on the play. Hold on now, folks, this thing might not be over yet."

"Pass interference," Cousins said abruptly. "Pass interference on Darius Frazier."

Massey motioned excitedly for his teammates to move closer to the end zone, while Frazier threw his hands into the air in disbelief and argued with the nearest referee. Derek stole a quick glance at his head coach. Teddy Morgan simply nodded encouragingly and drew circles with his finger, indicating his desire to stay focused on the next play and ignore the mayhem on the field and the boos from the crowd.

"Look at this! Randy Thompson is halfway onto the field, waving his hand over his head and complaining to the refs!" Mays exclaimed. "I think he's arguing that the ball was uncatchable, which would negate the penalty and end the game."

"Yeah, they're going to huddle and make sure they get this one right."

Replays on the video board showed Bookworm rushing towards the field-level camera angle, with Frazier reaching out and bumping his shoulder as they both made a play for the ball. Then a brown blur whizzed by over their heads, and Bookworm tumbled into the camera, causing the video to spiral out of control.

"It's a judgment call," Cousins explained. "Tough to say from that angle."

"And let's remind our viewing audience that college football pass interference rules are different from the NFL. It's a 15-yard penalty no matter where it happens. So that would move the ball all the way to the 11!"

"There are also just 12 seconds left," added Cousins. "So forget about getting first downs. The Beavers have got two shots at the end zone."

The boos reached a peak as the referee confirmed the call. Then they morphed into the usual yells and jeers as the ball was spotted at the 11.

Derek shouted the call with a little more bounce in his step, a little more confidence. The new set of downs breathed determination and poise into his teammates. The Gargoyles were standing in their own end zone now. They had them right where they wanted. All they had to do was pounce.

"*HUT!*"

He surveyed his options, hesitated, then heaved the football towards Mad Max, who had the height advantage on the defending safety. Max reached up to stop the ball's momentum with one hand and cradle the catch with the other. But it spun away before he could corral it, and ricocheted off the safety's helmet, then Max's shoulder pad, then Bowser's knee. Bowser reached out and almost snagged it, but the football eluded his grasp and tumbled to the ground.

"Wow! I counted three players who had a shot at that ball!" Cousins remarked. "Not a bad throw by Bell, although it could have been a tad lower for an easier catch by Maxwell. But the Beavers are fortunate that one didn't end up in the hands of a Gargoyle."

"So with five seconds left, there's one last chance for the Beavers."

"Great clock management and execution on this last drive, whatever happens here," Cousins commended. "And they've done it without two of their best players."

"Here we go."

They had another chance, and that was all that mattered. Derek strode to the line eagerly, still riding the energy wave that had jolted them after the penalty. He knew he had it in him. Just a few more yards, and the odds against them wouldn't matter. It wouldn't matter what the total yards looked like, or the time of possession, or the odds in Vegas. Once he fired that deadly bullet, it was over. Nothing else needed to be said.

Bookworm stared his defender down. He felt the spongy grass beneath his cleats and the warm August air under the stadium lights. He sensed the importance of the moment, the magnitude of the play. And he decided, right then and there, that he would not be denied...

Everything seemed to happen in slow motion. His legs began churning automatically, like clockwork in sync with Derek's yell. He was running down the field, with Massey right beside him and the Gargoyle safety eying him down like a predator ready to attack. He didn't even think about where the other defenders were or how many were covering him. He knew exactly where he was going and nobody was going to stop him.

Bookworm didn't see his feet cross the white line so much as feel it. He knew he was in the end zone subconsciously, like an intuitive sense ingrained in him from years and years of playing ball. He turned to see Derek finishing his release and the football zooming towards him in a perfect spiral, threading through a tiny gap where no defenders could reach out and tip it. In that moment, nothing existed except the two of them and the ball.

He jumped and snatched the pigskin from the air just as Darius Frazier's muscular arms reached over his shoulders from behind. He was falling, with Frazier's hands nearly touching the ball and the two of them intertwined as the world rushed by in a blur. He felt the laces and the smooth surface, and held on so tight that it might have been glued to his fingers. He hit the soft grass with a thud, and squeezed the football desperately as Frazier nearly crushed him on the way down.

Time stopped.

The fans in the stadium—and everyone watching on TV—seemed to hold their collective breath for one unforgettable second. Then the end zone referee threw his hands into the air.

The lights flashed. The cameras rolled. The away crowd in the corner erupted.

Bookworm heard the cheers, and that's when the best feeling in the world hit him. Frazier jumped to his feet, and for a brief moment he was alone on the turf, the center of attention in the biggest stadium in college football. Then the avalanche arrived.

Z was falling on him, almost suffocating him as he lay there with the football extended high above his head in triumph. Cody was pulling him to his feet with both arms so he could embrace him in a giant bear hug. Derek was hugging him, and Bulldog was hugging him, and Mozart was hugging him, and Garfield was nearly squashing him, and Playboy was trying to pull him back to the ground, and Mad Max was dancing around one of the pylons with his long blonde hair flying all over the place...

The Beaver fans were going wild, brandishing their homemade signs at the TV cameras and showing the world what their university meant to them. They, too, were hugging each other, even fans they didn't know. They were one big family, though Bookworm couldn't see any of that through the crowd of teammates surrounding him.

He didn't see as their friends and family back home ran around the house, cheering and celebrating and jumping on each other with happiness, or the students of St. Bruno's as they ran from their dorms and into the campus streets victoriously.

He didn't hear Mike Mays after they finally made the extra point attempt, shouting, "And that's it! The St. Bruno Beavers have defeated the Keystone State Gargoyles, 24 – 21, and have knocked off the No. 1 team in the country!"

He didn't see as Randy Thompson hurled his headset to the ground in frustration, so hard that it shattered to pieces and skidded across the sideline. He didn't see him roar in anger, his hair a mess, his black collared shirt disheveled. He looked like a madman as he stormed into the tunnel, his face red, his fists clenched. His team's national championship run was over before it had even begun...but he didn't see any of that.

All he saw were his teammates, hugging and shouting and crying all at the same time, and he was in the middle of everything. He had never felt so good in his entire life—not on Christmas morning, not on his birthday, not when Coach Morgan had called to tell him he'd be getting a full scholarship to play football. This, right here, was the absolute best, and his head coach had been right. The real thing was better than the dream.

Back at Blue Ridge Hospital, Adam finally told Roadrunner the news. And the running back didn't only give his first smile since getting hurt—he gave the biggest smile Adam had ever seen from him. And that made the waiting so much easier.

It was almost fun as Doctor Crawford came back with the test results, and explained that there were no other serious injuries. It was definitely fun as Adam, Coach Morgan and Doctor Hunt tried their best to get Roadrunner from the room to the back seat of the head coach's car without actually carrying him. It felt surreal as they dropped the team doctor off at his own car and drove towards the highway at 3 a.m., beginning their long journey back to western Pennsylvania.

As scared as he was to fall sleep, even Roadrunner couldn't fight it off after half an hour.

"Adam," he called drowsily just before drifting off, and his teammate turned around in the passenger seat.

"What's up?"

"We won today," the running back beamed, and Adam's thoughts flashed back eight hours in time, as they were suiting up to take the field, and Roadrunner was standing there begging the question that Joey always used to ask...

"We won."

Afterword

"Don't cry because it's over, smile because it happened."

--Anonymous proverb

Hey everyone!

Trevor Hart here, but most of you probably know me as Bookworm. I have decided to write the afterword in first-person, to give it more of a personal touch. The actual novel needed to be in third-person, because I wanted it to feel like a story and not just a biography of what happened from my perspective.

Yeah, in case you haven't guessed by now, I'm the one who wrote all that. Yep, I finally did it! I wrote a real book, and now I'm a published author!

It's been nearly five years since that amazing game at Keystone Stadium, and a ton of stuff has happened since then. Don't worry, I'll fill you in on all the details shortly. But first, let me tell you a bit about how this book came to be.

If you remember, I always had the dream of publishing a book, but hadn't written any good material when *Fifteen Minutes* was actually taking place. Well, the game hadn't been over for three hours when the idea popped into my head—what if I wrote a book about this?

I remember it like it was yesterday. The whole team was partying on the bus ride back to St. Bruno's. The guys kept getting phone calls and texts from literally everyone they knew, and we kept getting updates on the TV headlines and highlights from SportsNetwork. I was at the center of attention, getting treated like a hero and receiving dozens of congratulatory phone calls myself! It was definitely the loudest, happiest bus ride of my life.

That's when it hit me. I knew that moment had the makings of a great story. And after catching the winning touchdown pass and having a front-row seat to the whole experience, who better to write it than me?

Once that idea had been planted, I couldn't let it go. It simply grew and grew, and as the season wore on it gained momentum with the rest of the team, until they were practically begging me to start writing.

Of course, I had to do an extensive amount of research first, most of which was just sitting down with Adam and Roadrunner and having them recount every little memory as I transcribed everything on my laptop. I talked to pretty much every player, and added my own tidbits as well. I even got Coach Morgan into the act when we met in his office, and I had him recount some memories from his interactions with Adam. Unfortunately, I wasn't able to get Coach Thompson or DT to participate. But I pulled most of their lines from Adam's memory—he did really well with the scene in Thompson's office.

So the whole process of researching and gathering specifics took about a year. I completed most of the work during the spring and summer following the 2013 season. But then I had to put it all together, and that was the hard part. That took two years, and then another two for the editing and logistics of getting it published. But the hard work has definitely paid off, as you've seen.

Enough said on how this book came to be. Now I'll tell you what happened after we beat the Gargoyles.

The 2013 and 2014 Seasons

We finished the 2013 regular season with a record of 12 – 1. Our only loss came on the road to the North Virginia Colonials. Ironically, we ended up playing them again (and beating them) in the conference title game.

Adam returned from his injury in Week 4 and had a stellar performance with three touchdown passes and no picks. Roadrunner returned in Week 5. We couldn't be stopped once we got those two back, and our offense got better as the season wore on.

We capped that year by winning the FCS national championship, where Adam threw for four touchdowns in a come-from-behind win. After that, we enjoyed tons of national attention and received more TV exposure than a St. Bruno's sports team ever had. Part of it had to do with the championship, but the win against the Gargoyles really put us in the national spotlight, not to mention the fact that we had a projected first-round draft pick at quarterback.

Adam decided to return for his senior season, and the hype surrounding our team reached a feverish pitch that August. So it only seemed fitting when our offense exploded for record numbers of points and yardage that year—more than any other Beaver offense in the school's history. We went 13 – 0 and were overwhelming favorites to repeat. But we were upset in the semifinals, and so the season ended on a bad note.

Adam says that those two years were the best of his life so far. I know he really enjoyed his time with the Gargoyles, but he says he never realized what he had back then, and that made his time with the Beavers so much more meaningful.

He and I both agree that his first Beaver team—the one that knocked off Keystone State and won the championship—was special. Don't get me wrong, it was fun to go undefeated and score 50 points a game! But given the choice, we would both take the team that *didn't* go undefeated, but beat the No. 1 team in the country and won the championship, over the offensive fireworks of Adam's senior year. That first year was magical, if only because we weren't sure what we had. It had been a rough transition for Adam, and we weren't sure if everything would come together. The second time around all the outsiders expected us to win, and we came up short anyway.

Adam and the NFL

Adam was drafted by the Portland Pirates with the second overall pick of the 2015 NFL draft, and he became the starter that year. As a new expansion franchise, the Pirates struggled to get their feet off the ground, and went 4 – 12 in Adam's rookie year.

They were a team on the rise in his sophomore season, and they improved to 10 – 6, won their division and entered the playoffs. They lost in the first round, but came back stronger than ever in Adam's third year.

That season, the Pirates cruised to a 13 – 3 regular season record and won two tough playoff games to reach the Super Bowl.

That was an awesome experience, mainly because Roadrunner and I got to sit in the first row of the stadium (thanks to Adam!) He jogged over to chat before the game, and I asked him how it felt to fulfill his life-long dream. He replied that it felt amazing, but that it wouldn't have been half as good if Roadrunner, half the Beaver team and I hadn't come to watch him play, because he never would have gotten there without us.

Unfortunately, the Pirates lost that game to the Maryland Monsters. Most of the critics agree that Adam played well in defeat, but he insists that he'll play even better if he gets a second chance in the big game. It's just a hunch, but I've got a feeling it could be as soon as this upcoming year. NFL camps are back in action as I write this, and Adam's Pirates are favored to repeat as conference champs.

As for his love life, he has a new girlfriend and they seem like a great fit. She isn't turned off by all the publicity and handles it very well. Adam claims he's going to take his time and make sure she's "the one," but I've got a hunch they'll be getting married soon.

The Players and Coaches

Roadrunner finished his Beaver career near the top of the school list in rushing yards and touchdowns. Coach Morgan kept him on as a graduate assistant coach after his senior year, and he helped mentor a young Beaver offense after Adam departed for the draft. Currently, he's an assistant coach at nearby Mount Washington University. That was where Coach Morgan worked before coming to St. Bruno's, (in fact, the staff's familiarity with

Teddy helped Roadrunner land the job). He's well on his way to fulfilling his dream of becoming a head coach, and I know he'll get there eventually.

Z now manages a beverage factory near his hometown in southeastern PA. He and Lindsey aren't together anymore—the last time I heard from her, she was attending graduate school for a master's degree in education.

Mad Max just finished grad school and is now a chemical engineer at a big company in New York.

Mozart left for southern California after he graduated and is now a producer. He's making a name for himself, and I think he'll be pretty famous someday.

Playboy moved back to his hometown after getting his degree, and I think he just lived off his parents' savings initially. But then we started hearing rumors about him starting a business, and it turns out he invested a large amount of the money into his own beer company. He hired Bulldog to be his marketing assistant (Bulldog was a marketing major), and now they're even brewing their own lagers. It's still a very small business, but they're headed in the right direction.

As for the offensive linemen, Garfield now works at St. Bruno's food and catering service and loves it. Jason is an engineer at a company in D.C. Cody is a construction manager for a contractor in Virginia. Bigfoot works at a local delivery company. Graham Cracker got a job as a bartender back in his hometown. Tight end Jermaine Thomas is a physical education teacher for his alma mater high school.

Antonio Coronado (or Tonio) is now a chef at his uncle's authentic Mexican restaurant. Tony Ferrari left for the Navy after graduation. And Brian Massey now works as an assistant in the athletic office of a smaller college near his hometown. He wants to be an athletic director eventually.

As for Derek Bell, he became a successful starter in his junior and senior years, and led the Beavers to four total playoff wins. He replaced Roadrunner as the offensive graduate assistant on Coach Morgan's staff, after Roadrunner left for Mount Washington.

Randy Thompson was fired from Keystone State two years ago. They finished the 2013 season with a 7 – 6 record—Thompson's worst ever at the school. Things didn't get any better in DT's junior and senior years, as the team struggled to another 7 – 6 and then 8 – 5 mark.

Randy's pedigree probably would have saved him, were it not for the school's new athletic director that third year. Rumors are that he and Coach Thompson met privately before the season, and the new AD left a strong impression that he wasn't going to let Randy maintain his untouchable status at the university. He gave the coach an ultimatum to start winning big again, and anything less than a BCS bowl would cost him his job. Well, the team didn't even come close. Personally, I think the new AD never liked Thompson in the first place, but wanted one more subpar year to gain leverage and justify the firing.

Randy's back in the NFL now, but as a quality control coach. DT was still unemployed the last time I heard about him. Guess "the plan" didn't work out too well for them.

Pat Peterson was retained by the new staff and is still the quarterbacks coach for the Gargoyles. He and Adam still have a relationship, and he even attended the Super Bowl to watch him play.

Meanwhile, Teddy Morgan remains the St. Bruno's head coach. Many say he'll retire a Beaver, and I've got a feeling that he wants one more national championship, which would give him four and put him in a truly elite group of coaches. In true Teddy Morgan fashion, he'll deny that the pursuit of one last title is a driving force for him. But I also think he's waiting for the right time to pass the baton to his successor—he's looking for that year when there are a ton of seniors, and the roster will be young enough that the new coach can come in with low expectations and a fresh start.

The Beavers Today

This year's Beaver team—now the fourth one since Adam, Roadrunner and I graduated—has a real shot at the championship (something I know Teddy's excited about!) We've got a senior quarterback and some really outstanding receivers, probably even a better group than the one I was a part of. They lost in the semifinals last year and are really itching to get the job done this time around.

It's so fulfilling to see the team succeed like this even without a top NFL prospect at quarterback, and I think it's a testament to the job Teddy has done and the foundation we built by putting the Beavers on the national stage in Adam's first year. Whoever the new coach is, he'll have a heck of a program on his hands!

My Future

As for me, I currently work in the archives department at the St. Bruno school library. That place was my second home as a student, and the staff knew me so well that they offered me a job when the former guy retired!

I'm also working hard to promote my book, and would definitely like to have a dual career as an author. There's another story out there for me to write—trust me! I've really been itching to write the ultimate fantasy series. And by "ultimate" I mean something that will really blow you away. It'll be a creative explosion combined with an intense, relentless rush of energy and emotion. I'm thinking it will be a fantasy at its core, with a good helping of mystery, sci-fi and mythology. I might even mix in some romance, who knows?

But as far as this story goes, it's time to turn the stadium lights out, if you will. Thanks for sharing the journey with me.

Until next time,

Trevor Hart